The Divine Comedy

Simplified & Modernised

Alighieri Dante

B&S Books

Copyright

Copyright © 2024 B&S Books. All rights reserved.

No part of this book may be reproduced, stored in a retrieval system, or transmitted in any form or by any means—electronic, mechanical, photocopying, recording, or otherwise—without the express written permission of the publisher.

Cover design by: B&S Books

Table of Contents

Part 1 Inferno — 1

Chapter 1: The Dark Forest. The Hill of Difficulty. The Panther, the Lion, and the Wolf. Virgil. — 2

Chapter 2: The Descent. Dante's Protest and Virgil's Appeal. The Intercession of the Three Ladies Benedight. — 5

Chapter 3: The Gate of Hell. The Inefficient or Indifferent. Pope Celestine V. The Shores of Acheron. Charon. The Earthquake and the Swoon. — 8

Chapter 4: The First Circle, Limbo: Virtuous Pagans and the Unbaptized. The Four Poets: Homer, Horace, Ovid, and Lucan. The Noble Castle of Philosophy. — 11

Chapter 5: The Second Circle: The Wanton. Minos. The Infernal Hurricane. Francesca da Rimini. — 14

Chapter 6: The Third Circle: The Gluttonous. Cerberus. The Eternal Rain. Ciacco. Florence. — 17

Chapter 7: The Fourth Circle: The Avaricious and the Prodigal. Plutus. Fortune and her Wheel. The Fifth Circle: The Irascible and the Sullen. Styx. — 19

Chapter 8: Phlegyas. Filippo Argenti. The Gates of the City of Dis. — 22

Chapter 9: The Furies and Medusa. The Angel. The City of Dis. The Sixth Circle: Heresiarchs. — 25

Chapter 10: Farinata and Cavalcante de' Cavalcanti. Discourse on the Knowledge of the Damned. — 28

Chapter 11: The Broken Rocks. Pope Anastasius. General Description of the Inferno and its Divisions. — 31

Chapter 12: The Minotaur. The Seventh Circle: The Violent. The River Phlegethon. The Violent against their Neighbours. The Centaurs. Tyrants. — 33

Chapter 13: The Wood of Thorns. The Harpies. The Violent against themselves. Suicides. Pier della Vigna. Lano and Jacopo da Sant' Andrea. — 36

Chapter 14: The Sand Waste and the Rain of Fire. The Violent against God. Capaneus. The Statue of Time, and the Four Infernal Rivers. — 39

Chapter 15: The Violent Against Nature. Brunetto Latini. — 42

Chapter 16: Guidoguerra, Aldobrandi, and Rusticucci. The River of Blood — 45

Chapter 17: Geryon. The Violent Against Art. Usurers. The Descent into the Abyss of Malebolge. — 48

Chapter 18: The Eighth Circle, Malebolge: The Fraudulent and the Malicious. The First Bolgia: Seducers and Panders. Venedico Caccianimico. Jason. The Second Bolgia: Flatterers. Allessio Interminelli. Thais. — 51

Chapter 19: The Third Bolgia: Simoniacs. Pope Nicholas III. Dante's Reproof of corrupt Prelates. — 54

Chapter 20: The Fourth Bolgia: Soothsayers. Amphiaraus, Tiresias, Aruns, Manto, Eryphylus, Michael Scott, Guido Bonatti, and Asdente. Virgil reproaches Dante's Pity. Mantua's Foundation. — 56

Chapter 21: The Fifth Bolgia: Peculators. The Elder of Santa Zita. Malacoda and other Devils. — 58

Chapter 22: Ciampolo, Friar Gomita, and Michael Zanche. The Malabranche quarrel. — 61

Chapter 23: Escape from the Malabranche. The Sixth Bolgia: Hypocrites. Catalano and Loderingo. Caiaphas. — 64

Chapter 24: The Seventh Bolgia: Thieves. Vanni Fucci. Serpents. — 67

Chapter 25: Vanni Fucci's Punishment. Agnello Brunelleschi, Buoso degli Abati, Puccio Sciancato, Cianfa de' Donati, and Guercio Cavalcanti. — 70

Chapter 26: The Eighth Bolgia: Evil Counselors. Ulysses and Diomed. Ulysses' Last Voyage. — 73

Chapter 27: Guido da Montefeltro. His Deception by Pope Boniface VIII. — 76

Chapter 28: The Ninth Bolgia: Schismatics. Muhammad and Ali. Pier da Medicina, Curio, Mosca, and Bertrand de Born. — 79

Chapter 29: Geri del Bello. The Tenth Bolgia: Alchemists. Griffolino d'Arezzo and Capocchio. — 81

Chapter 30: Other Falsifiers or Forgers. Gianni Schicchi, Myrrha, Adam of Brescia, Potiphar's Wife, and Sinon of Troy. — 83

Chapter 31: The Giants, Nimrod, Ephialtes, and Antaeus. Descent to Cocytus. — 86

Chapter 32: The Ninth Circle: Traitors. The Frozen Lake of Cocytus. First Division, Caina: Traitors to their Kindred. Camicion de' Pazzi. Second Division, Antenora: Traitors to their Country. Dante questions Bocca degli Abati. Buoso da Duera. — 88

Chapter 33: Count Ugolino and the Archbishop Ruggieri. The Death of Count Ugolino's Sons. Third Division of the Ninth Circle, Ptolomaea: Traitors to their Friends. Friar Alberigo, Branco d' Oria.   90

Chapter 34: Fourth Division of the Ninth Circle, the Judecca: Traitors to their Lords and Benefactors. Lucifer, Judas Iscariot, Brutus, and Cassius. The Chasm of Lethe. The Ascent.   93

Part 2 Purgatorio   96

Chapter 1: The Shores of Purgatory. The Four Stars. Cato of Utica. The Rush.   97

Chapter 2: The Celestial Pilot. Casella. The Departure.   99

Chapter 3: Discourse on the Limits of Reason. The Foot of the Mountain. Those who died in Contumacy of Holy Church. Manfredi.   101

Chapter 4: Farther Ascent. Nature of the Mountain. The Negligent, who postponed Repentance till the last Hour. Belacqua.   104

Chapter 5: Those who died by Violence, but repentant. Buonconte di Monfeltro. La Pia.   107

Chapter 6: Dante's Inquiry on Prayers for the Dead. Sordello. Italy.   109

Chapter 7: The Valley of Flowers. Negligent Princes.   112

Chapter 8: The Guardian Angels and the Serpent. Nino di Gallura. The Three Stars. Currado Malaspina.   115

Chapter 9: Dante's Dream of the Eagle. The Gate of Purgatory and the Angel. Seven P's. The Keys.   118

Chapter 10: The Needle's Eye. The First Circle: The Proud. The Sculptures on the Wall.   121

Chapter 11: The Humble Prayer. Omberto di Santafiore. Oderisi d' Agobbio. Provenzan Salvani.   124

Chapter 12: The Sculptures on the Pavement. Ascent to the Second Circle.   126

Chapter 13: The Second Circle: The Envious. Sapia of Siena   129

Chapter 14: Guido del Duca and Renier da Calboli. Cities of the Arno Valley. Denunciation of Stubbornness.   132

Chapter 15: The Third Circle: The Irascible. Dante's Visions. The Smoke.   135

Chapter 16: Marco Lombardo. Lament over the State of the World.   138

Chapter 17: Dante's Dream of Anger. The Fourth Circle: The Slothful. Virgil's Discourse of Love. 141

Chapter 18: Virgil further discourses of Love and Free Will. The Abbot of San Zeno. 144

Chapter 19: Dante's Dream of the Siren. The Fifth Circle: The Avaricious and Prodigal. Pope Adrian V. 147

Chapter 20: Hugh Capet. Corruption of the French Crown. Prophecy of the Abduction of Pope Boniface VIII and the Sacrilege of Philip the Fair. The Earthquake. 150

Chapter 21: The Poet Statius. Praise of Virgil. 153

Chapter 22: Statius' Denunciation of Avarice. The Sixth Circle: The Gluttonous. The Mystic Tree. 155

Chapter 23: Forese. Reproof of immodest Florentine Women. 158

Chapter 24: Buonagiunta da Lucca. Pope Martin IV, and others. Inquiry into the State of Poetry. 161

Chapter 25: Discourse of Statius on Generation. The Seventh Circle: The Wanton. 164

Chapter 26: Sodomites. Guido Guinicelli and Arnaldo Daniello. 167

Chapter 27: The Wall of Fire and the Angel of God. Dante's Sleep upon the Stairway, and his Dream of Leah and Rachel. Arrival at the Terrestrial Paradise. 170

Chapter 28: The River Lethe. Matilda. The Nature of the Terrestrial Paradise. 172

Chapter 29: The Triumph of the Church. 174

Chapter 30: Virgil's Departure. Beatrice. Dante's Shame. 177

Chapter 31: Reproaches of Beatrice and Confession of Dante. The Passage of Lethe. The Seven Virtues. The Griffon. 179

Chapter 32: The Tree of Knowledge. Allegory of the Chariot. 181

Chapter 33: Lament over the State of the Church. Final Reproaches of Beatrice. The River Eunoe. 184

Part 3 Paradiso 187

Chapter 1: The Ascent to the First Heaven. The Sphere of Fire. 188

Chapter 2: The First Heaven, the Moon: Spirits who, having taken Sacred Vows, were forced to violate them. The Lunar Spots. 190

Chapter 3: Piccarda Donati and the Empress Constance. — 193

Chapter 4: Questionings of the Soul and of Broken Vows. — 195

Chapter 5: Discourse of Beatrice on Vows and Compensations. Ascent to the Second Heaven, Mercury: Spirits who for the Love of Fame achieved great Deeds. — 197

Chapter 6: Justinian. The Roman Eagle. The Empire. Romeo. — 200

Chapter 7: Beatrice's Discourse of the Crucifixion, the Incarnation, the Immortality of the Soul, and the Resurrection of the Body. — 203

Chapter 8: Ascent to the Third Heaven, Venus: Lovers. Charles Martel. Discourse on diverse Natures. — 205

Chapter 9: Cunizza da Romano, Folco of Marseilles, and Rahab. Neglect of the Holy Land. — 208

Chapter 10: The Fourth Heaven, the Sun: Theologians and Fathers of the Church. The First Circle. St. Thomas of Aquinas. — 211

Chapter 11: St. Thomas recounts the Life of St. Francis. Lament over the State of the Dominican Order. — 214

Chapter 12: St. Buonaventura recounts the Life of St. Dominic. Lament over the State of the Franciscan Order. The Second Circle. — 216

Chapter 13: Of the Wisdom of Solomon. St. Thomas reproaches Dante's Judgement. — 219

Chapter 14: The Third Circle. Discourse on the Resurrection of the Flesh. The Fifth Heaven, Mars: Martyrs and Crusaders who died fighting for the true Faith. The Celestial Cross. — 222

Chapter 15: Cacciaguida. Florence in the Olden Time. — 225

Chapter 16: Dante's Noble Ancestry. Cacciaguida's Discourse of the Great Florentines. — 228

Chapter 17: Cacciaguida's Prophecy of Dante's Banishment. — 231

Chapter 18: The Sixth Heaven, Jupiter: Righteous Kings and Rulers. The Celestial Eagle. Dante's Invectives against ecclesiastical Avarice. — 233

Chapter 19: The Eagle discourses of Salvation, Faith, and Virtue. Condemnation of the vile Kings of A.D. 1300. — 236

Chapter 20: The Eagle praises the Righteous Kings of old. Benevolence of the Divine Will. — 239

Chapter 21: The Seventh Heaven, Saturn: The Contemplative. The Celestial Stairway. St. Peter Damiano. His Invectives against the Luxury of the Prelates. 242

Chapter 22: St. Benedict. His Lamentation over the Corruption of Monks. The Eighth Heaven, the Fixed Stars. 245

Chapter 23: The Triumph of Christ. The Virgin Mary. The Apostles. Gabriel. 248

Chapter 24: The Radiant Wheel. St. Peter examines Dante on Faith. 251

Chapter 25: The Laurel Crown. St. James examines Dante on Hope. Dante's Blindness. 254

Chapter 26: St. John examines Dante on Charity. Dante's Sight. Adam. 257

Chapter 27: St. Peter's reproof of bad Popes. The Ascent to the Ninth Heaven, the 'Primum Mobile.' 260

Chapter 28: God and the Angelic Hierarchies. 263

Chapter 29: Beatrice's Discourse of the Creation of the Angels, and of the Fall of Lucifer. Her Reproof of Foolish and Avaricious Preachers. 265

Chapter 30: The Tenth Heaven, or Empyrean. The River of Light. The Two Courts of Heaven. The White Rose of Paradise. The great Throne. 268

Chapter 31: The Glory of Paradise. Departure of Beatrice. St. Bernard. 271

Chapter 32: St. Bernard points out the Saints in the White Rose. 273

Chapter 33: Prayer to the Virgin. The Threefold Circle of the Trinity. Mystery of the Divine and Human Nature. 276

Introduction

Dante Alighieri's *The Divine Comedy* is one of the most significant works in Western literature, standing as a timeless epic that has influenced writers, thinkers, and artists for over seven centuries. Written between 1308 and 1320, the poem is widely regarded as Dante's magnum opus and one of the great literary achievements of the Middle Ages. It is much more than a mere tale of an individual's journey through Hell, Purgatory, and Heaven—it is a reflection of the political, philosophical, theological, and cultural values of Dante's time, and an exploration of universal themes that resonate across ages.

The Divine Comedy is structured as an allegorical journey through the three realms of the Christian afterlife: Hell (*Inferno*), Purgatory (*Purgatorio*), and Paradise (*Paradiso*). Over the course of 100 cantos, the poem guides readers through these realms, with each part presenting its own unique spiritual and moral lessons. The work is written in the Tuscan dialect of Italian, which Dante helped elevate to literary prominence, and in a strict poetic structure known as *terza rima*, consisting of three-line stanzas with an interlocking rhyme scheme. This form mirrors the poem's thematic focus on the divine order, unity, and the Christian concept of the Trinity.

Dante Alighieri: The Poet and the Exile

To understand *The Divine Comedy*, it is important to understand the life of Dante Alighieri, the man behind the masterpiece. Born in Florence in 1265, Dante lived during a period of intense political turmoil in Italy. He was deeply involved in the politics of his city-state, serving in various public roles, but his political involvement led to his eventual exile. Florence was divided between two factions—the Guelphs, who supported the papacy, and the Ghibellines, who supported the Holy Roman Emperor. Within the Guelph party, there was further division between the White and Black Guelphs. Dante belonged to the White Guelphs, who sought more autonomy from the papacy. When the Black Guelphs gained power in Florence, Dante was exiled, an event that had a profound impact on his writing.

Exiled from his beloved Florence in 1302, Dante spent the remaining years of his life wandering through various courts in Italy. This experience of political injustice and personal loss permeates much of *The Divine Comedy*, particularly in *Inferno*, where Dante's bitterness toward his political enemies is palpable. Yet Dante's exile also deepened his spiritual and philosophical reflections, as he sought to reconcile his personal misfortunes with the broader moral and theological order of the universe. This inner conflict is central to *The Divine Comedy*, where Dante not only explores the fate of souls in the afterlife but also grapples with his own moral and spiritual journey.

The Structure of *The Divine Comedy*

At the core of *The Divine Comedy* is Dante's allegorical journey through the realms of the dead, guided first by the Roman poet Virgil and later by his beloved Beatrice, who represents divine love and grace. The journey begins in Hell (*Inferno*), where Dante confronts the consequences of sin; it continues through Purgatory (*Purgatorio*), where souls are purified before entering Heaven; and it culminates in Paradise (*Paradiso*), where Dante experiences the beatific vision of God.

The three parts of the poem—*Inferno*, *Purgatorio*, and *Paradiso*—each represent a stage in the soul's journey toward salvation, reflecting Dante's deep engagement with Christian theology. The structure of the poem is highly symbolic, with each part corresponding to one of the three theological virtues: faith (*Paradiso*), hope (*Purgatorio*), and charity (*Inferno*). The number three, representing the Holy Trinity, recurs throughout the work, both in its content and in its form.

Inferno: The Descent into Sin

The *Inferno* is arguably the most famous and widely read section of *The Divine Comedy*, and it offers readers a vivid portrayal of Hell as a place of retributive justice. Hell is depicted as a vast, funnel-shaped pit, descending in a series of concentric circles, each representing different types of sin. As Dante descends through the circles of Hell, he encounters sinners who are punished in ways that reflect the nature of their transgressions. This concept, known as *contrapasso* (the idea that punishment mirrors the sin), is central to Dante's moral vision. For example, the lustful are eternally buffeted by winds, symbolising how they were swept away by their passions in life, while the greedy are forced to push heavy weights, reflecting the burden of their material desires.

What makes *Inferno* so compelling is not just the imaginative nature of the punishments, but Dante's portrayal of sin as a self-destructive force. The souls in Hell are not merely victims of divine wrath; they are active participants in their own damnation. Their choices in life have led them to their eternal fates, and their punishments serve as extensions of their own actions and desires. Dante's Hell is a place where the moral and spiritual consequences of sin are laid bare for all to see, and it serves as a powerful reminder of the importance of moral integrity.

Throughout *Inferno*, Dante encounters historical and mythological figures, as well as many of his contemporaries, including political enemies. His personal vendettas against these figures are part of what makes *The Divine Comedy* such a deeply personal and, at times, controversial work. Yet, beyond these personal grievances, Dante's vision of Hell is ultimately about the consequences of moral choices and the inherent justice of the divine order.

Purgatorio: The Path to Redemption

Purgatorio offers a stark contrast to the despair of *Inferno*. While Hell is a place of eternal punishment, Purgatory is a realm of hope and transformation. Souls in Purgatory are not condemned but are undergoing purification so that they may eventually enter Heaven. The mountain of Purgatory, which Dante and Virgil must ascend, is divided into seven terraces, each corresponding to one of the seven deadly sins: pride, envy, wrath, sloth, greed, gluttony, and lust. On each terrace, souls atone for their sins through suffering that reflects their moral failings in life.

Dante's portrayal of Purgatory is deeply compassionate. The souls here are not suffering because of divine wrath, but because they recognise the need to be cleansed of their sins. They willingly endure their purification, understanding that it is a necessary step toward salvation. This idea of spiritual progress is a key theme in *Purgatorio*, and it reflects Dante's belief in the possibility of moral growth and redemption.

In *Purgatorio*, Dante also continues his exploration of human psychology and emotion, particularly through his encounters with the souls undergoing purification. These souls are more relatable than the damned in Hell, as they express regret for their sins and a desire for redemption. Dante's own character undergoes a transformation in this section as well, as he learns from the souls he encounters and begins to shed the pride and anger that characterised his earlier journey through Hell.

Paradiso: The Vision of Divine Love

In *Paradiso*, the final section of the poem, Dante reaches the culmination of his spiritual journey: the vision of God. This section of the poem is the most abstract and theological, as Dante attempts to describe the ineffable beauty and harmony of Heaven. Paradise is depicted as a series of concentric spheres, corresponding to the planets and stars, through which Dante ascends with the help of Beatrice. Each sphere is inhabited by souls who have achieved different levels of virtue, and the higher Dante ascends, the closer he comes to God.

While *Paradiso* lacks the dramatic tension of *Inferno* and *Purgatorio*, it is nevertheless a powerful meditation on divine love and the nature of human happiness. Dante's vision of Heaven is one of perfect order and harmony, where every soul finds its place according to its degree of love and virtue. The souls in Paradise are not jealous of those who occupy higher spheres, for they are fully content in their love of God and their knowledge of the divine will.

At the heart of *Paradiso* is Dante's understanding of divine love as the force that moves the universe. In one of the most famous passages of the poem, Dante describes God as the "Love that moves the sun and the other stars" (*L'amor che move il sole e l'altre stelle*). This vision of a cosmos ordered by love is the ultimate message of *The Divine Comedy*, and it reflects Dante's deep faith in the possibility of redemption and the power of divine grace.

The Universal Appeal of *The Divine Comedy*

One of the reasons *The Divine Comedy* continues to resonate with readers today is its universal themes of sin, redemption, and the search for meaning. Dante's exploration of the human soul's journey toward God is not limited to the religious context in which it was written; it speaks to the fundamental human desire for understanding, purpose, and moral clarity. The moral and ethical questions that Dante raises—about the consequences of our actions, the nature of justice, and the possibility of forgiveness—are as relevant today as they were in the 14th century.

Moreover, *The Divine Comedy* offers readers a richly layered text that can be interpreted on multiple levels. It is a political allegory, a spiritual journey, a psychological exploration, and a philosophical treatise all at once. This complexity makes it a work that rewards careful study and re-reading, as new insights and meanings emerge with each encounter.

Dante's influence on literature, philosophy, and art has been profound and far-reaching. Writers from Geoffrey Chaucer to T.S. Eliot have drawn inspiration from *The Divine Comedy*, and its themes of moral struggle and redemption continue to inspire new interpretations in contemporary culture. The poem's vivid imagery and symbolic depth have also made it a fertile source for visual artists, from Botticelli's illustrations to Gustave Doré's famous engravings.

Overall, Dante Alighieri's *The Divine Comedy* is a work of unparalleled imagination, moral depth, and literary brilliance. It is a poem that speaks to the eternal human concerns of sin, suffering, and redemption, while also offering a deeply personal reflection on the political and spiritual challenges of Dante's own time. Through his journey from the depths of Hell to the heights of Heaven, Dante invites us to reflect on our own moral choices, the nature of justice, and the possibility of salvation.

In this epic poem, Dante's voice transcends the boundaries of time and place, offering us a vision of a universe governed by divine order and love. As we read *The Divine Comedy* today, we are reminded that the questions it raises about the human condition—our capacity for both good and evil, our longing for meaning and redemption—are as relevant now as they were in Dante's time. The journey Dante takes us on is not just his own; it is a journey for every reader who seeks to understand the nature of existence and the possibility of grace.

Preface

Ever since I was young, I have loved reading books. The classic works of literature, which have stood the test of time, held a special place in my heart. However, as much as I wanted to immerse myself in these books, I often found their old and complicated language difficult to understand. Even though I put in the effort, it wasn't always easy to grasp the true meaning of these texts.

This experience made me think about others who might face similar struggles. What about young readers, people for whom English is not their first language, or those who simply find reading difficult? More importantly, what about neurodivergent individuals who may have unique needs when it comes to reading? I wanted to ensure that these timeless stories could be enjoyed by everyone, no matter their background or abilities.

This desire inspired me to start a project aimed at making classic books more accessible, while still keeping their original messages intact. I've created this collection for readers of all ages, with a special focus on neurodivergent individuals. For those who may experience challenges such as ADHD, dyslexia, or autism, reading complex and archaic language can be particularly daunting. By simplifying these texts, I hope to make them more engaging and less overwhelming, allowing neurodivergent readers to fully appreciate the wisdom and beauty these works have to offer.

One such classic is *The Divine Comedy* by Dante Alighieri. This monumental work has shaped literature, philosophy, and even our modern understanding of morality. It explores profound themes such as sin, redemption, and the human quest for meaning. However, Dante's original text, written in the early 14th century, can feel distant and impenetrable for modern readers. The language, filled with references to medieval theology and politics, combined with the poem's intricate structure, can make it challenging to approach for many.

In translating and simplifying *The Divine Comedy*, I've undertaken a task that is both humbling and inspiring. My goal is to bring this masterpiece closer to readers who might be daunted by its original form while preserving the essence of what makes it so powerful, thought-provoking, and timeless. By simplifying the language and making the themes more accessible, I hope to open up Dante's vision of Hell, Purgatory, and Paradise to a wider audience—especially those who may have found it out of reach before.

Through this project, I aim to invite more people into the world of classic literature, making it easier for them to explore and enjoy these great works. By focusing on clarity and simplicity, I hope to create versions of these timeless books that are not only more accessible but also more enjoyable for everyone, including neurodivergent readers. With this edition of *The Divine Comedy*, I want to ensure that all readers can embark on Dante's journey and discover the insights that have resonated with so many across the centuries.

Part 1 Inferno

Chapter 1: The Dark Forest. The Hill of Difficulty. The Panther, the Lion, and the Wolf. Virgil.

Halfway through my life's journey, I found myself in a dark forest. I had lost the clear and straight path. It is hard to explain how wild, rough, and scary this forest was. Just thinking about it fills me with fear again. It was so terrible that death felt like a small thing compared to it. But I will talk about the good I found there, along with everything else I saw.

I don't even remember how I got into that forest. I was so tired and sleepy when I strayed from the right path. But after some time, I reached the base of a mountain. The valley ended there, and it made my heart feel heavy with fear. I looked up and saw the mountain's slopes, lit up by the sun. Its rays gave me some hope and helped guide me.

At that moment, my fear eased a little. It had troubled me through the night, which I had spent in so much distress. I felt like a person who escapes from the sea, breathing hard, and then looks back at the dangerous waters. My soul, still frightened, turned back to look at the dark path I had just come through—a path no living person had ever survived before.

After I rested my tired body, I began climbing the steep slope again. My feet moved carefully, with each step uphill. But just as I started, I saw a panther. It was quick and covered in spotted fur. It blocked my way, refusing to let me pass. I turned back many times, uncertain if I could continue.

It was early morning, and the sun was rising with the stars. These stars had shone on that first beautiful creation when Divine Love set everything into motion. This gave me some hope—the light of the new day, the beauty of the season, and even the panther's colorful fur. But my fear returned when I saw a lion appear.

The lion seemed to be coming right toward me, its head held high. It looked hungry and fierce, so much that the very air around it seemed afraid. Then came a wolf, looking thin and starved. She had a hunger that nothing could satisfy. Many people had lost hope because of her. Seeing her filled me with dread, and I lost all hope of climbing the hill.

I felt like someone who gains wealth, only to lose it all, and then weeps and feels hopeless. That was how I felt because of that restless beast. Slowly, she forced me back to the dark valley, away from the sun. As I rushed down, filled with fear, I saw someone in the distance. He looked like he hadn't spoken in a long time.

When I saw him in that vast desert, I cried out, "Have pity on me, whoever you are—whether you're a man or a spirit!"

He answered, "I am not a man now, but once I was. Both my parents were from Lombardy, and they lived in Mantua. I was born during Julius Caesar's time, though it was late in his rule. I lived in Rome when Augustus was in power, during the days of false gods. I was a poet, and I sang about Aeneas, the noble son of Anchises, who came from Troy after the great city fell in flames."

"But why are you turning back to this misery?" he continued. "Why don't you climb the mountain of joy, the source of every happiness?"

I replied, "Are you the great Virgil, the source of such wise words? I have studied your works with great love. You are my master, the one who showed me the beautiful style of writing that has honored me. See that beast behind me! I have turned back because of her. Please, wise Sage, protect me, for she makes my blood run cold."

"You need to take another path if you want to escape this wild place," he said when he saw my tears. "This beast will not let anyone pass. She harasses and destroys anyone who tries. She is so evil and hungry that no amount of food can satisfy her. In fact, after eating, she becomes even hungrier. She mates with many other creatures, and more will come, until the Greyhound arrives to put an end to her suffering."

He will not live on wealth or the things of this world. Instead, he will live on wisdom, love, and virtue. His nation will rise between Feltro and Feltro. He will be the savior of lowly Italy, the place for which Camilla died. Euryalus, Turnus, and Nisus also fell there. He will hunt this beast through every city until he drives her back to Hell, where she first came from, released by envy.

So, I think it's best for you to follow me. I will be your guide and lead you through the eternal place. There, you will hear cries of despair and see ancient spirits full of sorrow, each one mourning for death a second time. You will also see those who are content within the flames, because they hope to join the blessed souls one day. If you want to reach that place, another soul, more worthy than I, will guide you. When I leave, she will take my place.

The Emperor who rules above does not allow me to guide you all the way because I rebelled against his law. He rules everywhere and sits on his high throne in the city of Heaven. How happy is the one he chooses!

I replied, "Poet, I beg you, by the God you never knew, help me escape this pain and worse. Lead me to where you said, so I may see Saint Peter's gate and the people who suffer so."

Then he moved on, and I followed behind him.

Chapter 2: The Descent. Dante's Protest and Virgil's Appeal. The Intercession of the Three Ladies Benedight.

Day was ending, and the darkened sky freed the animals of the earth from their work. But I, alone, was getting ready to face the struggle, both of the path and the sorrow. I would remember this clearly forever.

"O Muses, O great genius, help me now! O memory, you wrote down what I saw. Here, your true power will be shown!"

I began to speak: "Poet, my guide, look at my strength and decide if I am ready before you lead me on this hard journey. You said that the father of Silvius went to the immortal world while still alive.

If the enemy of all evil was kind, thinking of the great result that would come from it, it doesn't seem impossible to wise men. He was of great Rome and chosen to be a father of her empire in Heaven, where the holy seat of Peter was established. On his journey, he heard things that led to both his success and the papal power.

Later, the Chosen Vessel went there to bring back strength to the Faith, the beginning of the path to salvation. But why am I here? Who allows it? I am not Aeneas. I am not Paul. I do not think I am worthy of this.

So, if I go, I fear I might be making a mistake. You are wise and know more than I can say."

I started to change my mind, just like someone who changes his intention when new thoughts arise. I lost my courage on that dark hillside, thinking deeply. The task that I was so eager to start now seemed impossible.

"If I understand you right," said the noble shade, "your soul is trapped by fear. This fear can often stop people from achieving honor, just like false sights scare a timid animal.

To free you from this fear, I will tell you why I came and what I heard when I first felt sorry for you. I was among those who are in suspense when a beautiful, saintly Lady called to me. She spoke so gently that I begged to follow her command.

Her eyes shone brighter than the stars, and she began to speak softly, with an angelic voice in her own language:

'O kind spirit of Mantua, whose fame still lives in the world and will last as long as the world exists. A friend of mine, who is not a friend of fortune, is blocked on the desert slope. Fear has made him turn back. I worry that he might already be lost, so I have come to help, though I fear it may be too late.'"

Get moving now, and use your elegant speech and whatever is needed to help him. Help him so that I may be comforted. I am Beatrice, and I am sending you. I came from the place where I long to return. Love moved me, and now I must speak. When I stand before my Lord, I will often praise you for your help." She paused, and then I began to speak:

"O noble Lady, you are the one through whom humans surpass all that exists in the heavens. Your command is so precious to me that I would obey it even if it were already too late. You do not need to explain your wish any further. But tell me, why are you not afraid to come down to this place from the vast heaven you wish to return to?"

"If you want to understand," she replied, "I will tell you briefly why I am not afraid to enter here. One should only fear things that can harm others. The rest are not to be feared, as they have no power. God created me in His mercy, so your misery does not affect me, nor can these flames touch me.

There is a kind Lady in Heaven who is sad about your trouble. That is why I am sending you. Her prayers softened the harsh judgment in Heaven. She turned to Lucia and said, 'Your faithful follower is in need of you, and I recommend him to you.' Lucia, who is an enemy of all cruelty, hurried to the place where I was sitting with the ancient Rachel.

'Beatrice,' she said, 'you are the true praise of God. Why do you not help him who loved you so? He left the common crowd for your sake. Do you not hear his cries of sorrow? Do you not see that he is fighting against death by the river where the sea has no power?'

No one in the world was ever as quick to act for their own good or escape their troubles as I was after hearing those words. I came down from my blessed seat, trusting in your noble speech, which brings honor to you and those who hear it.

6

After she spoke to me, she turned away, her eyes shining with tears. This made me hurry to you even more. I came here to help you, as she wished. I have saved you from the wild beast that blocked the short path up the mountain.

So what is it now? Why do you hesitate? Why is such weakness in your heart? Why do you not have the courage you need, knowing that three blessed Ladies are caring for you in Heaven and that my words promise you so much good?"

Just like flowers that droop and close in the cold night but then open again when the sun shines on them, my strength returned. Courage flowed into my heart, and I began to feel brave again.

"O, kind Lady who helped me, and you, who quickly obeyed her words of truth," I said, "your words have filled my heart with a strong desire to continue this journey. I am now ready to follow my first intention. Let's go, for now, we have one single will. You are my leader, my lord, and my master." After I said this, he moved forward, and I followed him into the deep, wild path.

Chapter 3: The Gate of Hell. The Inefficient or Indifferent. Pope Celestine V. The Shores of Acheron. Charon. The Earthquake and the Swoon.

"Through me is the way to the city of sorrow; through me is the way to eternal pain; through me is the way among the lost people. Justice moved my high Creator. Divine power, highest wisdom, and first love created me. Before me, nothing was created except eternal things, and I will last forever. Abandon all hope, you who enter here!"

I saw these words written in dark colors above the top of a gate. "Master, what do they mean?" I asked. He, as someone experienced, replied, "Here, you must let go of all doubts and put an end to all fear. We have come to the place where I told you that you would see the sorrowful people who have lost the good of reason."

Then, after he placed his hand on mine, his cheerful look comforted me. He led me into the hidden things.

There, sighs, cries, and loud wails filled the air, which was without stars. Hearing this, I began to weep right away.

Different languages, strange accents, angry voices, cries of pain, and hoarse shouting mixed with the sound of hands beating together. This noise filled the air, spinning around endlessly in the darkness, like sand caught in a whirlwind. I was filled with horror and said, "Master, what is this sound? Who are these people that seem so beaten down by pain?"

He replied, "These miserable souls are the ones who lived without doing anything good or evil. They are mixed with that group of angels who were neither rebellious nor faithful to God. They only cared about themselves. Heaven rejected them to keep its beauty, and Hell did not accept them because even the damned do not want them."

I asked, "Master, what makes them suffer so much that they cry out in pain?" He answered, "I will tell you briefly. They have no hope of death. Their lives are so pitiful that they envy every other fate. The world will never remember them. Mercy and justice both reject them. Let's not talk about them anymore. Just look at them and move on."

I looked and saw a flag that was spinning around, moving so fast it seemed angry to stop for even a moment. Behind it came a long line of people. There were so many that I never would have believed that death had taken so many souls.

As I watched, I recognized some of them. I saw the shade of the one who made the great refusal out of cowardice. Right away, I understood that these were the souls hated by both God and His enemies.

These worthless souls, who never truly lived, were naked and tormented by swarms of flies and hornets. The insects stung them so badly that blood ran down their faces, mixing with their tears. At their feet, worms gathered to drink this mixture.

I looked farther and saw people by the bank of a great river. I asked, "Master, please tell me who these are, and what rule makes them so ready to cross over. I can barely see them in the dim light."

He replied, "You will learn everything once we reach the gloomy shore of the Acheron River." Ashamed of my questions, I looked down, afraid that my words might have annoyed him. I stayed silent until we got to the river.

Suddenly, I saw an old man coming toward us in a boat. His hair was white with age, and he shouted, "Woe to you, wicked souls! Give up hope of ever seeing Heaven! I am here to take you to the other shore, to the eternal darkness of heat and frost. And you, living soul," he pointed at me, "get away from these dead people!"

When he saw that I didn't move, he said, "You will not cross here. You must take another path and another boat. A lighter vessel will carry you."

But my guide spoke to him, "Do not trouble yourself, Charon. This is willed by the one who has the power to do so. Do not question it further."

At this, the old ferryman's fiery eyes calmed. He had circles of flame around his eyes, but his anger quieted. Meanwhile, all the souls, who were tired and naked, turned pale and gnashed their teeth when they heard his harsh words. They cursed God, their parents, the human race, the time, the place, and even their birth.

Then, weeping bitterly, they moved toward the cursed shore that waits for everyone who does not fear God. Charon, the demon with fiery eyes, gathered them together, hitting anyone who lagged behind with his oar.

Like leaves falling in autumn, one after another, until the tree is bare, these souls threw themselves from the shore, one by one, at Charon's signal, like birds obeying a call. They crossed the dark water. Before they even reached the other side, a new group was already gathering on this side.

"My son," my kind master said to me, "all those who die in God's wrath come here from every land. They are eager to cross the river because divine justice drives them, turning their fear into desire. No good soul ever comes this way. So, if Charon complains about you, now you know why."

After he finished speaking, the dark plain shook so violently that I still tremble with fear at the memory. The land of tears released a blast of wind and flashed a bright red light. It overwhelmed my senses, and I fell as if I were in a deep sleep.

Chapter 4: The First Circle, Limbo: Virtuous Pagans and the Unbaptized. The Four Poets: Homer, Horace, Ovid, and Lucan. The Noble Castle of Philosophy.

A loud thunder broke through my deep sleep, waking me up suddenly, like someone being shaken awake. I quickly stood up and looked around, trying to understand where I was. I realized I was at the edge of a dark and sorrowful valley, filled with the sound of endless cries. It was deep, foggy, and so dark that I couldn't see anything in its depths.

"Let's go down into this dark world," the Poet said. He was very pale. "I will go first, and you will follow." Noticing how pale he looked, I asked, "How can I go if you are scared? You're usually the one who comforts me."

He replied, "The sadness of the people here shows on my face. What you see is pity, not fear. Let's move on; we have a long journey ahead." With that, he led me into the first circle around the abyss.

It seemed quiet here, with no cries, only soft sighs that made the air tremble. These sighs came from sadness without pain, from a crowd of people: men, women, and children.

My guide said to me, "You may wonder who these spirits are. Before we go further, I want you to know that they did not sin. If they had any merit, it wasn't enough, because they were not baptized, which is the gateway to the Faith you believe in. If they lived before Christianity, they didn't worship God in the right way. I am among them. For these shortcomings, and not for any other fault, we are lost. Our only punishment is that we live without hope, though we still have desire."

Hearing this made my heart heavy with grief. I knew many people of great worth who were in this Limbo.

"Tell me, Master," I began, wanting to be certain about the Faith that overcomes all errors, "Has anyone ever left here by their own merit or by someone else's, who later became blessed?"

He understood my hidden question and replied, "I was new in this place when I saw a Mighty One come here, crowned with victory. He took the souls of the first man, Adam, his son Abel, Noah, Moses the lawgiver, Abraham the patriarch, King David, Israel with his father and children,

Rachel, for whom he worked so much, and many others. He made them blessed. You must know that before these souls, no others were ever saved."

We continued walking through the forest crowded with ghosts. We had not gone far from the summit when I saw a light that brightened a large area of the darkness. We were still a little distance from it, but I could make out that noble people were there.

"Who are these," I asked, "who are honored so much that they stand apart from the rest?"

He replied, "They are honored because their names are still remembered with respect in the world. This grace in Heaven gives them this special place." Just then, I heard a voice say, "All honor to the greatest Poet! His shade returns among us."

After the voice stopped, I saw four mighty shades coming toward us. They did not look sad or joyful. My kind guide said to me, "See the one with the sword in his hand who walks in front of the three? He is their leader. That is Homer, the greatest Poet. The next is Horace, the satirist. The third is Ovid, and the last is Lucan. They honor me because I share the title the voice just proclaimed."

I watched these great poets, who made up the noble group of the highest poet, Homer, who soars above the others like an eagle. They spoke among themselves for a while, then turned to me with a greeting. My guide smiled at this. They honored me even more by making me part of their group, so I became the sixth among such wise poets.

We walked toward the light, speaking of things that should remain unspoken, as those do who belong to this place. We came to the base of a noble castle, surrounded by seven high walls and a beautiful stream that served as a defense. We crossed over it as if it were solid ground. Passing through seven gates, I entered a green meadow with the wise sages.

There were people there with calm, serious expressions. They had great authority in their looks and spoke rarely, and even then, only in gentle voices. We moved to one side into an open, well-lit area where I could see them all clearly.

12

Across from us, on the green grass, I saw the mighty spirits. I felt honored just to look at them. I saw Electra with many companions, including Hector and Aeneas. There was Caesar, dressed in armor with eyes like a hawk. On the other side, I saw Camilla and Penthesilea. I also saw King Latinus sitting with his daughter Lavinia. I saw Brutus, who drove out Tarquin, and others like Lucretia, Julia, Marcia, and Cornelia. Saladin stood alone, apart from the rest.

After I looked up for a moment, I saw the Master of all who know, sitting with his group of philosophers. They all looked up to him and honored him. I saw both Socrates and Plato standing close to him, along with others like Democritus, who believed the world was shaped by chance, and philosophers like Diogenes, Anaxagoras, Thales, Zeno, Empedocles, and Heraclitus.

I also saw Dioscorides, who was a great collector of knowledge, as well as Orpheus, Tully, Livy, and the moral Seneca. Euclid, the master of geometry, was there, along with Ptolemy, Galen, Hippocrates, Avicenna, and Averroes, who wrote the famous commentary.

There were many others, but I can't name them all because our journey pushes me forward. The company of six poets divided into two groups. My wise guide led me away from this quiet place to an area where the air trembled, and we entered a place where no light shone.

Chapter 5: The Second Circle: The Wanton. Minos. The Infernal Hurricane. Francesca da Rimini.

We left the first circle and descended into the second, which was smaller but filled with more sorrow. Here, Minos stood, looking frightening as he snarled. He judged each soul that came to him, deciding where in Hell they should go.

When an evil soul comes before him, it confesses everything. Minos then wraps his tail around himself as many times as the level he wants to send the soul down. Many souls stand before him, waiting for their turn. They come forward, speak, listen, and then are thrown down.

When Minos saw me, he said, "You, who have come to this place of pain, be careful how you enter and who you trust. Don't be fooled by the size of the entrance."

But my guide replied, "Why do you shout? Do not stop him. His journey is meant to be. It is willed by the one who has the power to make it so. Do not ask further questions."

Now, the sad cries grew louder as we came to a place with no light. It roared like the sea during a storm, clashing with strong winds. This endless hurricane blew the souls around in chaos. It whirled and struck them, giving them no peace.

When they reached the edge of the storm, they cried out and wailed, cursing the power that condemned them. I understood that this torment was for those who let their desires rule over reason.

Just like starlings flying together in the cold season, the wind drove these souls here, there, up, and down. They had no hope of rest or even less pain. As cranes fly in long lines, singing as they go, I saw shadows of souls carried by the wind, crying out in sorrow.

I asked, "Master, who are these people punished by the dark wind?"

He answered, "The first one you want to know about was an empress who spoke many languages. She was so devoted to lust that she made it legal to excuse her own actions. She is Semiramis. Next is Dido, who killed herself for love and broke her promise to the ashes of Sychaeus. And then, there is Cleopatra, who lived in indulgence."

I also saw Helen, for whom so many years of misery happened. I saw Achilles, who fought against love at the end of his life. I saw Paris, Tristan, and more than a thousand others, whom my guide pointed out to me, all separated from life by love.

After listening to my guide name these women and knights of the past, I felt deep pity and was almost overwhelmed. I said, "Poet, I want to speak with those two who seem to float lightly on the wind as they move together."

He replied, "You'll see when they come closer. Then, call to them in the name of love, which leads them, and they will come to you."

As soon as the wind carried them nearer, I raised my voice, "O weary souls, come speak with us if no one stops you!"

Like doves called by their desire, flying with open wings to their nest, they came to us through the dark air. The power of my words brought them to us.

"O kind and gracious living soul," one of them said, "you travel through the purple air to visit us, who stained the world with our sins. If the King of the Universe were our friend, we would pray for your peace, since you feel pity for our twisted fate. Whatever you wish to hear or speak of, we will do so, as long as the wind is calm, as it is now."

"I was born in a city by the sea, where the river Po meets the ocean. Love, which quickly takes hold of a gentle heart, seized this man for my beauty, which was taken from me. And even now, it pains me. Love, which does not let anyone escape its power, captured me with the pleasure of this man so strongly that, as you see, it has not left me. Love led us to one death. The one who took our lives will be punished in the lowest circle of Hell."

When I heard these tormented souls, I bowed my head, filled with sadness, until my guide asked, "What are you thinking?"

I replied, "Oh, how many sweet thoughts and desires led them to such a painful end!" Then, I turned to the souls and spoke, "Your suffering, Francesca, makes me so sad that it brings me to tears. But tell me, during those moments of sweet sighs, how did love allow you to recognize your desires?"

She answered, "There is no greater sorrow than to remember happy times during misery, as your guide knows well. But if you want to know the first roots of our love, I will tell you, even though it brings tears.

One day, we were reading for our pleasure about Lancelot and how love conquered him. We were alone and had no reason to fear. Many times, our eyes met as we read, and our faces turned pale. But one moment overcame us. When we read how the longed-for smile was kissed by such a noble lover, this man, who will never be separated from me, kissed me on the mouth, trembling. The book and its writer were like a go-between for us. That day, we read no further."

While she spoke, the other spirit wept so bitterly that I fainted from pity. I fell to the ground as if I were a dead body.

Chapter 6: The Third Circle: The Gluttonous. Cerberus. The Eternal Rain. Ciacco. Florence.

When I woke up from my faint, caused by the sadness of those two souls, I saw new torments and new suffering around me. No matter where I turned or looked, I was surrounded by misery.

I had entered the third circle, a place of endless, cursed, cold, and heavy rain. The rain was mixed with huge hail, dark water, and snow that fell through the black air. The ground that absorbed it became foul.

Cerberus, a cruel and monstrous creature with three heads, barked like a dog over the souls buried here. His eyes were red, his beard was black and greasy, and his belly was large. His hands had claws that tore, skinned, and ripped the souls apart. The rain forced them to howl like dogs. They tried to cover themselves, one side shielding the other. The damned souls constantly turned, seeking shelter.

When Cerberus saw us, he opened his mouths and showed his fangs. Not a single part of him was still. My guide bent down, picked up some earth with his hands, and threw it into the creature's hungry mouths. Like a dog that quiets down when chewing on its food, Cerberus became calm, focusing only on devouring the dirt.

We walked past the shadows, stepping on their empty forms. They all lay flat on the ground, except for one, who sat up when he saw us pass by.

"O you who are being led through this Hell," he said to me, "remember me if you can. You were made before I was unmade."

I replied, "Your suffering may have erased you from my memory, so it seems I do not know you. But tell me, who are you, in such a terrible place and punishment? There may be worse sufferings, but none as displeasing as this."

He answered, "Your city, which is so full of envy that it spills over, held me in life. You citizens called me Ciacco. Because of the sin of gluttony, I am battered by this rain, as you see. And I am not the only one. All these souls here suffer the same penalty for the same sin."

I replied, "Ciacco, your misery saddens me and makes me want to weep. But tell me, if you know, what will happen to the people of our divided city? Is there anyone just left, and why has so much discord taken over it?"

He replied, "After long struggles, they will turn to bloodshed. The rural party will drive the other out with great violence."

After that, this one shall fall within three days, and the other shall rise by the power of the one who is now on the coast. The new leader will hold his head high for a long time, keeping the other under heavy burdens, no matter how much they cry and protest.

There are two just people in the city, but they are not understood. Envy, arrogance, and greed are the three sparks that have set all hearts on fire."

He finished speaking with tears in his eyes. I said to him, "I want to ask you more and hear you speak again. Tell me about Farinata and Tegghiaio, who were once so honorable, and about Jacopo Rusticucci, Arrigo, and Mosca, and others who focused on good deeds. Where are they now? Are they blessed in Heaven or suffering in Hell?"

He replied, "They are among the darker souls. They are weighed down by different sins at the very bottom of Hell. If you go deep enough, you will see them. But when you return to the world above, please remind others of me. I have no more to say, and no more answers to give."

Then he looked at me with straight eyes, glanced away, and bowed his head. After that, he fell flat, just like the other blind souls.

My guide then said to me, "He will not wake up again until the sound of the angelic trumpet. When the great enemy arrives, each soul will find its dark grave, take back its body, and hear the echoing cries for eternity."

We continued walking slowly over the mixture of shadows and rain, touching on the topic of life after death. I asked, "Master, will these torments get worse after the final judgment, or will they lessen, or remain the same?"

He replied, "Remember your teachings: as things become more perfect, they feel more joy and pain. Although these souls can never reach true perfection, they will feel more suffering in the future."

We walked in a circle, talking about many things that I do not repeat here. We came to the spot where the descent began, and there we found Plutus, the great enemy.

Chapter 7: The Fourth Circle: The Avaricious and the Prodigal. Plutus. Fortune and her Wheel. The Fifth Circle: The Irascible and the Sullen. Styx.

"Pape Satan, Pape Satan, Aleppe!" Plutus shouted in his clucking voice. My wise guide, who knew everything, said to me, "Do not be afraid. Whatever power he has will not stop us from going down this cliff."

Then he turned to the bloated creature and said, "Be silent, you cursed wolf! Let your anger consume you. Our journey is not without cause; it is willed from above, where Michael took revenge on the proud."

Just like sails collapsing when the mast breaks, Plutus fell to the ground.

We then descended into the fourth circle, moving along the sad shore that contains all the suffering of the universe. "Oh, God's justice! Who piles up so many new torments and sufferings? Why does our sin bring so much destruction?" I wondered.

Here, people were rolling huge weights with their chests. They moved in opposite directions, and when they collided, they turned around and rolled back, shouting, "Why do you hoard?" and "Why do you waste?"

They kept moving around the dark circle, returning to the opposite side and shouting their insults. When each reached their side, they turned and began their struggle again. Seeing this, my heart was pierced with sadness. I asked, "Master, who are these people, and were they all clerics, with shaved heads on the left side?"

He replied, "They were foolish in their first lives, so they wasted or hoarded without measure. You can hear it in their angry shouts when they reach the two points where their opposite sins separate them. The ones with shaved heads were clerics, including popes and cardinals, who let greed rule them."

I asked, "Master, should I not recognize some of them who had these vices?"

He answered, "You are thinking in vain. The lives they led have made them so dim that they cannot be recognized now. They will forever return to these clashes. When they rise again from their graves, some will have clenched fists, and others will have their hair shaved. Their poor use of wealth on earth has brought them to this pointless fight. No words can fully describe it."

He continued, "Now you can see, my son, how temporary the riches of Fortune are, which cause people to fight. All the gold beneath the moon could never give even one of these souls a moment's rest."

"Master," I said, "tell me, what is this Fortune you speak of, who controls the world's wealth?"

He replied, "Oh, foolish creatures! How much ignorance surrounds you! I will now explain my thoughts about her."

He who knows everything, in His wisdom, created the heavens and gave them guides to ensure every part shines equally. In the same way, He made Fortune a ruler over earthly things, so that wealth and power move from one people to another, from one family to another, beyond human control.

Because of this, one nation will rise while another falls, following her hidden decisions, which are as secret as a snake in the grass. Human knowledge has no power over her; she plans, judges, and carries out her rule like the other heavenly beings. Her changes never stop, and necessity forces her to act quickly. She moves things in turns without delay.

Fortune is often cursed by those who should praise her. They blame her unfairly, giving her a bad name. But she is happy and doesn't hear their insults. Among the other joyful heavenly creatures, she turns her wheel, rejoicing in her work.

"Now, let's go down to even greater suffering," my guide said. "The stars that were rising when we started are now setting, and we must not waste time."

We crossed the circle to the other side, near a spring that boiled and flowed into a dark, narrow ditch. The water was darker than black, and we followed it down a rough path. This sad stream forms a marsh called Styx when it reaches the base of the grim, gray shores.

I looked and saw people covered in mud. They were all naked, with angry expressions. They were not just hitting each other with their hands, but also with their heads, chests, and feet. They tore at each other with their teeth.

My guide said, "Look, my son, at the souls overcome by anger. But I also want you to know that under the water are others who sigh and make the water bubble, as you can see wherever you look."

These souls trapped in the mud said, "We were sullen in the bright, sunny world, keeping our anger inside. Now, we are stuck in this dark mire." They muttered this as they choked on the words, unable to speak them clearly.

We walked around the filthy swamp, staying on a path between the dry bank and the murky water. I kept my eyes on those who were stuck in the mud. Eventually, we reached the base of a tower.

Chapter 8: Phlegyas. Filippo Argenti. The Gates of the City of Dis.

Before we arrived at the tower, we looked up at its top and saw two small flames. From a distance, another flame answered them, though it was so far away it was hard to see.

I turned to my guide and asked, "What does this signal mean, and who is making it?"

He replied, "Soon you will see what is expected to come across the muddy waters, unless the fog hides it."

No arrow ever flew through the air as fast as I then saw a small boat speeding toward us, guided by a single pilot who shouted, "Have you come, wicked soul?"

"Phlegyas, you shout in vain this time," said my guide. "You won't have us any longer than it takes to cross this swamp."

Phlegyas reacted like someone who just realized they have been tricked and is filled with rage. My guide stepped into the boat and then motioned for me to follow. Only when I stepped in did it seem fully loaded.

As soon as we were on board, the boat started moving, cutting through more water than it usually does with others. While we were moving along the dark channel, a figure covered in mud rose in front of me and asked, "Who are you to come here before your time?"

I replied, "Even though I have come, I am not staying. But who are you, so filthy and full of sorrow?" He answered, "You can see, I am one who weeps."

I replied, "Then keep weeping and wailing, cursed soul. I know who you are, even though you are covered in filth."

He stretched out his hands toward the boat, but my guide pushed him back, saying, "Away with you, you dog!"

Then, my guide put his arms around my neck, kissed my face, and said, "Blessed is the woman who bore you. That soul you just spoke to was an arrogant person in life. No goodness remains to honor his memory, so his spirit is filled with fury here.

How many people on earth are seen as great kings, but here they will be like pigs in the mud, leaving behind a legacy of shame!"

"Master," I said, "I would be very pleased if I could see him thrown into this swamp before we leave this lake."

He replied, "Before we reach the shore, you shall be satisfied. It is right for you to enjoy this desire."

Soon after, I saw the spirits in the mud turn on Filippo Argenti, attacking him fiercely. Even now, I thank God for witnessing that. They all screamed, "Get him, Filippo Argenti!" The angry Florentine spirit turned on himself, biting his own flesh in rage.

We left him there and moved on. I'll say no more about him. But soon, I heard cries that made me focus and open my eyes wide.

My guide said, "Now, my son, we are approaching the city of Dis. Here, you'll find its grave citizens and large crowds."

I replied, "Master, I can already see its towers in the valley. They glow red, as if they were burning."

He answered, "That's because the eternal fire inside makes them glow red. That's how it looks here in the depths of Hell."

We reached the deep moats surrounding the sorrowful city. The walls looked as if they were made of iron. We circled the area before finding a place where our boatman shouted, "Get out here; this is the entrance!"

I saw more than a thousand spirits near the gates. They had fallen from Heaven, and they angrily asked, "Who is this who walks through the realm of the dead while still alive?"

My guide made a secret gesture, signaling that he wanted to speak with them privately. They calmed down a bit and then said, "You, come alone! Let the one who entered these lands so boldly go back the way he came. Let him try if he can; you shall stay here since you've led him through these dark regions."

Imagine, dear reader, how terrified I was at those cursed words. I truly thought I would never return to the world above.

I cried out, "O my dear guide! You have saved me from danger many times before. Don't leave me now. If we cannot go further, let's quickly retrace our steps together."

The guide who had brought me this far said, "Do not be afraid. No one can take our passage from us. It is willed by a Higher Power. Wait here and let your spirit find hope again. I will not leave you in this world below."

With that, he moved forward and left me there. I was filled with doubt, as conflicting thoughts of 'yes' and 'no' fought in my mind.

I could not hear what he said to them, but it wasn't long before they ran back inside. Then they shut the gates in my guide's face. He turned back to me slowly, his steps heavy, his head down, and his boldness gone.

With a sigh, he said, "Who has denied me entry to these sorrowful houses?" Then, looking at me, he added, "Do not fear because I'm angry. I will win this fight, no matter what they try to do. Their arrogance is nothing new. They've shown it before at a less hidden gate, which still remains unlocked. You saw the warning written on it. Now, someone is coming down the steep path from above to open this city for us."

Chapter 9: The Furies and Medusa. The Angel. The City of Dis. The Sixth Circle: Heresiarchs.

The fear that had turned my face pale earlier disappeared when I saw my guide's determination. He stood still, like a person listening carefully, because his eyes couldn't see far through the thick fog and darkness.

"We must win this fight," he began. "Otherwise..." He paused, then added, "I wish someone would arrive to help us!"

I understood that he was worried, even though he tried to cover it up with his words. This only made me more afraid, as I imagined the worst outcome.

I asked, "Does anyone ever come down to this bottom part of Hell from the first circle, where hope is lost but pain is not as harsh?"

He replied, "It rarely happens that someone makes this journey. Once, the cruel witch Erictho called me to come down here to summon a spirit from the Circle of Judas—the lowest and darkest part of Hell, farthest from the heavens above. I know the way well, so don't worry. This foul-smelling swamp surrounds the city of sorrow, which we cannot enter without a fight."

He continued speaking, but I didn't catch everything he said. My eyes were fixed on the tall tower with its flaming top. In that moment, I saw three terrifying figures rise up. They were the Furies, stained with blood, looking like women but with snakes wrapped around their heads.

My guide, who knew these servants of the Queen of Eternal Sadness, said to me, "Look, those are the Furies. The one on the left is Megaera, the one on the right is Alecto, and the one in the middle is Tisiphone."

Each of them tore at their chests with their nails, beating themselves, and screaming so loudly that I clung to my guide in fear.

"Call Medusa! Let's turn him to stone!" they shouted, looking down at me. "We should have punished Theseus for his attack!"

My guide quickly turned me around, saying, "Close your eyes! If you look at the Gorgon, you will never return to the surface." He covered my eyes with his hands to make sure I couldn't see.

O you with clear minds, pay attention to the meaning hidden beneath these mysterious words!

Now, a loud noise came across the dark waters, so terrifying that both sides of the riverbank trembled. It was like a wild wind, caused by clashing hot and cold air, that rips through forests, breaking branches, and scattering dust. It drives away animals and shepherds as it moves.

My guide uncovered my eyes and said, "Look toward that old foam over there, where the smoke is thickest."

I looked, and just like frogs scatter across the water when a snake appears, I saw more than a thousand souls fleeing from a figure walking over the Styx. His feet stayed dry as he walked on the surface.

He waved his left hand to push the foul air away from his face, and that seemed to be the only effort he made. I quickly realized he was sent from Heaven. I turned to my guide, who signaled for me to stay quiet and show respect.

This figure reached the gates of the city and opened them with a small rod; there was no resistance.

"O you who are banished from Heaven!" he called out at the threshold. "Where does this arrogance come from? Why do you fight against a will that you can't escape? This has only increased your suffering many times over. Why do you try to defy fate?

Remember Cerberus, who still has scars on his chin and throat!"

Then he turned back along the muddy path, without speaking to us, looking like someone with concerns far more serious than those in front of him. Confident from his words, we continued toward the city.

We entered without any trouble. Curious to see what kind of place this was, I looked around. Inside, I saw a vast plain filled with suffering and torment.

It was like the cemetery at Arles, where the Rhone River flows, or the one near Pola by the Quarnaro, but here, it was far worse. The ground was covered with tombs, and flames scattered between them, making the stone graves so hot that they looked like red-hot iron.

The lids of all the tombs were lifted, and from each came dreadful cries, sounding like those in deep agony.

I asked my guide, "Who are these people in these tombs, crying out in such pain?"

He answered, "These are the heretics, along with their followers. The tombs are filled with many more souls than you think. Here, they are buried with others who shared their beliefs, and the heat varies depending on their guilt."

We turned right, moving between the tormenting flames and the high walls of the city.

Chapter 10: Farinata and Cavalcante de' Cavalcanti. Discourse on the Knowledge of the Damned.

We continued along a narrow path between the walls of the city and the suffering souls. I followed behind my guide.

"O great power that leads me through these circles of the damned," I began, "please answer my questions and satisfy my curiosity. These souls lying in their tombs, can we see them? The covers are all open, and no one seems to guard them."

He replied, "They will be sealed again when the souls return from the Valley of Jehoshaphat, bringing their bodies back from the world above. This cemetery belongs to Epicurus and his followers, who believed that the soul dies with the body. Soon, you will get the answers to your questions, including the one you haven't yet asked."

I said, "Good guide, I have not spoken everything on my mind because I want to speak less. But you seem to know this already."

Then, suddenly, a voice came from one of the tombs, "O Tuscan, who walks through this city of fire while still alive, please stop here a moment. Your words show you are from my noble homeland, which I may have treated harshly."

The voice startled me, and I stepped closer to my guide in fear. He said to me, "Turn around and look. That is Farinata, who has risen from the grave. You will see him from the waist up."

I fixed my eyes on the speaker. He stood tall with his chest and head held high, as if he had no fear of Hell itself.

My guide moved me closer, saying, "Speak clearly to him now."

When I reached the foot of his tomb, he looked me over and, with some disdain, asked, "Who were your ancestors?"

Willing to answer, I told him everything about my family. He raised his eyebrows slightly and said, "They were fierce enemies to me and my forefathers. Twice, I scattered them from the city."

I replied, "They returned both times, though your side never learned that skill."

Another spirit, who had risen to his knees beside Farinata, looked around, searching to see if anyone was with me. When his suspicions faded, he asked, weeping, "If you are traveling through this blind prison by your intellect, where is my son? Why isn't he with you?"

I answered, "I am not here by my own will. He who waits over there leads me. Your son, Guido, may have treated him with disdain."

Hearing my words and the punishment he faced, I realized who he was. My answer made him tremble.

He cried out, "You said, 'had'? Is he not alive? Does he no longer see the sweet light of day?"

When I hesitated to reply, he fell back into his tomb and did not appear again.

Farinata, who had kept his proud stance, remained still, not moving his neck or turning away.

Continuing his speech, he said, "If they have not learned that lesson correctly, it torments me more than this bed of fire. Before the Lady who reigns here rises fifty times again, you will know how serious that is.

Since you will return to the world above, tell me why my people face such cruelty in your city's laws?"

I answered, "It's because of the bloodshed at the Arbia River. That battle is the reason prayers are still offered in our temples."

He sighed and shook his head. "I was not alone there," he replied, "nor did I act without reason. But I was the only one who stood openly against the destruction of Florence when others agreed to it."

"Hoping that your descendants find peace," I said, "please explain something that confuses me. It seems, if I heard you correctly, that you can see the future, but not the present. Is that true?"

"We see the future," he replied, "as people with weak eyesight see things far away. This much is granted to us by the Supreme Ruler. But when events get closer or happen in the present, we know nothing unless someone brings us the news. From the moment the future is closed to us, our knowledge will be completely dead."

Feeling sorry for not understanding this sooner, I said, "Please tell that fallen soul that his son is still among the living. If I was silent before, it was because I was already thinking about what you've now explained to me."

By this point, my guide was calling me back, so I urgently asked the spirit to tell me who else was with him.

He replied, "I lie here with more than a thousand others. Within these tombs are Emperor Frederick II and the Cardinal. I won't mention the rest."

With that, he disappeared. I turned back to my guide, still thinking about what he had said, which seemed troubling to me. As we walked, my guide asked, "Why are you so confused?" I explained my thoughts to him.

"Remember what you have learned here," the wise guide instructed, raising his finger. "When you stand before her whose eyes see all, she will reveal the path of your life."

He then turned to the left, and we left the wall, heading toward the center. We walked down a path that led into a valley, where a foul stench filled the air.

Chapter 11: The Broken Rocks. Pope Anastasius. General Description of the Inferno and its Divisions.

On the edge of a steep cliff, surrounded by broken rocks in a circle, we encountered an even worse crowd of souls. The foul stench rising from the deep abyss forced us to step back and take cover behind a large tomb. On the tomb was an inscription that read, "Here lies Pope Anastasius, who was led astray by Photinus."

"We need to go slowly here," my guide said, "so that we can get used to the awful smell. Then, it won't bother us as much."

I replied, "Can we do something to pass the time while we wait?" He answered, "I am already thinking of that."

"My son," he began, "inside these rocks are three smaller circles, layered like the ones we just passed. They are full of cursed souls. To help you understand what you will see, I'll explain why they are here.

All forms of evil that Heaven hates involve harm to others, either through violence or deceit. Since deceit is a uniquely human trait, it angers God the most, and those who practice it suffer in the lowest circle of Hell.

The first circle we will enter punishes the violent. Violence can be committed against three targets: God, others, and oneself. This circle is divided into three sections accordingly.

You can harm others or their property, which includes murder, assault, theft, arson, and extortion. This first section punishes murderers, thieves, and those who harm others unjustly.

One can also harm oneself or one's own belongings. Those who do this, such as suicides and wasters of property, find no comfort here. They must remain in the second section, filled with regret for their actions.

Violence against God includes blasphemy, denying His existence, and scorning Nature and its gifts. This third and smallest section punishes those who speak against God, including those from Sodom and Cahors.

Fraud, on the other hand, affects both those who trust you and those who don't. The first type breaks only natural bonds of love and honesty, so the second circle of Hell holds hypocrites, flatterers, magicians, falsifiers, thieves, and other deceivers.

The second type, the worst, breaks trust and betrays those who rely on it. This deepest circle of Hell is where Satan sits, and it consumes those who betray others."

I said, "Master, your explanation is clear and helps me understand this terrible place and those within it."

"But tell me," I said, "those souls in the swampy waters, who are blown around by the wind and beaten by the rain, and who argue with such bitter words—why are they outside the red city if God is angry with them? And if He isn't, why do they suffer like this?"

He replied, "Why does your mind wander from what it usually understands? Where is your thinking focused? Don't you remember what your Ethics discusses about the three conditions Heaven cannot tolerate—Incontinence, Malice, and Insane Bestiality? And how Incontinence offends God less and attracts less blame?

If you understand this point and recall who the souls are that suffer outside the city, you will see why they are separated from these worse sinners and why divine justice punishes them less harshly."

"O guiding Sun, you clear up my confusion so well that I almost enjoy doubting as much as knowing! But please go back for a moment," I said, "and explain how usury offends divine goodness."

"Philosophy," he answered, "shows how Nature follows the divine intellect and its art. If you study your Physics, you will see that human work follows Nature as closely as a student follows a teacher. Your work, then, is like God's grandchild.

Genesis tells us that humans should earn their lives and grow through honest work. But the usurer takes another path, putting his hope in money instead. By doing this, he scorns both Nature and its follower, human work.

Now, let's keep moving, for the Fish are trembling on the horizon, and the Wain lies across the northwest. We have a long way down to go."

Chapter 12: The Minotaur. The Seventh Circle: The Violent. The River Phlegethon. The Violent against their Neighbours. The Centaurs. Tyrants.

The place where we reached the edge of the cliff was steep and rugged. It was so rough that anyone would hesitate to descend.

It looked like the landslide that struck the side of the Adige River near Trent, caused either by an earthquake or the natural collapse of the mountain. The rock shattered from the top down to the plain, forming a path for anyone trying to cross.

The descent of this ravine was similar. There, at the edge of the broken chasm, lay the infamous creature from Crete—the Minotaur, born from the false cow. When he saw us, he bit himself in rage, just like someone overcome by anger.

My guide shouted at him, "Do you think this is Theseus, the Duke of Athens, who killed you in the world above? Go away, beast! This man has not come here because of your sister. He is here to see your punishments."

Like a bull that breaks free after receiving a fatal blow, stumbling and staggering, the Minotaur reacted the same way. My guide called out, "Quick! Run to the path while he's distracted. It's best to descend now!"

We began our descent over the pile of stones. They shifted under my feet from the weight they were not used to carrying.

I walked with deep thought, and my guide said, "You're thinking about this landslide, which is guarded by that beast I just silenced. Let me explain. The last time I came down to the lower Hell, this cliff had not yet collapsed.

But not long before He came, who carried away the great prize from Dis, the deep and dreadful valley shook so violently that I thought the whole universe was falling into chaos. At that moment, this ancient rock split here and in other places.

Now, look below, for the river of blood draws near. In it boil all those who used violence to harm others."

O blind greed! O insane rage! These things push us forward in our short lives, only to throw us into eternal suffering.

I saw a wide, bow-shaped ditch, surrounding the plain as my guide had described. Along its inner edge, centaurs ran in a line, holding bows and arrows, just like they did when hunting in the world above.

When they saw us approaching, they stopped. Three of them came forward, carrying their bows and arrows. One called out from a distance, "Why are you coming down this slope? Speak, or I'll draw my bow!"

My guide answered, "We will give our answer to Chiron, who stands among you. Your rashness has always been your downfall."

Then he touched me and said, "This one is Nessus, who died for the lovely Dejanira and took his revenge on himself. The one staring at his chest is the great Chiron, who taught Achilles. The other is Pholus, known for his wrath.

Thousands of them patrol the moat, shooting arrows at any soul that rises too far out of the blood."

We approached the fast-moving creatures. Chiron took an arrow and used the notch to push his beard back.

After opening his large mouth, Chiron said to his companions, "Do you notice that whatever he touches moves? Dead men's feet do not do that."

My guide, who had now reached Chiron's chest, where the human and horse forms meet, replied, "Yes, he is alive, and I am here to guide him through this dark valley. We are here because we have to be, not because we want to be. Someone who left singing 'Hallelujah' gave me this task. He is not a thief, nor am I a spirit of darkness.

But by the power that allows me to travel through this wild place, please give us one of your own to show us the way across the river and to carry him on his back. He is not a spirit and cannot walk on air."

Chiron turned to Nessus, who was standing nearby, and said, "Go with them, guide them, and warn them if you meet any other bands."

With Nessus as our guide, we moved along the edge of the boiling red river, where those trapped inside cried out in pain. I saw people sunk in the blood up to their eyebrows. Nessus said, "These are tyrants who shed blood and stole. Here they suffer for their cruel deeds. This is Alexander and the fierce Dionysius, who brought years of suffering to Sicily. The one with the black hair is Azzolino, and the blond one is Obizzo of Este, who was killed by his own stepson."

I turned to look at my guide, and he said, "Let Nessus lead, and I will follow behind you."

A little farther on, Nessus stopped above a group of souls who were only visible from the neck up, sticking out of the boiling river. He pointed to one and said, "That one split open the heart of a man who is still honored in London."

Then I saw other souls lifting their heads and chests out of the river. I recognized many of them. The river gradually became shallower until it only covered their feet. This was where we crossed over to the other side.

"As you see the river here becoming shallower," Nessus said, "know that it continues to get shallower on the other side until it reaches the place where tyrants must suffer. Divine justice punishes them here. It tortures Attila, who was a scourge on earth, along with Pyrrhus and Sextus. It also draws tears from Rinier da Corneto and Rinier Pazzo, who caused much bloodshed on the highways."

Then Nessus turned around and crossed back over the river.

Chapter 13: The Wood of Thorns. The Harpies. The Violent against themselves. Suicides. Pier della Vigna. Lano and Jacopo da Sant' Andrea.

Nessus had not yet reached the other side when we entered a thick forest. There was no path through it. The trees were not green but dark and twisted. The branches were gnarled and tangled, covered in sharp thorns instead of leaves or fruit.

Even the wild areas between Cecina and Corneto, avoided by farmers, were not as dense as this. Here, the dreadful Harpies made their nests. These creatures once drove the Trojans from the Strophades, warning them of disaster. They had broad wings, human faces, clawed feet, and feathered bellies. They made sad, haunting cries from the strange trees.

My guide said, "Before you go any further, know that you're now in the second round. You'll stay here until we reach the dreadful sand. Look around, and you'll see things that confirm what I say."

I heard cries of pain from all directions, but I saw no one. This made me freeze in confusion. I think my guide guessed what I was thinking—that the voices came from people hiding among the trees. So, he said, "If you break a small branch from one of these trees, your thoughts will be proven wrong."

I stretched out my hand and broke a twig from a large thorn. The trunk cried out, "Why do you hurt me?" As dark blood oozed from the break, it continued, "Why do you tear me apart? Don't you have any pity? We were once humans, now turned into trees. Even if we were snakes, your hand should be kinder."

Like a burning green branch that hisses as it leaks sap, blood and words flowed from the splinter. Shocked, I dropped the twig and stood frozen in fear.

My guide spoke to the wounded tree, "If he had believed what he read in my poems earlier, he wouldn't have harmed you. But since the truth seemed unbelievable, I encouraged him to do something that now grieves me. Please tell him who you were, so he can share your story in the world above."

The trunk replied, "Your kind words draw me to speak. I was once the keeper of both keys to Frederick's heart, carefully locking and unlocking secrets so

36

that few people knew his mind. I was so loyal to my duty that I lost my sleep and health. But the wickedness of the court, always watching Caesar with greedy eyes, turned others against me. They twisted Augustus's mind, and my honored life turned into sorrow.

In my pride and pain, I thought death was the only escape. In taking my own life, I acted unjustly against myself. But I swear to you, by the roots of this twisted wood, I never betrayed my lord who was so worthy of honor. If one of you returns to the world, please restore my memory, which still lies in ruin due to envy's blow."

The tree went silent. My guide urged me, "Don't waste this chance. Ask more if you wish to know."

I hesitated, so I said, "Please, you ask for me. I feel too much pity to speak."

So, my guide asked, "Since our words seem to move you, please tell us how the soul is bound within these trees. And can anyone ever be freed from them?"

The tree breathed deeply, then turned its breath into a voice, "I will answer briefly. When a tormented soul leaves the body in suicide, Minos sends it to the seventh circle. It falls randomly into this forest, like a seed, and grows into a tree. The Harpies feed on its leaves, causing pain, which is the only way it can express its suffering.

When Judgment Day comes, we will retrieve our bodies, but we won't wear them again, as it's not right to reclaim what we rejected. Instead, our bodies will hang on these trees, a reminder of our suffering."

We listened, thinking the tree might say more when suddenly a loud noise broke through the silence. It was like hearing the crash of beasts and branches as hunters approach.

Then, on our left, we saw two souls running wildly through the forest. They were naked and covered in scratches, so frantic that they broke every branch in their path.

The one running ahead shouted, "Help me, Death! Help!" The one lagging behind yelled, "Lano, you weren't this slow at the jousts of Toppo!" Then, as if he could no longer run, he huddled up next to a bush.

Behind them came a pack of black she-mastiffs, fierce and fast, like greyhounds unleashed. They attacked the man who had crouched down, tearing him apart piece by piece and carrying away his bloody remains.

My guide took my hand and led me to the bush that was weeping in pain from its own wounds. The bush cried out, "O Jacopo da Sant' Andrea, what good did it do you to use me as a shield? What did I do to deserve being dragged into your wicked life?"

My guide then approached and asked, "Who were you, that your voice is filled with such suffering as blood pours from your wounds?"

The bush answered, "O souls who have come to witness this shameful destruction, see how my leaves have been torn away. Please, gather them and place them under this wretched bush.

"I was from the city that changed its first patron to the Baptist, and because of that, he will forever make it suffer. If some trace of him did not still remain along the Arno River, the people who rebuilt it after Attila's attack would have worked in vain. I, myself, caused my own death, hanging from my own house."

Chapter 14: The Sand Waste and the Rain of Fire. The Violent against God. Capaneus. The Statue of Time, and the Four Infernal Rivers.

Out of pity for him and my hometown, I gathered the scattered leaves and gave them back to the wounded bush. Then we reached the edge of the second circle, where a terrifying form of divine justice was revealed.

To describe this new sight clearly, we came upon a plain where no plant could grow. The gloomy forest surrounded it, like a garland, just as a moat encircles a castle. We stopped at the edge.

The ground was made of dry, thick sand, similar to the deserts once crossed by Cato. The vengeance of God is truly fearsome to anyone who witnesses what I saw.

The plain was filled with groups of naked souls, all crying out in misery. Different rules seemed to apply to each group. Some lay flat on the ground, others sat huddled up, while the rest wandered around endlessly. There were far more wandering than lying down, but the ones on the ground screamed louder in their suffering.

A rain of wide, fiery flakes fell over the entire sand plain, like snow falling in the Alps without wind. Just as Alexander the Great saw fire rain down on his army in India, so these flames fell continuously, burning everything they touched. The sand caught fire instantly, doubling the agony of the souls there.

The souls moved their hands without rest, trying to brush off the burning embers, shaking them off constantly, but to no relief.

"Master," I began, "you have overcome everything so far, except for the demons at the gate. Who is that powerful soul lying there, completely ignoring the fire and looking defiant, as if the rain doesn't affect him?"

The soul, noticing I was asking about him, cried out, "As I was in life, so I am in death. Even if Jove himself exhausted his blacksmith—who forged the thunderbolt that struck me—and called upon every other smith in the fiery forges of Mount Etna to help him, he still wouldn't find joy in taking revenge on me."

At this, my guide spoke with a force I had never heard before. "Capaneus, your arrogance isn't extinguished, even in death. That is why your punishment is even greater. Your rage is the true source of your torment."

Then he turned to me with a calmer expression and said, "That was one of the seven kings who besieged Thebes. He held God in contempt during life, and even now, his defiance is what causes his suffering."

"Now follow me," my guide said, "and be careful not to step on the burning sand yet. Keep close to the edge of the forest."

Without speaking further, we walked until we came to a small stream flowing out of the woods. Its water was red, a sight that still makes my hair stand on end. The stream reminded me of the Bulicame, a spring whose waters were once divided among sinful women. This little stream ran down through the sand, and its banks and bed were made of stone, showing us the way forward.

My guide said, "In all that I've shown you since we entered the gate of Hell, nothing is as remarkable as this river. It quenches all the flames falling above it."

I asked him to explain more, eager to understand what he meant.

"In the middle of the sea," he began, "there is an island called Crete. Long ago, under its king, the world was pure. On this island, there is a mountain called Ida, which was once lush with water and trees. Now, it is barren. Rhea chose it as the cradle for her son. To hide his cries, she had the place filled with noise.

On this mountain stands an old man, facing Rome as if it were his mirror. His back is turned toward Damietta. His head is made of pure gold, his chest and arms of silver, his waist down to his thighs of brass, and from there down to his feet of iron. One of his feet, however, is made of clay, and he leans more on that foot than the other. Except for the gold part, every section is cracked and tears flow out. These tears run down into the valley, forming rivers like Acheron, Styx, and Phlegethon, until they reach a point where they can't go any deeper. There, they become the pool of Cocytus, which you will see later."

I asked, "If this stream has its source in our world, why do we only see it at the edge of this forest?"

He replied, "You know this place is a circle. Although you've traveled far down and to the left, you haven't yet seen the whole circle. So, if something new appears, it shouldn't surprise you."

I continued, "Master, where are Lethe and Phlegethon? You haven't mentioned one, and you said the other is made of this rain."

"You're asking good questions," he answered. "But the boiling red water you see here should answer one of them. You will see Lethe outside this pit, where souls go to wash away their sins once they've repented."

He then said, "It's time to leave the forest. Follow me carefully. We can walk on these stone edges that are not burning, and the vapors here will protect us from the flames."

Chapter 15: The Violent Against Nature. Brunetto Latini.

We walked along the stony path, covered by the mist from the stream, which shielded us from the fire. It was like the dikes built by the Flemings between Cadsand and Bruges to keep the sea away, or the barriers the people of Padua built along the Brenta River to protect their homes. Whoever made these paths must have used a similar idea, though they weren't as tall or thick.

By now, we were so far from the forest that even if I turned around, I wouldn't have been able to see it. We soon encountered a group of souls walking beside the stream. They stared at us, much like people do when a new moon appears in the sky.

Among them, one soul recognized me. He grabbed the hem of my clothes and cried out, "What a surprise!"

When he stretched out his arm, I focused on his burned face. Despite the scars, I recognized him and bowed my head respectfully, saying, "Are you here, Ser Brunetto?"

He replied, "Yes, it's me, Brunetto Latini. Would you mind if I walk alongside you for a bit?"

I answered, "I would be honored. If you wish, I'll sit down here with you, as long as my guide allows it."

"O my son," he said, "if anyone from this group stops walking, they must lie here for a hundred years, unable to brush away the flames. So keep moving, and I will follow close behind. I'll rejoin my group later, who continue to walk in sorrow."

I didn't dare step down to walk at his level, so I kept my head bowed out of respect as I walked on the raised path.

He asked, "What brings you down here before your time? Who is this that guides you?"

"Up in the world above," I explained, "I lost my way in a dark valley. Before I had lived my full life, this guide appeared to lead me home along this path."

He said to me, "If you follow your star, you can't miss a glorious destiny. I could see this when we were together in the beautiful world. If I hadn't died so early, I would have gladly helped you in your work.

But the ungrateful and wicked people who came down from Fiesole long ago and still carry the roughness of the mountains will become your enemies because of your good deeds. And they will be right to do so, for among bitter crab apples, the sweet fig cannot grow.

People say they are blind, greedy, envious, and proud. Make sure you keep yourself free from their habits. Your future holds such honor that both political parties will fight over you, but neither will truly support you.

Let those from Fiesole act as they always do, but don't let them harm the seed of the Romans who stayed behind when Florence became a nest of evil."

I replied, "If my wish could be granted, you would not be here, cut off from human life. The memory of you still touches my heart. You taught me so much about how a person can leave a lasting mark. I am grateful, and as long as I live, I will show it in my words.

What you say about my future, I will remember. I will share it with a Lady who will interpret it, if I ever reach her. I just want you to know that I will face whatever fate brings, as long as my conscience is clear.

I've heard similar warnings before, so let Fortune spin her wheel as she wants. Let the farmer keep digging with his hoe."

My guide turned to me, looking over his right cheek, and said, "He listens well who understands." I continued walking with Ser Brunetto, asking him about the others who were most known and respected among his group.

He replied, "It's good to know some, but there are others better left unnamed, for we don't have time to mention them all. To summarize, they were all scholars and men of great fame, but they were tainted by the same sin.

Over there is Priscian, among that wretched crowd, and Francis of Accorso. And if you had wanted to look deeper, you would have seen the one who was moved by the Pope from the Arno to the Bacchiglione, where he now suffers for his sins.

I would say more, but I see new smoke rising from the sand. I can't stay any longer. Please take care of my 'Tesoro,' where I still live. That's all I ask."

Then he turned away, running like those who race for the Green Mantle in Verona. He looked like one of the runners who wins, not the one who loses.

Chapter 16: Guidoguerra, Aldobrandi, and Rusticucci. The River of Blood

Now I was near where I could hear the echo of water falling into the next circle. It sounded like the buzzing of a beehive.

Suddenly, three shadows came running toward us from a group suffering under the burning rain. They cried out to me, "Stop! You look like someone from our twisted city!"

Oh, the wounds I saw on their bodies—both fresh and old, burned by the flames. Just remembering it now still pains me.

My guide listened to their cries and turned to me. "Wait," he said. "We should be polite to them. If it weren't for the fire here, I'd say you should hurry more than them."

As soon as we stopped, they caught up to us and formed a circle around us.

The three souls circled around me, moving like wrestlers looking for an opening before a fight. They kept their faces turned toward me while their feet moved in the opposite direction. One of them spoke, "If the misery of this place makes us look burnt and ugly, please don't let that stop you from telling us who you are. You seem to walk through Hell confidently, still alive.

The one walking behind me, though now skinless and naked, was once more important than you might think. He was the grandson of the good Gualdrada. His name was Guidoguerra, known for his wisdom and bravery in battle.

The one beside me is Tegghiaio Aldobrandi, a name that should be honored in the world above. I am Jacopo Rusticucci, and my harsh wife is the cause of my suffering more than anything else."

If I hadn't feared the fire, I would have thrown myself down among them, and I think my guide would have let me. But since I would have burned, fear overcame my desire to embrace them.

I began, "Your suffering makes me sad, not disgusted. My guide told me about people like you, so I knew who was approaching. I am from your city and have always respected your noble names and deeds.

I seek the sweet rewards promised to me by my guide, but first, I must travel to the center of Hell."

"So may your soul carry you for a long time," one of them replied, "and may your name shine after you. Please tell us, do valor and courtesy still exist in our city, or have they completely disappeared? Guglielmo Borsier, who suffers here with us, has lately filled us with grief through his words."

"Newcomers and sudden wealth have brought pride and extravagance to Florence," I answered. "The city weeps because of this."

Hearing my reply, they looked at each other as if I had spoken the truth.

"If it's always this easy for you to speak your mind," they replied, "you are fortunate. If you escape these dark places and see the beautiful stars again, please remember to tell others about us."

With that, they broke their circle and ran off so quickly it seemed like they had wings. They disappeared so fast that I couldn't even say "Amen" before they were gone. My guide decided it was time to move on.

I followed him, and we hadn't gone far when the sound of rushing water became so loud we could barely hear each other speak.

It was like the river that flows from Monte Veso toward the east, known as the Acquacheta, before it descends into its lower bed near Forli. There, it plunges down in a single waterfall that could fill a huge space. Just like that, the dark water rushed down from a steep bank with a roar that almost hurt the ears.

I had a cord tied around my waist. I had once planned to use it to catch a panther with a spotted coat. Following my guide's command, I untied the cord, gathered it up, and handed it to him.

He turned to the right, moved a little away from the edge, and then threw the cord down into the deep abyss.

I thought to myself, "Something new must be coming. My guide is watching so closely."

Oh, how careful we should be around those who can see not just what we do, but what we think as well!

He said to me, "Soon, what I'm expecting will appear, and you will see what you have been wondering about."

When something that seems false is actually true, it's best to keep quiet, even if you have nothing to be ashamed of. But here, I can't stay silent. So, reader, by the notes of this story, I swear to tell the truth.

Through the dark, thick air, I saw a shape rising up, something that would amaze even the bravest heart. It looked like a person coming up from the sea, stretching his legs to swim up after freeing an anchor caught on the ocean floor.

Chapter 17: Geryon. The Violent Against Art. Usurers. The Descent into the Abyss of Malebolge.

"Look," my guide said, "at the creature with the pointed tail! He breaks through mountains and destroys walls. He spreads corruption everywhere." He then motioned for the creature to come ashore near the edge of the stone path.

This hideous symbol of deceit came forward, showing its head and chest, but kept its tail on the edge of the cliff. Its face looked like that of a kind man, but the rest of its body was like a serpent. It had two hairy paws up to the armpits. Its back and sides were covered with intricate designs of knots and shields. No tapestry made by the Tartars, Turks, or even Arachne could compare to its patterns.

It lay on the edge, like a boat partially in water and partially on land, or like a beaver waiting to attack. Its tail hung in the air, twisting and turning, ending in a stinger like that of a scorpion.

My guide said, "We need to go a bit closer to that wicked creature."

We moved to the right, taking ten steps along the edge to avoid the burning sand and fire. As we got closer to the beast, I saw a group of people sitting in the sand, near a hollow area.

"Go and see who they are," my guide said, "so you can understand this part of Hell better. Keep it brief, though. While you're there, I'll speak with this creature and convince it to carry us on its back."

So, I walked alone to the farthest part of the seventh circle, where the sorrowful souls sat. Tears flowed from their eyes as they moved their hands, trying to shield themselves from the fire and the hot ground. They looked like dogs in summer, scratching at fleas and flies with their feet and noses.

I looked closely at some of them but didn't recognize any faces. Each had a pouch around their neck, with a specific color and symbol. Their eyes were fixed on these pouches.

As I scanned them, I noticed a yellow pouch with a blue lion on it. Then I saw another, red as blood, displaying a white goose. A third pouch, marked with a blue sow on a white background, caught my eye. The man wearing it said, "What are you doing here in this pit? Go away! Since you're still alive, know that a neighbor of mine, Vitaliano, will soon join me here. I'm from Padua, among these Florentines, and they keep shouting for the man who brings the pouch with three goats."

He twisted his mouth and stuck out his tongue like an ox licking its nose. Fearing I had stayed too long, I turned away and went back to my guide.

I found him already sitting on the back of the monstrous creature. "Be brave now," he said. "We must go down on this beast. You get on in front of me. I'll sit behind to protect you from its tail."

I trembled like someone with a fever, teeth chattering and nails turning blue. But shame made me gather my courage in front of my guide. I climbed onto the creature's shoulders, wanting to say, "Hold on to me," but no sound came out.

My guide, who had saved me before, put his arms around me to hold me steady. "Now, Geryon, start your descent," he ordered. "Remember, this is a new burden for you."

Geryon slowly moved away from the edge, just like a small boat pushing off from the shore. As soon as it felt free, it turned its tail where its chest had been, and glided through the air like an eel, using its paws to propel itself.

I felt a fear greater than Phaethon did when he lost control of the sun's chariot, scorching the heavens, or Icarus when his wings melted and his father cried out in despair. I was surrounded by nothing but air, and I could see nothing except the monstrous creature carrying me.

Geryon moved forward, slowly and steadily, spiraling downwards. I felt the motion only from the rush of air on my face and the movement below.

I heard a terrible crashing noise to my right; it was the whirlpool beneath us. I leaned out to look down, and what I saw made me even more afraid of the dark pit. I saw fires burning and heard cries of suffering, which made me cling even closer to my guide.

Now I could see us turning and descending, surrounded by terrifying sights on all sides. It felt like a falcon that, after flying high for a long time without spotting prey, finally swoops down quickly, circling and landing far from its master, tired and sullen. In this way, Geryon lowered us to the bottom of the rocky cliff, dropped us off, and sped away like an arrow released from a bowstring.

Chapter 18: The Eighth Circle, Malebolge: The Fraudulent and the Malicious. The First Bolgia: Seducers and Panders. Venedico Caccianimico. Jason. The Second Bolgia: Flatterers. Allessio Interminelli. Thais.

There is a place in Hell called Malebolge, made entirely of stone and dark like iron. In the middle of this area is a wide, deep well. The surrounding area has ten deep valleys, like moats around a castle. Around the well, high cliffs form the outer edge.

Like castles with many moats, this place has high walls with small bridges. The bridges extend from the cliffs and cross over the moats to the well in the center. Geryon had placed us down here, and my guide led me to the left, with me following close behind.

On my right, I saw new suffering, new torments, and new punishments. The first valley was filled with naked sinners, some walking toward us and others away, depending on which side of the valley they were on. They moved like crowds on a bridge during a Roman Jubilee year, where people walk in opposite directions.

Demons with horns and whips stood along the stone path, beating the sinners from behind. The poor souls lifted their legs at the first strike and didn't wait for a second or third lash.

As I walked, I spotted a familiar face. I stopped to get a better look, and my guide agreed, pausing with me. The man tried to hide his face, but it didn't work. I said, "You there, with your head down—if I'm not mistaken, you are Venedico Caccianemico. What brought you here to such painful punishment?"

He replied, "I don't want to admit it, but your clear words force me to remember the past. I am the one who convinced Ghisola to give in to the Marquis's desires, as shameful as it is to say. I'm not the only one from Bologna here, though; this place is filled with my kind. There are more of us here than there are people back in Bologna who say 'sipa,' which means 'yes.' If you need proof of our greed, just think of our greedy hearts."

As he spoke, a demon struck him with a whip and shouted, "Move along, pimp! There are no women here to sell for money."

I rejoined my guide, and after a short walk, we reached a rocky ledge sticking out from the cliff. We climbed it easily and turned to the right along its ridge, leaving those endless circles of torment behind us.

When we reached a spot where the path was hollowed out below to allow the beaten souls to pass, my guide said, "Wait and look at the faces of those coming toward us. You haven't seen them yet because they've been walking alongside us."

From the old bridge, we looked down at the group moving along the other side of the valley. They were being whipped, just like the others.

Without me asking, my guide pointed to a tall man approaching. "See that one?" he said. "Despite his suffering, he doesn't shed a tear. Look at his proud face; that's Jason, who used his cunning to steal the Golden Fleece from the Colchians. He passed through the island of Lemnos, where the women, filled with rage, killed all the men."

There, with sweet words and false promises, he deceived Hypsipyle, the maiden who had already tricked others. He left her pregnant and abandoned. This is why he suffers here, and it's also punishment for his betrayal of Medea. All who deceive in such ways are punished here. That is enough for you to know about the first valley and those it holds."

We had now reached the point where a narrow path crosses the second ditch, forming a bridge to another arch. From there, we could hear moaning from the next Bolgia. The people trapped there were snorting like pigs and beating themselves with their hands.

The walls around the ditch were coated with a mold, rising from below, which attacked the eyes and nose. The pit was so deep that we couldn't see the bottom unless we climbed the arch and leaned over where the rock jutted out.

When we reached the top and looked down, I saw people submerged in filth that seemed to come straight from a sewer. As I peered into the pit, I noticed a man with a head so covered in muck that I couldn't tell if he was a priest or a layman.

He shouted, "Why are you staring at me more than the others?" I replied, "Because I think I recognize you. Aren't you Alessio Interminei of Lucca? That's why I'm looking at you more than the others."

He nodded and hit his head in frustration, saying, "Flattery buried me here. My tongue never got enough of it."

Then my guide said, "Look a bit further ahead and see that filthy woman who scratches herself with dirty nails. Sometimes she crouches, sometimes she stands."

"That's Thais, the harlot," he added, "who once told her lover, 'Yes, I am full of gratitude, and even more.' Let's be satisfied with just this look."

Chapter 19: The Third Bolgia: Simoniacs. Pope Nicholas III. Dante's Reproof of corrupt Prelates.

"Oh, Simon Magus! Oh, your misguided followers! You who sell God's gifts, which should be devoted to holiness, for gold and silver! Now the trumpet sounds for you because you belong in this third Bolgia."

We had reached the part of the cliff that hung over the middle of the ditch. I looked down and saw that the sides and bottom of the ditch were filled with round holes of the same size. They reminded me of the holes for baptismal fonts in my lovely Saint John's church, one of which I once broke to save a drowning child.

Out of each hole, a sinner's legs stuck out up to the calves. The rest of their bodies were inside the stone. Flames burned their feet, causing their legs to quiver violently, as if they might snap.

The flames moved over their feet like burning oil on water. I noticed one of them twisting more frantically than the others, his feet writhing in a redder flame. I asked, "Master, who is that one twisting so much more than the others? And why is his flame redder?"

He answered, "If you want, I can take you down to him. Then you can learn about his wrongdoings."

I said, "Whatever you think is best. You are my guide. I'll follow your lead."

So, we went down the narrow path of the fourth ditch, moving to the left. When we reached the bottom filled with holes, my guide put me down near the hole of the one who was crying out in pain.

"O miserable soul, upside down like a stake," I began, "if you can, speak up!"

I stood over him like a friar who listens to a criminal's confession. He cried out, "Is that you already, Boniface? The records lied to me by several years! Are you so quickly satisfied with the wealth you took by deceit and trickery?"

I was confused, not understanding his words. I stood there, not knowing what to say. Then Virgil said, "Tell him, 'I am not who you think I am.'"

I repeated Virgil's words. The spirit twisted his feet again and, sighing, said, "What do you want from me? If you're so eager to know who I am, know that I once wore the Pope's mantle. I was a member of the Orsini family and worked to advance my own relatives, both with wealth in the world above and here below."

"Beneath my head are other popes who were guilty of simony before me. I will fall below them when the one I mistook you for arrives. But I will stay here longer with my feet burning than he will, for an even worse shepherd will come from the west to cover us both in shame."

This one will be like the Jason we read about in the Maccabees. Just as that king obeyed him, so will the ruler of France.

I might be bold here, but I answered him: "Please tell me, what price did our Lord ask from Saint Peter before giving him the keys? The truth is, he asked for nothing except, 'Follow me.' Neither Peter nor the others asked for gold or silver when Matthias was chosen to replace the fallen soul. So, stay here and guard the money you got through deceit, which made you so defiant against Charles."

"If it weren't for my respect for the sacred keys you held in life, I would use even harsher words. Your greed causes suffering in the world, trampling on the good and lifting up the wicked. The Bible warned you pastors about this when it spoke of the woman who sat upon many waters, sinning with kings. She had seven heads and ten horns, symbols of power, until her virtue was no longer pleasing."

"You have made gold and silver your gods. How are you any different from idol worshipers, except that they worship one, and you worship hundreds? Ah, Constantine! Your conversion was not the cause of evil, but rather the wealth you gave to the Church."

While I was saying these words, he began to struggle violently with his feet, as if stung by anger or guilt. I think my words pleased my guide, for he listened with a content smile. Then, he lifted me up and carried me back the way we came. He didn't tire as he carried me up to the top of the arch that led from the fourth ditch to the fifth. Gently, he set me down on the steep, uneven rock, which even goats would struggle to climb.

From there, I could see into another valley.

Chapter 20: The Fourth Bolgia: Soothsayers. Amphiaraus, Tiresias, Aruns, Manto, Eryphylus, Michael Scott, Guido Bonatti, and Asdente. Virgil reproaches Dante's Pity. Mantua's Foundation.

Now I must speak of a new torment in the twentieth canto of this song about those in the depths of Hell. I was ready to look down into this new pit, filled with the agony of those suffering there. I saw people in the circular valley, walking slowly and weeping, just like mourners in a procession.

As I looked more closely, I noticed that each one was twisted. Their heads were turned backward to their bodies, so they could only walk in reverse. They couldn't look forward. I've never seen or even imagined something so strange, except maybe if someone had been twisted by a terrible disease.

Think about this, dear reader, and imagine how I could keep from crying when I saw our own human form so distorted. Tears ran down their backs from their twisted faces. I wept as I leaned on the hard rock. Seeing me, my guide asked, "Are you also one of these foolish people? Pity lives here only when it's completely dead. Who could be more lost than one who feels sorry for those facing divine punishment?"

"Lift your head," he continued, "and see that man for whom the earth opened before the Thebans' eyes, making them shout, 'Where are you rushing, Amphiaraus? Why are you leaving the war?' He fell until he reached Minos, who judges all souls. Now, his shoulders are twisted because he wanted to see too far ahead. So now he looks behind and walks backward."

"Look at Tiresias," my guide went on. "He changed his appearance from male to female when all his body parts were transformed. Later, he had to strike two entangled serpents with his staff to become a man again."

"And there is Aruns, who walks backward and faces the other's belly. He lived in the hills of Luni, in a cave among the white marble quarries. From there, he could see the stars and the sea without anything blocking his view."

The woman you see there, covering her chest with her loose hair and with a body part covered in fur, is Manto. She wandered through many lands after her father died and the city of Bacchus was taken over. Eventually, she settled in the place where I was born, and I want to tell you more about it.

After her father passed away, Manto traveled the world for a long time. In northern Italy, near the Alps, there is a lake called Benaco. It's fed by over a thousand streams that come from the surrounding mountains. The water flows through a valley where the borders of Trento, Brescia, and Verona meet. There's a fortress called Peschiera that sits by the lake, protecting the area from the neighboring cities.

From this lake, a river starts to flow. As it leaves, it's no longer called Benaco; it becomes the Mincio River. The river runs through green fields until it reaches a swampy plain, often turning unhealthy in summer.

When Manto came to this place, she saw a deserted patch of land in the middle of the swamp. To avoid people, she stayed there with her servants, practicing her magic. Eventually, she died there. Later, people gathered around this area, which was protected by the marsh. They built a city on her remains and named it Mantua, after her.

The city was once full of people until a foolish leader named Casalodi was tricked by Pinamonte. So, if you ever hear someone tell the story of my city differently, don't believe them.

I said, "Master, your words are so clear and trustworthy that they burn away any doubts I have. But tell me, do you see any noteworthy people among those passing by? My mind is focused on that."

He replied, "The man with the beard that reaches his dark shoulders was an augur back in the days when Greece was almost empty of men. He, along with Calchas, decided the moment to cut the first cable at Aulis. His name is Eryphylus, as mentioned in my great tragedy, which you know well.

"The thin man next to him is Michael Scott, a master of magical illusions. See also Guido Bonatti and Asdente, who now regrets leaving his leather and thread to become a soothsayer. Look at those poor souls who abandoned their sewing needles to tell fortunes with herbs and charms.

"But now, let's move on. Time is passing; it is already past midnight. The moon was full yesterday, so let's continue our journey through this dark forest."

With these words, we continued walking.

Chapter 21: The Fifth Bolgia: Peculators. The Elder of Santa Zita. Malacoda and other Devils.

As we went from bridge to bridge, talking about other things not part of this story, we finally reached the top of another chasm in Malebolge. We stopped to look at another dark pit filled with cries of agony.

It was as dark as the Venetian shipyard in winter, where pitch boils to repair old ships. They can't sail during that season, so some build new ships, while others fix the worn-out ones. Some hammer the bow, others the stern, while others make oars and twist ropes. Some repair the main sail and others the mizzen. But here, it wasn't fire heating the pitch; it was a divine force boiling it, coating the banks on every side.

I could see the thick pitch bubbling up and then flattening back down, but I couldn't see anything inside it. While I stared down into the pit, my guide suddenly shouted, "Watch out! Be careful!" He pulled me back from the edge.

I quickly turned around, wanting to see what danger we needed to escape. My heart raced in fear as I saw a black devil running along the ridge toward us. He looked fierce and ruthless, with open wings and light steps. His shoulders were sharp and high, and he carried a sinner slung over them, holding him by his legs.

From our bridge, the demon said, "Hey, Malebranche! Here's one of the elders from Saint Zita. Throw him into the pit! I'm heading back to that town where more of them are waiting. Everyone there is corrupt, except Bonturo. They'll turn 'No' into 'Yes' for the right price."

He tossed the man into the pit, then turned back quickly, like a dog chasing a thief. The sinner sank and then surfaced face down. The demons hiding under the bridge shouted, "This is not a holy place! Here, you swim differently than in the Serchio River. Stay under the pitch, or our hooks will get you."

They grabbed him with their rakes and said, "You'll dance under the pitch, and maybe you'll steal some peace if you can." Like cooks dipping meat into a pot to keep it from floating, they pushed him down.

My guide turned to me and said, "To avoid being seen, crouch down behind this rock for cover. And don't worry about what they do to me. I know how to handle this; I've been through this before."

He walked ahead past the bridge, and when he reached the edge of the sixth pit, he stood firm. Suddenly, a group of devils came rushing out from under the bridge, shouting and waving their hooks. They were like dogs charging at a beggar who suddenly appears.

"Don't harm me," my guide said. "Let one of you step forward to talk, then decide what to do." They all yelled, "Let Malacoda speak!" One of them stepped forward while the rest stayed back. "What do you want?" he asked.

"Do you think I got this far without Heaven's will?" my guide said. "It's destined for me to show this man the way. Let us pass."

Malacoda lowered his hook, dropped his pride, and told the others, "Don't touch him." My guide turned to me and said, "You can come out now; it's safe." I hurried to him, but the devils moved forward, and I feared they might break their promise.

I remembered the fear on the faces of the soldiers at Caprona when they found themselves surrounded by enemies despite having safe passage. I pressed close to my guide and didn't take my eyes off the devils' grim faces.

"Shall I hit him on the back?" one devil asked another, and they replied, "Yes, give him a little nick." But the demon talking to my guide quickly turned and said, "Quiet, Scarmiglione."

He then told us, "You can't go any further on this path; the sixth bridge is broken at the bottom. If you want to keep going, take the rocky path ahead. There's another bridge that still stands. Just yesterday, it was 1,266 years since that bridge collapsed. I'll send some of my demons to check if anyone is trying to escape. You can go with them; they won't harm you."

Then he shouted, "Alichino, Calcabrina, step forward! And you, Cagnazzo and Barbariccia, lead the ten! Libicocco, Draghignazzo, Ciriatto, Graffiacane, Farfarello, and Rubicante, search the boiling pitch and make sure these two stay safe until the next bridge."

"Oh no! What are we doing, Master?" I said nervously. "Can't we go alone without their help? Do you see how they gnash their teeth and look at us with hatred?"

"Don't be afraid," he replied. "They're only doing that for the souls boiling in the pitch, not us."

The devils turned to the left, each sticking out their tongues at their leader as a signal. The leader then blew a trumpet sound using his rear.

Chapter 22: Ciampolo, Friar Gomita, and Michael Zanche. The Malabranche quarrel.

I've seen soldiers breaking camp, preparing for battle, and sometimes rushing to escape. I've seen scouts and messengers on the move, tournaments fought, and jousts held. There were trumpets, drums, and all kinds of signals. But I have never seen anything as strange as the way these demons moved with their bagpipes.

We went along with the ten demons. What a savage group! It felt like being in a church with saints but in a tavern with drunks at the same time. My eyes stayed fixed on the pitch, watching the souls being burned there.

Just like dolphins show their backs above water to warn sailors of danger, some of these sinners would occasionally arch their backs above the pitch to ease their pain. But just as quickly, they'd sink back down.

The souls were like frogs sitting at the edge of a ditch with just their heads above water. They would quickly disappear under the boiling pitch whenever Barbariccia, the demon, came near.

I saw one soul hesitate, just like a frog that stays above water while the others dive. Then Graffiacan, one of the demons, grabbed him by the hair, pulling him up until he looked like an otter coming out of the water. I recognized him because I had learned the names of all the demons when they were chosen. They called out to Rubicante, "Use your claws and skin him!"

I said to my guide, "Please find out who this unlucky soul is." My guide moved closer to the sinner and asked him where he was from. The man replied, "I was born in Navarre. My mother made me a servant to a lord because she had me with a scoundrel who ruined himself and his possessions. Later, I served King Thibault and became corrupt, for which I now pay in this heat."

Ciriatto, a demon with boar-like tusks, tore at the man's skin. He was like a mouse among hungry cats. But Barbariccia grabbed him and said to the others, "Hold off while I question him."

Then Barbariccia turned to my guide and said, "Ask him more questions if you want before they rip him apart."

My guide asked, "Do you know any other Italians in the pitch?" The sinner answered, "I just left one who was nearby. I wish I were still with him because then I wouldn't fear these claws or hooks!"

Libicocco, one of the demons, shouted, "Enough of this!" and tore the man's arm with his hook. Draghignazzo tried to grab his legs, but their leader made an angry face and stopped him.

When they calmed down a bit, my guide asked, "Who was that one you left?"

The man replied, "It was Friar Gomita from Gallura, full of tricks. He held his lord's enemies in his grasp but let them go for a bribe. He was a master of corruption. With him is Michael Zanche of Logodoro. Those two can never stop gossiping about Sardinia."

He noticed one of the demons grinding his teeth and said, "I would say more, but I'm afraid he'll scratch my itch."

The chief demon, turning to Farfarello, who looked ready to strike, shouted, "Stand back, you malicious bird!"

"If you want to see more sinners," the frightened man continued, "Tuscans or Lombards, I can make them come. Just let these demons step back a bit so they don't take their revenge on me. I'll sit right here and call seven of them by whistling, which is our signal."

Cagnazzo raised his snout and shook his head. "Listen to him! It's just a trick to escape," he said.

But the sinner, cleverer than them all, replied, "I know how to trick my enemies."

Alichin, one of the demons, could no longer hold back. He said, "If you dive, I won't chase you, but I'll fly above the pitch and watch."

"Get ready for some action!" I thought. The demons looked at each other with reluctance. The Navarrese picked his moment, planted his feet, and leaped into the pitch, escaping their grasp.

The demons were suddenly filled with shame, especially Alichin, who yelled, "You're caught!"

But it was too late. The sinner had already dived under the pitch, swimming away like a duck escaping a falcon. Alichin, furious at the escape, turned on Calcabrina, who had followed him, and attacked his fellow demon right above the pit.

Both of them fell into the boiling pitch, clawing at each other like two fierce hawks. The heat was quick to punish them, and their wings got stuck in the thick tar, so they couldn't rise.

Barbariccia, one of the demons, quickly sent four others with hooks to fish them out. They flew to the other side of the pit and began pulling the sinners out, who were already coated in the sticky pitch. That was the last scene we saw before we left them.

Chapter 23: Escape from the Malabranche. The Sixth Bolgia: Hypocrites. Catalano and Loderingo. Caiaphas.

My guide and I walked on in silence, one behind the other, like monks following their path. I started thinking about Aesop's fable of the frog and the mouse. This scene was so similar that it made me uneasy, and I began to worry.

I thought, "The demons are mocking us and might be angry because of what just happened. If they come after us, they'll be as relentless as a dog chasing a rabbit."

Fear gripped me, and I felt my hair stand on end. I looked back and said, "Master, if we don't hide now, the Malebranche demons will catch up to us! I can already sense them behind us."

My guide replied, "I can read your thoughts as if I were looking into a mirror. Just now, I had the same worry. But if we can find a slope on the right, we might be able to get down to the next pit and escape."

He hadn't finished speaking when I saw them—wings spread, flying towards us to capture us. In an instant, my guide scooped me up, just like a mother who wakes up to find her house on fire and grabs her child without stopping to think about herself.

He slid down the steep bank, holding me close against his chest. We raced down faster than water rushing through a mill's sluice.

We reached the bottom of the ravine just before the demons got to the top of the hill. But my guide wasn't afraid, because divine power had put the demons in charge of the fifth pit, and they couldn't leave it.

At the bottom, we saw people moving slowly, weighed down and exhausted. They wore heavy, hooded cloaks, just like the ones worn by monks in Cologne. The cloaks were dazzling on the outside, but inside, they were lined with lead, weighing the people down.

We walked alongside them, listening to their sad cries. They moved so slowly that with every step we caught up with a new group.

I turned to my guide and said, "Can you find someone here who might tell us who they are?"

One of them, hearing my Tuscan accent, called out, "Wait, you who walk so quickly through this dark air!"

My guide replied, "Stop and let's hear what he has to say."

We stopped, and two figures hurried to catch up with us, although their heavy cloaks slowed them down. They studied me with intense eyes before one of them spoke: "You seem alive, but if you are dead, how are you walking without a heavy cloak like ours?"

I answered, "I was born and raised in Florence, by the river Arno, and I am still alive. But who are you? And what punishment makes you suffer so much that I see tears running down your cheeks?"

One of them replied, "We were called the 'Jovial Friars,' both from Bologna. I am Catalano, and this is Loderingo. We were chosen by your city to keep the peace, but we failed, and now we pay the price."

I was about to speak when I saw something that made me stop—a man nailed to the ground with three stakes. When he saw me, he writhed and groaned.

Catalano noticed and said, "This man you see nailed here advised the Pharisees that it was better for one man to die for the people. Now he lies here, suffering, and every passerby feels his weight. His father-in-law and the others who agreed with him are also punished in this pit."

Virgil, my guide, looked in surprise at the man crucified on the ground, horrified by his eternal torment.

Then my guide spoke to the friar: "Don't be upset if I ask you this. Is there a path to the right that we can take to get out of here without forcing some of the demons to help us escape?"

The friar replied, "There's a rock not far from here that crosses all the valleys, except this one, where it is broken. You can climb up the slope of that broken rock to get out."

My guide stood still for a moment, deep in thought. Then he said, "The one who controls the sinners over there didn't tell us the truth."

The friar responded, "I heard in Bologna that one of the Devil's tricks is lying. He is, after all, the father of lies."

With anger in his eyes, my guide strode forward, and I quickly followed in his footsteps, leaving the friar and the burdened souls behind.

Chapter 24: The Seventh Bolgia: Thieves. Vanni Fucci. Serpents.

It was early in the year when the sun moves into Aquarius, and the nights are nearly equal to the days. Frost covered the ground, looking like a layer of snow, but it melted quickly under the morning sun.

A farmer, who was worried about his crops, woke up and saw the fields covered in white frost. He went inside, worried about what to do. But when he came out again and saw the frost had melted, his hope returned. He grabbed his shepherd's staff and took his sheep out to graze.

Similarly, I felt alarm when I saw the concern on my guide's face. But soon, my worry was eased. As we reached the broken bridge, he turned to me with a gentle look, the same one I saw at the base of the mountain. He opened his arms, and after a moment of thought, he grabbed hold of me.

Like someone who carefully plans each step, he lifted me towards the top of a large rock. He then looked at another crag and said, "Grab onto that one next, but test it first to see if it will hold you."

Climbing in a cloak was not easy. My guide was light and nimble, but I struggled to follow him, climbing from one jagged rock to another. If this climb had been as steep as the last one, I would have been too tired to make it. But since the valley slopes downwards, one side of the path rises and the other descends, making it easier.

At last, we reached the point where the last stone breaks apart. I was so out of breath that I couldn't go any further. I sat down as soon as I got there.

"You need to push through this tiredness," my guide said. "You can't achieve fame by sitting comfortably. If you live your life without effort, you will leave no mark on the world, just like smoke vanishing in the air or foam dissolving in water."

He continued, "So get up! Fight through this pain with the spirit that wins every battle. A longer climb still awaits you. Leaving this place is just the start."

Hearing this, I gathered my strength and said, "Let's go on. I'm ready."

We climbed up a narrow, jagged, and even steeper path than the one before. I kept talking as we went to hide how exhausted I felt. Then a voice came from the next ditch. I couldn't understand the words, but it was angry.

I leaned over the arch to look, but it was too dark to see the bottom. "Master," I said, "let's go to the next ditch and climb down the wall. I can hear voices, but I can't make out the words. I can't see anything down there."

He replied, "The only answer I will give is action. When you ask modestly, it's best to respond with deeds rather than words."

We climbed down from the bridge to the eighth ditch. There, I saw a horrifying sight: the ditch was filled with serpents, so many that my blood freezes just thinking about them.

Libya can no longer boast of its deadly serpents. Even with all its snakes—chelydri, jaculi, and amphisbaena—it has nothing as terrifying as what I saw here. Not even Ethiopia or the shores of the Red Sea had ever seen such a monstrous sight!

In this grim and dark crowd, people were running around, terrified and naked. They had no hope of escape or hiding. Snakes coiled around their hands, tying them behind their backs. The snakes' heads and tails wrapped around their bodies tightly.

Suddenly, a serpent sprang out and struck one of the people near us, biting him right where the neck meets the shoulders. In an instant, he burst into flames and burned completely, turning to ashes on the ground. But then, just as quickly, the ashes came together, and he was restored to his original form.

It was like the story of the phoenix, the bird that burns itself and rises again every 500 years. The phoenix lives on nothing but incense and spices, and when it dies, it wraps itself in nard and myrrh before being reborn.

The man who had just risen looked confused, like someone who has been knocked down by a demon. He glanced around in pain and sighed, bewildered by his suffering.

"God's justice is harsh!" I thought. "What a severe punishment this is!"

My guide then asked the man who he was. The man replied, "I was just thrown into this pit from Tuscany. I lived like a beast, not a human. I am Vanni Fucci, a brute. Pistoia was my home."

I said to my guide, "Tell him not to move, and ask what crime brought him here. I remember him as a violent and angry man."

The sinner heard me, looked up, and his face showed sadness and shame. He said, "It hurts me more that you see me in this misery than it did when I died. I'm here because I stole treasures from the church. I even blamed it on someone else. But since you're here, listen to this: First, Pistoia will suffer. Then, Florence will change its people and ways. Mars will send a storm over Val di Magra, covering it with clouds. A fierce battle will rage over Campo Picen, and every 'Bianco' will be struck down. I tell you this to make you feel pain."

Chapter 25: Vanni Fucci's Punishment. Agnello Brunelleschi, Buoso degli Abati, Puccio Sciancato, Cianfa de' Donati, and Guercio Cavalcanti.

After finishing, Vanni Fucci raised his hands and made an obscene gesture toward the sky, shouting, "Take that, God! This is aimed at you!"

Right then, the snakes became my allies. One coiled around his neck as if to say, "You will speak no more." Another wrapped tightly around his arms so he couldn't move.

"Pistoia, why don't you burn to ashes and perish?" I thought. "You are unmatched in your wickedness."

As Vanni fled without another word, I saw a furious Centaur approach, shouting, "Where is that mocker?" His back was covered in serpents, even more than those found in the swamps of Maremma. On his shoulders, just behind his neck, lay a dragon with its wings spread wide, setting fire to everything it touched.

My guide then told me, "That is Cacus. He lived under the rock on Mount Aventine and often turned the place into a lake of blood."

He doesn't go on the same path as his brothers because of the deceitful theft he committed with the herd he had near him. His tricks finally ended under the blows of Hercules, who may have struck him a hundred times, even though he only felt ten."

As he spoke, three spirits appeared below us. Neither I nor my Guide noticed them until they shouted, "Who are you?" This interrupted our conversation, and we turned our attention to them.

I didn't recognize them, but it happened as it often does, where one ends up naming another. One of them called out, "Where is Cianfa?" I raised my finger from my chin to my nose so my Guide would pay attention.

If you, Reader, are slow to believe what I say, I wouldn't blame you, for even I find it hard to accept what I saw. As I stared at them, a six-legged serpent jumped forward and latched onto one of them.

It wrapped its middle feet around his stomach, grabbed his arms with its front legs, and bit both of his cheeks. Its hind legs stretched over his thighs, and its tail slipped between them, spreading over his back.

Never had ivy wrapped so tightly around a tree as this monstrous creature coiled itself around the man's body. Then, they began to merge as if made of hot wax. Their colors blended, and they no longer looked like themselves.

It was like watching flames spread across a sheet of paper, turning it brown before it fully burns. The two other spirits watched and cried out, "Oh no, Agnello! How you've changed! You're now neither two nor one!"

The two heads had already merged into one, and two figures became one face. Their four limbs turned into two arms, while their legs, thighs, belly, and chest transformed into something entirely new and unseen.

The original forms were erased, replaced by a twisted shape that slowly walked away.

Just like a lizard darting across a road in the heat of summer, a small, fiery serpent, dark as pepper, came rushing toward the other two. It struck one of them in the stomach. The man collapsed, his eyes locked on the serpent. He stayed still, yawning like he was in a fever or deep sleep.

The serpent stared back at him. Smoke began to pour out of the man's wound and the serpent's mouth, mixing together in the air.

Let Lucan and Ovid be silent now. What I'm about to describe is far more extraordinary than anything they wrote about.

The snake split its tail into a fork, and the wounded man's feet started to join together. The man's legs merged, and the snake's split tail began to take the shape of human legs.

I saw the man's arms shrink into his body, while the short legs of the serpent grew longer. The snake's back legs twisted into the shape of what a man usually keeps hidden. Meanwhile, the man's limbs reshaped into something more reptilian.

Their colors changed, hair grew on one, while the other lost its hair. One stood up, while the other fell. They didn't take their eyes off each other as their faces transformed.

The one standing pulled his face back towards his temples. The excess flesh formed into ears, while the rest became a nose, and his lips thickened.

The one on the ground pushed his head forward, drawing his ears into his head like a snail pulling back its horns. His tongue split into two, while the snake's forked tongue sealed up. The smoke around them ceased.

The soul that had become a serpent slithered away, hissing down the valley. The man who turned into a reptile spat out words as he fled.

He then turned his new shoulders and said to the other, "Now Buoso will crawl down this path just like I did."

This is how I saw the seventh pocket of Hell shift and change. Forgive me, Reader, if my writing struggles to capture the strange sight.

Even though my mind was confused, I could still clearly see Puccio Sciancato. He was the only one of the three who didn't change. The other was the one mourned by you, Gaville.

Chapter 26: The Eighth Bolgia: Evil Counselors. Ulysses and Diomed. Ulysses' Last Voyage.

Rejoice, Florence! You are so great that you spread your fame across land, sea, and even through Hell! I found five of your citizens among these thieves, and it brings me shame. Your name is not honored here.

If dreams tell the truth before dawn, you will soon learn what Prato wishes upon you, Florence. And if it happened now, it wouldn't be too soon. It must happen, and it will grieve me more the older I get.

We continued on our way, climbing the stairs that had brought us down before. My Guide led me back up.

Following the lonely path among the rocks and ridges, I found it difficult to move without using both hands and feet. I felt sorrow then, and I feel it again now as I remember what I saw. I need to hold back my thoughts more than usual so they don't stray unless guided by virtue. If some good fortune has been granted to me, I should not waste it.

As many as the fireflies that a farmer sees down in the valley while resting on the hill during the time when the sun hides its face from us, I saw flames flickering in the eighth pit. I noticed this as soon as I could look down into its depths.

Just as the man who avenged himself on the bears watched Elijah's chariot rise to heaven, seeing only the flame like a small cloud in the sky, so did each fire move along the trench. Each flame hid a sinner within it.

I stood on the bridge, leaning forward to see better. If I hadn't grabbed onto a rock, I would have fallen off. My Guide, noticing my focus, said, "Inside those flames are souls. Each one wraps itself in its own fire."

"Master," I replied, "I thought so already, but now I'm certain because of what you said. I wanted to ask who is in that flame, the one split at the top, almost like the pyre where Eteocles and his brother were placed."

He answered, "Inside that flame are Ulysses and Diomed. They are being punished together for their deeds. They suffer here for the ambush of the Trojan horse, which led to the fall of Troy. They also suffer for the trick that still makes Deidamia mourn Achilles and for stealing the Palladium."

"If they have the power to speak inside those flames," I said, "please, Master, I beg you, let us wait until that split flame comes closer. I am eager to hear them."

He responded, "Your request is worthy of praise, so I accept it. But let me speak to them. They might not appreciate your words, as they were Greeks."

When the flame came near enough, my Guide spoke, "O you who are two souls in one fire, if I earned your respect while I was alive, or if my writing meant anything to you, stop and tell us how you met your end."

The larger horn of the ancient flame began to sway back and forth, like a flame caught in the wind. Then, as if it were a tongue, it spoke.

"When I left Circe, who kept me hidden for more than a year near Gaeta, neither my love for my son nor respect for my father, nor even my longing for Penelope could overcome my desire to experience the world and learn about human vices and virtues.

I set out on the open sea with one ship and my faithful crew. I saw both the coasts of Spain and Morocco and the islands that surround the sea.

My crew and I were old and slow when we reached the narrow passage where Hercules set his warnings, telling man not to venture further. We left Seville behind on the right and Ceuta on the left.

'Brothers,' I said, 'you have faced a hundred thousand dangers to reach the West. Do not waste the little time left to you. Seek knowledge and explore the uncharted world. Remember your noble origins; you were not made to live like beasts, but to pursue virtue and knowledge.'

My words inspired my crew so much that I could hardly have held them back. We turned our ship toward the morning sun and spread our sails for this mad journey.

We had sailed through the night, seeing all the stars of the other pole, while ours had sunk too low to be seen. Five times the moon had waxed and waned since we entered this deep passage. Then we saw a mountain in the distance, taller than any we had ever seen.

We rejoiced, but soon our joy turned to sorrow. A whirlwind came from the new land and struck the front of the ship. Three times it spun us around; on the fourth, it lifted the stern and sank the bow, until the sea closed over us."

Chapter 27: Guido da Montefeltro. His Deception by Pope Boniface VIII.

The flame stood tall and quiet, speaking no more, and moved away from us with the permission of my gentle Guide. However, another flame behind it caught our attention with a strange noise.

Just like the Sicilian bull that roared with the cries of the man trapped inside it, this flame seemed to speak in a way that made its suffering clear, even though it was just fire.

Then, after some time, the flame found a way to form words as it rose to its tip. We heard it say, "O you who spoke in the Lombard dialect, saying 'Go your way; I do not press you further,' don't be annoyed that I come late to speak with you. Stay a moment, for you see how I burn and suffer."

If you have just fallen into this dark world from that beautiful land of Italy, where I committed my sins, tell me, are the people of Romagna at peace or war? I came from the mountains between Urbino and the ridge where the Tiber River starts."

I was still listening closely when my Guide touched my side and said, "Speak to him; this one is Italian."

I already had my answer ready, so I began, "O soul hidden in the flames below, Romagna has never been without wars, and it's the same now with its rulers. However, I left no open wars there at this moment.

Ravenna stands as it has for many years. The Eagle of Polenta watches over it, protecting even Cervia with its wings. The city that once resisted and defeated the French now finds itself under the 'Green Paws' again. The old and young Mastiff of Verrucchio, who once treated Montagna so cruelly, use their sharp teeth to control their lands.

The cities of Lamone and Santerno are ruled by the Lion of the white den, who changes sides between summer and winter. And the city on the Savio River, lying between the plains and the mountains, lives in a constant struggle between tyranny and freedom.

Now, I ask you to tell us who you are. Don't be stubborn like others. That way, your name might still have honor in the world above."

After the fire roared a little more, it moved its pointed tip back and forth, then spoke:

"If I thought that my reply would reach someone who would return to the world above, I would stay silent, fearing disgrace. But since no one ever leaves this place, if I've heard correctly, I will answer without fear.

I was a soldier, then I became a friar, thinking that wearing the robe would make up for my sins. And it would have, if not for the high priest—the Pope—who led me back to my old ways. I'll tell you how and why.

While I was still flesh and blood, my deeds were not brave like a lion's, but cunning like a fox. I knew all the tricks and deceptions, using them so well that my reputation spread everywhere.

When I reached the age where I should have slowed down and retired, what I once loved now displeased me. I repented and confessed my sins. I would have found peace, if not for the Pope, the leader of modern Pharisees, who was fighting a war near the Lateran. It was not against Saracens or Jews; it was against other Christians.

Neither my religious status nor his sacred role stopped him from seeking me out, just like Emperor Constantine sought out Saint Sylvester to cure his leprosy. The Pope came to me for help to cure his pride. I hesitated at first, as his words were mad with arrogance.

Then he said, 'Don't be afraid. I absolve you now. Tell me how I can destroy Palestrina. I have the power to open and close Heaven's gates, as you know. The two keys are mine, which my predecessor didn't value.'

His strong arguments pushed me to speak, where silence would have been better. I said, 'Father, since you cleanse me of the sin I am about to commit, a long promise with a short fulfillment will bring you victory.'

After I died, Saint Francis came for me. But a black cherubim stopped him, saying, 'Don't take him. He belongs to my servants. He gave fraudulent advice, and I've been after him ever since. Those who do not repent cannot be forgiven. One cannot both repent and willfully continue sinning. It's a contradiction.'

Oh, how I trembled when he seized me, saying, 'Did you not think I could reason?' He brought me to Minos, who wrapped his tail around me eight times. Then, in great anger, Minos bit his tail and said, 'This one is meant for the thieving fire.' That's how I ended up here, suffering in this flame."

When the flame finished speaking, it left us, twisting and shaking its sharp tip as it went. My Guide and I continued our journey, climbing over the crag and crossing another arch. This bridge covered the next trench, where those who cause discord receive their punishment.

Chapter 28: The Ninth Bolgia: Schismatics. Muhammad and Ali. Pier da Medicina, Curio, Mosca, and Bertrand de Born.

Who could ever describe in full the blood and wounds that I now saw? Even with the clearest words, no one could fully tell the horror of it. Our memory and language simply cannot capture so much pain.

If you gathered everyone who once lamented their wounds on the cursed land of Puglia—those who suffered at the hands of the Romans and the long war that left behind spoils of rings, as Livy records correctly; those who resisted Robert Guiscard's attacks; and all the rest whose bones lie at Ceperano, where every Apulian was a traitor, or at Tagliacozzo, where the unarmed Alardo won—you still wouldn't see anything as terrible as the sight in the Ninth Bolgia.

Never had a barrel burst as violently as I saw a man split open from his chin to where the body breaks wind. His intestines hung between his legs; his heart was visible, and the disgusting bag that turns food into waste was wide open.

As I stared in horror, he looked at me, opened his chest with his hands, and said, "Look at how I tear myself apart! See how mangled I am! Ahead of me, Ali walks, his face split from his forehead to his chin. Everyone you see here spread lies and caused division while alive; that's why we are cut open like this.

Behind us is a demon who cuts us open with his sword as we walk around this pit. By the time we circle back to him, our wounds heal, and he slices us open again. But who are you, standing there on the crag, just watching? Are you delaying your own punishment?"

My Guide answered, "He is not dead, nor is he here because of guilt. He is here to gain experience; I, who am dead, must lead him through Hell from circle to circle. This is true, as I now speak to you."

Over a hundred souls stopped in the pit to look at me, forgetting their own pain in their amazement.

"Tell Brother Dolcino to stock up on supplies," said Muhammad to me, "if he doesn't want to join me soon. The snow will otherwise hand victory to his enemies, the people of Novara." Then he lifted one foot to leave but stopped to say this, and finally stretched out his leg to walk away.

Another soul, with his throat cut, his nose sliced off, and one ear missing, stood staring at me in surprise. His throat was red with blood. "You who are not condemned by sin," he said, "and who I saw alive in the land of Latium—unless I'm mistaken—remember Pier da Medicina if you ever return to the fair plains that slope from Vercelli to Marcabo.

Tell the best men of Fano, Messer Guido and Angiolello, that they will be betrayed. They will be thrown overboard and drowned near Cattolica by a cruel tyrant. Neptune, between Cyprus and Majorca, never witnessed such a crime among pirates.

The traitor, who only sees with one eye, holds the land that someone here wishes never to see again. He will trick them into a meeting, and the wind from Focara won't save them."

I asked, "Tell me who this person is, so I can bring news of you."

Pier then grabbed another soul's jaw and opened his mouth. "This is him," Pier said, "but he can't speak. He was exiled and advised Caesar to strike first, never delay."

I saw Curio, the one who boldly urged Caesar to cross the Rubicon, now standing stunned, his tongue cut from his slit throat.

Then, another figure, his hands cut off, lifted his stumps into the air, his face smeared with blood. "Remember me," he cried. "I am Mosca, who said, 'A thing done is an end!' That phrase sowed the seeds of war in Tuscany."

"Yes," I added, "and death to your family." He left, drowning in sorrow and rage.

I continued to look around and saw something so terrifying that I hesitate to recount it. If my conscience didn't reassure me, I would not speak of it. I saw a headless body walking, carrying its own head by the hair, like a lantern. The head stared at us, saying, "Oh, misery!"

It was like a lamp, both the head and the body in one. When it reached the bridge's foot, it lifted its arm, bringing the head closer to us to speak. "Look at this terrible punishment," it said. "I am Bertrand de Born, the one who caused a son to rebel against his father. For sowing discord between people so close, my brain is now separated from my body. This is the justice I now endure."

The Divine Comedy

Chapter 29: Geri del Bello. The Tenth Bolgia: Alchemists. Griffolino d'Arezzo and Capocchio.

The many people and their various wounds overwhelmed me. My eyes wanted to stop and weep. But Virgil said, "Why are you still staring at these sad, mutilated souls? You didn't do this at the other pits. Remember, the valley is twenty-two miles long, and now the moon is beneath our feet. We have little time left, and there's still much to see."

"If you knew why I was looking," I replied, "you might allow a longer pause." While I spoke, my guide walked ahead, and I quickly followed, adding, "In that pit where I was staring, I think a spirit of my family suffers for his sins."

The Master replied, "Don't worry about him anymore. Focus on what lies ahead. I saw him earlier under the little bridge, pointing at you and angrily gesturing. He was called Geri del Bello. You were so focused on another soul then that you didn't notice him, and he left."

I said, "His violent death, which hasn't yet been avenged, made him angry. That's probably why he walked away without speaking to me. It makes me pity him even more."

We spoke like this until we reached a place on the crag where the next valley came into view. If there were more light, we could see to the bottom. When we stood above the last trench of Malebolge, the damned souls could now be seen.

The cries of suffering pierced my heart. I covered my ears with my hands. It was like the pain in hospitals during a plague, where the air is thick with disease, as in Valdichiana in the summer, or in Maremma or Sardinia. The stench from this pit was like that of rotting flesh.

We moved to the farthest bank, to the left, and I could see more clearly the punishment below. Here, Justice punished the forgers. It was a terrible sight. It reminded me of the ancient plague in Aegina, where all creatures died, and later the people were restored from ants, as the poets say. The spirits lay scattered on the ground in various positions. Some lay on their backs, others on their bellies, while some crawled along the filthy path.

We walked quietly, listening to the sick souls who didn't have the strength to lift themselves. I saw two leaning against each other like two pots leaning together. Their bodies were covered in scabs. I never saw a stable boy work as hard with a currycomb as these souls scratched at their itching skin with their nails. They scraped the scabs down their bodies like one would scrape fish scales with a knife.

My guide spoke to one of them, "You, who scratch yourself like that, tell me if there are any Italians here. May your nails keep working forever."

"We are Italians, as you see," one of them replied through tears. "But who are you who asks about us?"

The guide replied, "I'm here with this living man, traveling down cliff by cliff to show him Hell."

They suddenly stopped supporting each other and turned to me, trembling. My guide encouraged me, "Tell them whatever you want." I began, "May your names not be forgotten on earth. Tell me who you are and where you come from. Don't let your suffering stop you from speaking."

"I am from Arezzo," one of them answered. "I was burned at the stake by Albert of Siena. But that isn't why I'm here. I once joked that I could fly. Albert believed me, so he made me try to prove it. When I failed, he had me burned. But for my practice of alchemy, Minos condemned me to this last pit."

Then I said to the poet, "Are the people of Siena more foolish than the French?"

The other leper overheard and replied, "Except for Stricca, who was wise with money, and Niccolo, who discovered the luxury of using cloves, and Caccia d'Asciano, who wasted his vineyards and woods, and Abbagliato, who flaunted his wit."

Then he added, "But if you want to know who agrees with you against the Sienese, look at me. I am Capocchio, who falsified metals with alchemy. You must remember me; I was good at imitating nature."

Chapter 30: Other Falsifiers or Forgers. Gianni Schicchi, Myrrha, Adam of Brescia, Potiphar's Wife, and Sinon of Troy.

It was during the time when Juno was furious at Thebes for Semele's actions that Athamas, driven mad, saw his wife walking with their two children. He yelled, "Set the nets to catch the lioness and her cubs!" Then, without pity, he grabbed his son Learchus and smashed him against a rock. His wife, carrying the other child, drowned herself.

In another tragic moment, when Troy fell, Hecuba, once a queen, became a prisoner. When she saw her daughter Polyxena dead and found her son Polydorus' body washed ashore, she lost her mind and howled like a dog in her grief. But neither Athamas' madness nor Hecuba's suffering was as cruel as what I saw next.

Two pale and naked spirits came running towards us, biting like wild boars. One of them seized Capocchio by the neck and dragged him along the ground, scraping his stomach against the rocky floor. The Aretine, who was trembling nearby, told me, "That crazy spirit is Gianni Schicchi. He roams around attacking others in his madness."

I said to him, "Before it attacks you, please tell me who the other spirit is." He replied, "That is the ghost of Myrrha, who fell in love with her own father in a way that was far beyond right. She disguised herself to sin with him. Gianni Schicchi did something similar; he pretended to be Buoso Donati to forge a will and claim an inheritance."

After those two mad spirits passed, I turned my eyes to look at another tormented soul. This one looked like a distorted lute, bent at the waist. His body was swollen with dropsy, which caused his limbs to be mismatched with his bloated belly. He kept his lips apart, gasping for air like someone burning with thirst.

He noticed us and said, "You who are here without suffering, I don't know why, look at my misery. I am Master Adam. When I was alive, I had everything I wanted, but now, I crave just a drop of water. I keep thinking of the cool streams flowing down from the hills of Casentino into the Arno River. Their memory dries me up more than this disease that has wasted my body.

"In life, I was punished for forging the coins stamped with Saint John the Baptist's image. For this crime, I was burned alive in Romena. Now, if I could see even one of the Guidos or Alessandro here, I'd give anything for that sight—even Branda's fountain wouldn't be enough. I heard that one of them is already here, but I can't move to find him since I'm chained to this spot."

I asked him, "Who are those two lying there, smoking like a wet hand on a cold day?" He replied, "When I fell into this pit, I found them already here. They haven't moved since. One is the woman who falsely accused Joseph, and the other is Sinon, the Greek who tricked the Trojans. Their terrible fever makes them stink."

One of them, hearing his name mentioned, punched his swollen belly with his fist, making it sound like a drum. Master Adam responded, swinging his arm, "Even though I can't move my limbs, I still have one free arm for hitting." Sinon retorted, "You didn't fight back when you were thrown into the fire for forging coins. But now you want to hit me?"

Master Adam replied, "True, but at least I wasn't a liar like you, deceiving people at Troy."

"If I lied, you forged money!" said Sinon. "I'm here for one crime, but you're here for more than any other sinner."

"Remember the Trojan horse, liar!" Adam shot back. "The whole world knows about your trick."

"And may your endless thirst torment you forever," Sinon snapped. "May the dirty water before your eyes mock you as you suffer."

Adam hissed, "Your mouth is always open for evil. If I'm thirsty and swollen, you have a burning fever and an aching head. You'd do anything to see yourself in Narcissus' mirror."

I was so absorbed in their argument that my guide, Virgil, had to break my focus. He sternly said, "Now look at what you're doing. Pay attention!" Hearing the anger in his voice, I turned towards him, filled with shame. That feeling still lingers within me.

As one who dreams of their own suffering, hoping it's just a dream and wishing it would go away, I stood there, unable to speak. I wanted to explain myself, but I couldn't find the words.

"Feeling a little shame is better than letting it build up," my Master said. "So don't dwell on this. Remember, I am always by your side. If you ever find yourself in a similar situation, it's best not to listen to foolish arguments."

Chapter 31: The Giants, Nimrod, Ephialtes, and Antaeus. Descent to Cocytus.

The same voice that scolded me then offered me comfort, just like Achilles' spear, which both wounded and healed. We turned our backs on the valley, crossing the bank without speaking. It was neither day nor night, so I could barely see ahead. But I heard the sound of a horn so loud that it would have drowned out any thunder. Instinctively, I turned my eyes towards the sound.

It reminded me of the horn Orlando blew when Charlemagne was defeated. I turned my head and thought I saw tall towers in the distance. "Master, what city is that?" I asked.

"You're seeing things," he replied. "Those aren't towers; they're giants. The distance makes you think otherwise. When we get closer, you'll see the truth. Let's hurry up." He took my hand and said, "These giants are standing in the well, and from their waists up, they look like towers."

As the fog slowly lifted, I began to see more clearly. What I had mistaken for towers were indeed giants standing around the well's edge. Fear gripped me. They reminded me of the towers at Monteriggioni, except these were the giants whom Zeus still threatens with his thunderbolts.

I saw one giant's face, shoulders, chest, and part of his belly. His arms hung by his sides. Nature must have regretted creating these beings; they had strength, but not the wisdom to use it well.

His face was as large as the pine cone in Saint Peter's Square in Rome, and the rest of his body matched in size. Three men from Friesland wouldn't even reach his hair. I could see thirty palms' length of him above the ground.

The giant began to shout in a strange language: "Raphael mai amech izabi almi!"

My guide, Virgil, spoke sternly: "You foolish soul, stick to your horn. Let out your rage with that, not with your words. Check the strap around your neck. It holds your horn in place and keeps you tied down."

Then, turning to me, Virgil said, "This is Nimrod. Because of his actions, the world no longer speaks a single language. Let's leave him here; speaking to him is pointless since no one can understand his words."

The Divine Comedy

We continued our journey and came across another giant who was even more fierce. His right arm was chained in front, and his left arm was pinned behind him. Chains wrapped around his neck and body, leaving only a small part uncovered.

"This is Ephialtes," Virgil explained. "He once dared to challenge Zeus. Now, he suffers here, unable to move his arms."

"Can I see Briareus?" I asked.

"You will see Antaeus soon. He can speak and is free, unlike this one. Briareus is farther away, chained up like this one, but even more fearsome," Virgil replied.

Suddenly, Ephialtes shook so violently that it was like an earthquake. I was terrified, thinking we might die if not for the chains holding him.

We moved on and came to Antaeus. He stood five ells high, not counting his head, rising from the cave.

Virgil spoke to him, "You who once brought a thousand lions to the valley where Scipio defeated Hannibal, please help us. Place us gently at the bottom of this pit where the frozen river Cocytus lies. This man here can tell others about you when he returns to the world."

Antaeus reached out with his massive hands, which even Hercules once felt the weight of. Virgil called me to his side, and Antaeus lifted both of us as if we were light as feathers. I felt like I was looking up at the leaning tower of Carisenda with a cloud hanging over it.

Antaeus lowered us into the pit, placing us where Judas suffers alongside Lucifer. Then, without hesitation, he stood up straight again, like the mast of a ship.

Chapter 32: The Ninth Circle: Traitors. The Frozen Lake of Cocytus. First Division, Caina: Traitors to their Kindred. Camicion de' Pazzi. Second Division, Antenora: Traitors to their Country. Dante questions Bocca degli Abati. Buoso da Duera.

If I had words as harsh and strong as the dreadful place I'm about to describe, I would express my thoughts more fully. But I lack those words, so I hesitate. Speaking of the very bottom of the universe is no joke. This task is not for a child's voice. I hope the Muses, who helped build the walls of Thebes, will help me too so that I can tell the story correctly.

Oh, wicked souls, it would have been better if you had been born as sheep or goats rather than ending up here.

When we reached the dark pit below the giants' feet, even further down, I looked around at the high walls. Then I heard, "Watch your step! Don't trample on the heads of these miserable, tired souls!"

I turned and saw a frozen lake beneath me. It looked more like a solid sheet of glass than water. It was frozen so thick that even if a huge mountain fell on it, it wouldn't crack. Not even the Danube or the Don rivers freeze like this in winter.

Frozen in the ice, I saw pale, sad souls. They stood with their heads bent, their faces pointing down. Their tears froze as they fell, turning into ice on their faces.

I looked down and saw two figures so close that their hair was tangled together. I asked, "Who are you two?" They raised their faces to look at me. As their eyes filled with tears, the cold froze them, sealing their eyes shut. Their heads pressed together like stubborn goats.

One of them, who had lost his ears to the cold, spoke, "Why do you stare at us? If you want to know who we are, this valley belongs to us and our father, Albert. We are from one body, and you won't find any other soul in this whole icy area more deserving of this punishment. I am Camicion de' Pazzi, and I wait here for Carlino to join and ease my suffering."

I saw hundreds of faces, purple from the cold. A shiver ran through me that I'll never forget.

As we walked toward the center of the lake, where everything heavy sinks, I accidentally kicked someone's head.

The soul cried, "Why do you kick me? Are you here to make my suffering worse?"

"Master, wait for me," I said. "I need to clear up something with him."

My guide paused, and I turned to the soul, asking, "Who are you to curse others like this?"

He replied, "Who are you, walking through Antenora, kicking others? Even if you're alive, you've gone too far."

"I am alive," I answered. "If you tell me who you are, I can mention your name in the world above."

"I'd rather not!" he snapped. "Leave me alone. You're terrible at flattery."

I grabbed his hair and said, "Tell me who you are, or I'll rip your hair out!"

He screamed, "Even if you pull all my hair, I won't tell you my name!"

I had already twisted his hair in my hand when another voice shouted, "Bocca, what's wrong? Why do you yell? Who's bothering you?"

Now I knew who he was. "I don't need you to speak anymore, traitor. I'll make sure your name is known," I said.

"Go ahead," Bocca replied. "But don't leave out the one who spoke just now. He's here because he betrayed the French. You can say, 'I saw Buoso da Duera standing in the cold.' Also, if you're asked who else is here, say you saw Beccaria, whose throat was cut by the people of Florence. You'll also find Gianni del Soldanier, Ganelon, and Tebaldello, who betrayed Faenza while everyone slept."

As we walked away, I saw two souls frozen in the same hole. One was biting the other's head as if it were a piece of bread. Just like Tydeus in the story, gnawing on Menalippus's skull out of anger, this soul bit down viciously on the other's head.

Chapter 33: Count Ugolino and the Archbishop Ruggieri. The Death of Count Ugolino's Sons. Third Division of the Ninth Circle, Ptolomaea: Traitors to their Friends. Friar Alberigo, Branco d' Oria.

"Hey, you who show such hatred by chewing on this man," I said, "tell me why you hate him so much. If your complaint is justified, and you tell me who you both are and what he did, I'll make sure your story is known in the world above."

The sinner lifted his mouth from his gruesome meal, wiping it on the hair of the head he had been chewing on. Then he began, "You want me to relive this horrible pain that already haunts me? Fine. But if my words can bring shame to the traitor I'm devouring, then I'll tell you while I weep. I don't know who you are, or how you got down here, but you sound like a Florentine.

"Know this: I am Count Ugolino, and this here is Archbishop Ruggieri. Let me explain why I'm here. Because of his evil schemes, I was imprisoned and later put to death. But you might not know how cruel my death was, so listen closely.

"There was a small opening in the tower where I was held, now known as the 'Tower of Hunger.' I had been locked in there for many months when I had a terrible dream that hinted at the future. I dreamed that Ruggieri was hunting a wolf and its cubs on a mountain. He had set fierce, trained hounds on them. In my dream, I saw the father and his sons collapse from exhaustion, and the dogs tore them apart.

"When I woke up, I heard my sons crying in their sleep, asking for bread. If that doesn't make you cry, then what do you even cry about? They woke up, and the time came when we used to receive food, but no one brought us anything. I heard the door to the tower being locked, and I looked at my sons' faces. I didn't cry—I had turned to stone inside. They cried, and my little Anselm said, 'Father, why do you look at us like that?'

"I didn't shed a single tear. I stayed silent all day and all night until another day came. When a faint light finally shone into our prison, I looked at my sons and saw my own sadness on their faces. In despair, I bit both my hands. They thought I did it out of hunger, so they said, 'Father, if it would hurt less, eat us instead. You gave us this flesh; now you can take it away.'

"I calmed myself, so I wouldn't make them even sadder. We stayed silent for another day and the next. Oh, cruel earth, why didn't you just swallow us? On the fourth day, Gaddo fell down at my feet, crying, 'Father, why don't you help me?' And there he died. The other three died one by one between the fifth and sixth days. I was blind by then, groping around to touch their bodies. I called out to them for three days after they had died. Then hunger did what grief could not."

When he finished speaking, he resumed gnawing on the head with his teeth, like a dog tearing at a bone.

Ah, Pisa, shame of the land where people say "Si!" Since your neighbors are slow to punish you, let the islands of Capraia and Gorgona block the Arno River, so that everyone in you may drown! If Count Ugolino betrayed you, Pisa, you still had no right to punish his innocent sons. Their youth made them guiltless.

We moved on further to where the ice trapped other souls, but this time they were all upside down. Here, even tears freeze, turning back into the eyes and making their suffering worse. Though the cold had numbed my face, I thought I felt a breeze. "Master," I asked, "what's causing this wind?"

"You will soon see the answer," he replied. "When we get closer, you'll find out what's making the wind blow."

Then, one of the souls trapped in the ice called out, "Oh, cruel souls who have been sent to this final place, lift these frozen veils from my eyes so I can weep a little before my tears freeze again!"

I said, "If you tell me who you are, I'll help you. If I don't, may I end up at the very bottom of this ice!"

He replied, "I am Friar Alberigo, the one from the 'evil garden.' I am here getting a date in return for my fig."

"You mean you're dead already?" I asked.

"I don't know what's happening to my body in the world above," he answered. "Sometimes a soul falls here before death when a demon takes over the body. That's what happened to me, and that's why I'm here."

Down here, souls fall straight into this pit. The one behind me, Ser Branca d'Oria, still appears to be living up above. You should know this if you've just come down here."

I responded, "I think you're mistaken—Branca d'Oria isn't dead yet. He's alive, eating, drinking, sleeping, and wearing clothes."

"In the ditch above, among the Malebranche demons, where the sticky pitch boils, Michel Zanche hadn't even arrived yet when Branca left his body to a devil. That devil now rules his body, along with a relative of his who helped him betray others."

Then he begged, "Reach out your hand and open my eyes." But I didn't help him—I thought refusing him was the kindest thing to do.

Ah, Genoese! You are filled with every vice, and not a shred of virtue. Why aren't you wiped off the earth? Even here, in the lowest part of Hell, I found one of you already bathing in Cocytus, even though his body above still walks the earth!

Chapter 34: Fourth Division of the Ninth Circle, the Judecca: Traitors to their Lords and Benefactors. Lucifer, Judas Iscariot, Brutus, and Cassius. The Chasm of Lethe. The Ascent.

"'Vexilla Regis prodeunt Inferni'—the banners of the King of Hell advance," my Master said. "Look ahead, and see him if you can."

It was like seeing a windmill far away through a thick fog or in the darkening night. To escape the gusts, I stepped behind my Guide, for there was no other shelter.

By now, we were in the part of Hell where the souls were fully trapped in ice, shining through like straw embedded in glass. Some were lying down, others were standing, some with their heads, and others with their feet. Some were even curled up like bows, their faces touching their feet.

We had come so far that my Master thought it was time to show me the creature who once had a beautiful face. He moved in front of me and made me stop. "Behold Dis," he said, "and prepare yourself for what you'll see."

I was so frozen with fear that I can't even describe it in words. I didn't die, but I wasn't alive either—imagine, if you can, being stuck in that state between life and death.

The Emperor of this wretched realm stood halfway out of the ice. He was enormous—bigger than any giant I had seen before. If giants were to compare themselves to him, they'd be like children compared to a grown man.

If he was once as beautiful as he is now ugly, and if he dared to rebel against his Maker, then it's no wonder that all troubles come from him. It was shocking to see that he had three faces on one head: the face in the middle was red, the right face was a mix of white and yellow, and the left was as dark as the people who live near the Nile.

Under each face came two massive wings, as big as sails on a sea ship, but without feathers. They were like bat wings, and he flapped them, creating three separate winds that froze all of Cocytus. He cried with six eyes, and from each of his three mouths came tears and bloody drool. Each mouth gnawed on a sinner, chewing them as if they were food for his teeth.

The sinner in the middle mouth suffered the most; the chewing was nothing compared to the clawing, for sometimes his back was completely stripped of skin.

"That soul up there," said my Master, "is Judas Iscariot. His head is inside Lucifer's mouth, and his legs are outside, kicking. The two others who are being bitten head-first are Brutus and Cassius. You can see how Brutus twists in silence, and how strong Cassius looks. But the night is returning, and it's time for us to leave. We've seen all there is to see."

As my Master wished, I wrapped my arms around his neck, and he took advantage of the moment. When Lucifer's wings opened wide, my Master clung to the furry sides of the devil. He slowly climbed down between the thick hair and the frozen crust of the ice.

When we reached the point where Lucifer's thigh rotates, the Guide turned around and began to climb upwards, holding onto the hairy legs of the devil as one would climb a mountain. I thought we were heading back into Hell, but my Guide kept telling me to hold on tight; we were finally leaving all this evil behind.

We climbed through a narrow hole, and my Master seated me on the edge, then pulled himself up. I lifted my eyes, thinking I would still see Lucifer the way I had left him, but instead, I saw his legs pointing upwards.

If I felt disoriented then, let those who don't see what I saw understand how confused I was by what I had just experienced.

"Get up," said my Master, "there's still a long way to go, and the road is hard. The sun has already reached middle-tierce."

We weren't in any grand palace—this was a rough, natural dungeon with an uneven floor and little light.

"Before we leave this abyss," I said, getting up, "please clarify something for me: where's the ice? And how is Lucifer fixed like that upside-down? How did the sun cross the sky so quickly?"

"You still think you're on the other side of the center of the earth," my Guide explained. "You were, as long as I was descending. But when I turned around, you passed the point where all weight is drawn from every side. Now you are under the opposite hemisphere, below the land where Christ was crucified, standing on the little sphere that makes up the other face of the Judecca."

Here, it is morning when over there it's evening. The one who used his hair as our staircase still remains frozen in place, just as he was before.

On this side, he fell down from Heaven. The land that once rose here sank back into the sea out of fear of him, leaving this hemisphere behind. To escape him, the land over here retreated, leaving the space now filled by the ocean.

There is a place deep below, far from Beelzebub, extending as far as the grave. You can't see it, but you can hear a small stream running through a crack in the stone. The water has worn down the rock as it flows, winding and falling gently.

My Guide and I entered this hidden path to return to the bright world. Without stopping for rest, we climbed up. He led the way, and I followed, until I saw through a round opening some of the beautiful things the sky holds.

And so, we came out to see the stars again.

Part 2 Purgatorio

Chapter 1: The Shores of Purgatory. The Four Stars. Cato of Utica. The Rush.

Now, my little boat of genius sails toward calmer waters, leaving behind that sea of suffering. I will now sing about the second kingdom, where the human spirit cleanses itself and becomes worthy of heaven.

But let my poetry rise again. O holy Muses, this is your realm. Calliope, guide my song, with the sound that struck those poor magpies so hard they lost all hope of pardon.

The sweet color of the eastern sapphire filled the clear sky and brought joy to my eyes as soon as I left the gloomy air that had weighed down my spirit. The beautiful planet, which inspires love, lit up the eastern sky, covering the stars in her path. I turned to the right, looking at the opposite pole, and saw four stars never seen except by the first people. Heaven rejoiced in their flames. O northern world, how unlucky you are not to see these stars!

After looking at them, I turned slightly toward the other pole, where the Big Dipper had disappeared. There, I saw an old man standing alone. His presence was so dignified that he commanded more respect than any son owes his father. His long beard was mixed with white hair, and a double row of tresses fell onto his chest. The light from the four holy stars illuminated his face, making him appear like the sun.

"Who are you?" he asked, moving his white hair. "Who guided you here, fleeing the eternal prison and crossing the dark river? Who lit your path out of the endless night of Hell? Is the law of the abyss broken, or has Heaven made a new decree allowing the damned to come to my shores?"

My guide grasped me and, with words and gestures, made me bow in reverence. Then he answered, "I did not come on my own. A Lady from Heaven asked me to help this one. So, I guided him here. Since you wish to know more about our journey, I will tell you. This man has not yet faced death, but he was close to it because of his foolishness. There was no other way to save him than to take him through Hell. I have shown him all the tormented souls, and now I bring him to you, so he may see those who cleanse themselves under your care.

"It would take too long to explain every step, but know that a heavenly virtue aids me in guiding him. Please allow his passage. He seeks freedom, which is so precious that one would give their life for it. You know this because, for freedom's sake, you died in Utica, leaving behind the clothing that will shine on the last day.

"We do not break Heaven's law, for this one lives, and Minos does not bind me. I come from the realm where Marcia, your beloved, still prays for you to claim her. For her sake, let us pass through your seven realms. I will remember this favor for her if you permit us."

"Marcia was dear to me when I lived on the other side," he replied, "and I granted every wish she made. But now that she is beyond the evil river, she cannot move me, as the law established after my death forbids it. However, if a Lady from Heaven moves you, then I will not refuse. You need not flatter me. Just ask for her sake.

"But first, you must bind him with a smooth reed and wash his face, removing all stains, so he may meet the first angel of Paradise. This little island has only rushes growing on its shores; no other plant can survive here. Do not return this way again. The sun, now rising, will show you a gentler path up the mountain."

Then he vanished. I rose and turned to my guide. "Son, follow my steps," he said. "Let's go back; this way slopes down to lower ground."

The dawn was overcoming the early morning light. From afar, I could see the sea shimmering. We walked across the empty plain like travelers retracing their steps to find the lost road.

When we reached a place where the dew resisted the sun's rays, my guide gently placed both hands on the grass. Seeing his action, I offered my tear-streaked face to him. He then wiped away the dark stain left by Hell.

We then arrived at the deserted shore, where no one has sailed and returned. There, he tied the reed around me, and, as he plucked it, another sprouted immediately in its place.

Chapter 2: The Celestial Pilot. Casella. The Departure.

The sun had already reached the horizon, where it rises highest over Jerusalem. Night, on the other side of the world, was coming out from the Ganges, carrying the Scales in its hands. The bright cheeks of the beautiful dawn were turning orange. We were still standing by the sea, like people lost in thought, not yet ready to move.

Then, just as Mars appears fiery red in the west over the ocean at dawn, a light appeared to me, speeding over the sea faster than any bird could fly. I looked to my guide for answers, and when I looked back, the light had grown brighter and larger.

I began to see some white forms on either side of it, and something else was emerging underneath. My guide had not spoken a word yet, but as the first whiteness took the shape of wings, he recognized what it was and cried out, "Quick! Kneel down! It's the Angel of God. Fold your hands! You will see more like this from now on. Notice how he needs no oars or sails—just his wings—to cross such great distances. Watch how he points his wings toward Heaven. They never tire, unlike mortal wings!"

As the Divine Bird came closer, it became so bright that I had to look away. It came to the shore in a small, swift boat that barely touched the water. The angel stood at the stern, his face shining with joy, and inside the boat were more than a hundred souls.

"In exitu Israel de Aegypto!" they sang together, chanting the words of the Psalm. Then the angel made the sign of the cross over them, and they all jumped ashore. As quickly as he had come, the angel departed.

The souls, still unfamiliar with their surroundings, looked around as if trying to understand where they were. The day was breaking all around. The sun was high in the sky, chasing away the stars.

When the souls noticed us, they turned and asked, "If you know, show us the way to the mountain." My guide, Virgil, replied, "You may think we know this place, but we are strangers just like you. We came by another path, one that was rough and steep. Climbing from here will seem easy compared to that."

Hearing me breathe, the souls realized I was still alive. They turned pale with surprise. Like people rushing to hear news from a messenger carrying an olive

100

branch, they crowded around me. One soul moved forward as if to embrace me, so I reached out to do the same. But my hands passed through nothing but air. I felt confused, but the soul only smiled and drew back. I kept moving forward, trying to touch it again.

"Stop," the soul said gently. I then recognized who it was and begged it to stay and speak with me. "Just as I loved you in life, I love you now that I am free," it replied. "So I will stop. But why are you here?"

"My dear Casella," I said, "I am on this journey to return to the place I came from. But why has it taken you so long to get here?"

He answered, "I've suffered no wrong. The one who decides who comes here and when has denied me passage many times, but his will is righteous. For the last three months, though, he has allowed anyone who wished to come. I arrived here at the Tiber's mouth, and he welcomed me. His wing now points this way, where those who don't go to Acheron gather."

I asked, "If you still remember the songs of love that used to comfort me, could you sing one now to soothe my soul? It's struggling with the weight of my body on this journey."

"Love, which speaks with me in my mind," he began to sing so sweetly that the sound still echoes in me. My master, the other souls, and I stood there, as if nothing else could affect us. We listened, entranced.

Suddenly, the old man cried out, "What is this, you slow souls? Why are you standing still? Run to the mountain to shed the shell that hides God from you!"

It was like a flock of doves feeding in a field, calm and unafraid, but then suddenly startled by something that makes them scatter. That's how these souls reacted. They stopped singing and hurried toward the mountain, not knowing exactly where they were going. We, too, left in a rush.

Chapter 3: Discourse on the Limits of Reason. The Foot of the Mountain. Those who died in Contumacy of Holy Church. Manfredi.

The sudden rush had scattered everyone across the plain, heading toward the mountain that reason urges us to climb. I stayed close to my faithful guide. How could I have made this journey without him? Who else would lead me up the mountain? He seemed to feel some regret within himself. A pure conscience, even for the smallest fault, stings deeply.

Once he slowed his pace, which gave back the dignity that haste often ruins, my mind, which had been tense, began to relax. I looked up at the mountain that rises highest toward the heavens.

The sun was behind us, blazing red, casting my shadow ahead. I turned around, afraid I was alone. I looked and saw only darkness in front of me.

"Why do you still doubt?" my guide asked, turning to me. "Don't you trust that I'm with you and guiding you? It's already evening where the body that casts this shadow is buried. That body was taken from Brindisi and is now in Naples. So, don't be surprised that there's no shadow before me. The light of Heaven doesn't block itself."

He went on, "The power that makes these bodies suffer both cold and heat doesn't show us how it works. Anyone who thinks human reason can fully understand the mysteries of God is foolish. Stay content with what you can know. If we could understand everything, there would have been no need for Mary to give birth. Even great minds like Aristotle and Plato spent their lives seeking answers that only caused them grief."

He bowed his head and said no more. We walked until we reached the foot of the mountain. The rock wall there was so steep that even the most agile climber would have struggled. Compared to this, the most rugged paths between Lerici and Turbia would seem easy.

"Who knows which way the mountain slopes?" my guide wondered aloud, examining the rocky ground. I looked around, searching for a path.

Then, on the left, I saw a group of souls slowly moving toward us. They were walking so slowly, it almost seemed they were standing still.

"Look, Master," I said, "over there! Maybe they can give us advice if you can't find a way."

He looked at me, then said, "Let's go over to them. Keep hope in your heart, my son."

Even after a thousand steps, the souls were still far away, as far as a stone's throw from a skilled thrower. They gathered near the steep bank, standing close together, watching us.

"O blessed souls!" Virgil began, "By the peace you will one day enjoy, tell us where the mountain slopes, so we can climb it. Wasting time troubles those who know its value."

The souls moved toward us like sheep leaving their pen, timid and unsure, following the lead of the first one. One came forward, graceful and dignified.

When those in front saw my shadow on the ground, they stopped and pulled back. The others, not knowing why, also stopped.

Without waiting for a question, my guide spoke, "Yes, this is a human body you see. That's why his shadow breaks the sunlight on the ground. Don't be amazed. He has heavenly aid to help him climb this wall."

The souls, hearing this, stepped aside and gestured for us to go ahead. One of them called out, "Whoever you are, turn around and see if you recognize me."

I turned and looked closely. He was blond, handsome, and noble-looking, though one of his eyebrows was split. When I said I didn't recognize him, he showed me a wound high on his chest and smiled.

"I am Manfredi, grandson of Empress Constance," he said. "When you return, please tell my daughter, the mother of Sicily and Aragon's honor, the truth about me.

"After I was mortally wounded, I turned, weeping, to God, who willingly forgives. My sins were great, but God's infinite goodness has arms wide enough to welcome anyone who turns to Him.

"The Bishop of Cosenza, who chased me on orders from Pope Clement, didn't understand this. If he had, my body would still lie under the stone by the bridge near Benevento. Instead, the rain and wind now scatter my bones beyond the kingdom's borders.

"But know this: no curse is strong enough to block eternal love if there's still a glimmer of hope. True, anyone who dies opposing the Church, even if repentant, must wait outside this mountain's gates for thirty times the length of their rebellion, unless shortened by the prayers of the righteous.

"If you can, help me find peace by telling my daughter, Constance, what you've seen and my fate here. Those on earth can help us greatly from here."

Chapter 4: Farther Ascent. Nature of the Mountain. The Negligent, who postponed Repentance till the last Hour. Belacqua.

When something captures our mind, whether it's joy or pain, the soul focuses entirely on it. It feels like nothing else matters. This explains why, when we are fully absorbed in something we hear or see, we lose track of time. The mind can only handle one task at a time—if it's listening, it can't keep track of time. One part is busy, while the other is free.

I learned this lesson when I was so engrossed in listening to and looking at that spirit. The sun had already risen fifty degrees, but I hadn't even noticed it. Then, we heard voices cry out, "Here is what you seek!"

The path we took was so narrow and blocked by thorns that only my guide and I could fit through after that group of souls left us. It reminded me of the small gaps that farmers create with thorny branches when they harvest grapes.

Climbing here was more challenging than scaling the steep hills of San Leo, Noli, or Bismantova, where you can use your hands and feet. Here, you needed the wings of desire to lift you, following the one who gave me hope and lit the way.

We climbed through a crack in the rock. The narrow edges pressed on both sides, and we had to use our hands and feet to grip the ground as we climbed. When we finally reached the top of the ridge, I asked, "Master, which way should we go now?"

He replied, "Don't go down. Keep climbing behind me until we find a wise guide to show us the way."

The mountain peak was so high that I couldn't see the top. The slope was steeper than any line drawn from a circle's edge to its center. Exhausted, I called out, "Father, wait! I'm falling behind!"

He pointed to a small ledge ahead and said, "Pull yourself up there, my son." His words gave me the strength to push forward until I stood on that terrace.

We both sat down, facing the east where we had climbed up. Everyone likes to look back at where they've come from. I first looked down to the shore, then up at the sun, surprised that its rays were now hitting us from the left.

The poet noticed my confusion about the sunlight coming from a different direction. He said, "If you could picture this mountain and Mount Zion on opposite sides of the world, sharing the same horizon, you would see why the sun shines differently here. It's because of how the Earth turns."

"Master," I said, "I understand more now than ever before. The path the sun takes makes sense. But tell me, how much farther do we have to go? The mountain seems endless."

He answered, "This mountain is tough at first, but the higher you climb, the easier it gets. When climbing feels as natural as gliding downstream in a boat, you will have reached the end. Then you can rest. I know this to be true."

As he finished speaking, a voice nearby said, "You might need to sit down before then." We turned and saw a large rock on the left. We hadn't noticed it before.

We walked over and found people standing in the shadow of the rock, resting as if they were too lazy to move. One man, looking especially tired, was sitting down, holding his knees and resting his head on them.

"Look, Master," I said, "that man seems lazier than Sloth herself!"

He looked up at us, lifting his eyes just above his knees, and said, "Keep climbing, brave soul." I recognized him then, and even though I was short of breath, I approached him. He barely lifted his head as I came near and asked, "Have you noticed how the sun now shines over your left shoulder?"

His slow movements and brief words made me smile. "Belacqua," I said, "I don't feel sorry for you anymore. But tell me, why are you sitting here? Are you waiting for someone to guide you, or has your usual habit of laziness taken over?"

He replied, "Brother, what's the point of climbing? The Angel at the gate won't let me through yet. I have to wait here for as long as I delayed turning to God in my life, unless a prayer from a good heart helps me sooner. If not, I'll just stay here."

Meanwhile, my guide had already started climbing again. "Come on," he said to me. "The sun is at its highest, and night is already covering the shores of Morocco."

The Divine Comedy

Chapter 5: Those who died by Violence, but repentant. Buonconte di Monfeltro. La Pia.

I had already left those spirits behind and was following my guide when suddenly, someone pointed at me and shouted, "Look! It seems the sunlight doesn't shine on the left of him. He looks like a living person leading another!"

Hearing this, I turned and saw the group staring at me in astonishment, not at my guide, but at me and the shadow my body cast.

"Why do you let this distract you?" my guide said, noticing I had slowed down. "What does it matter what they say? Keep following me and let the people talk. Stand firm like a tower that doesn't sway with every wind. A person who lets too many thoughts cloud their mind loses focus and weakens themselves."

All I could say was, "I'm coming." I said it with a bit of shame, like someone asking for forgiveness.

As we continued along the mountainside, a group of people appeared ahead of us, singing the "Miserere" verse by verse. When they realized that my body blocked the sunlight, their song changed to a long, hoarse "Oh!"

Two of them rushed forward to meet us and asked, "Who are you?"

My guide replied, "Go back and tell those who sent you that this man is still alive, in a body of flesh. If they stopped because they saw his shadow, that should be enough of an answer. They should honor him; it might help them."

Never had I seen vapors or clouds move as fast as those two returning to their group. When they got back, they all rushed towards us like a wild, uncontrolled crowd.

"These people are coming to beg something of you," said my guide. "So keep walking and listen as you go."

"O soul," they called out, "you who are heading to heaven with the same body you were born in, please stop for a moment! Look at us! If you've seen any of us before, tell others about us when you return to the world. Why do you walk away? Why not stay?"

They continued, "We were all killed violently, and we were sinners until the very end. Then, a light from Heaven awakened us, and we repented. We died reconciled to God, and now we long to see Him."

I replied, "Though I look at you all, I don't recognize anyone. But if there's anything I can do for you, please tell me. I promise to help, for the peace I seek by following this guide."

One of them spoke up, "We trust your promise without any oath. I speak on behalf of the others. Please, if you ever go to the land between Romagna and the kingdom of Charles, ask the people of Fano to pray for me so I can be freed from my sins. That's where I'm from. I was struck down in the heart of the Antenori, where I thought I'd be safe. It was the lord of Este who did this to me, out of hatred beyond what was just. If I had escaped to Mira when I was overtaken at Oriaco, I'd still be alive."

Another spirit then said, "I hope you reach that blessed mountain you desire, as you show kindness to me. I am Buonconte from Montefeltro. No one, not even Giovanna, prays for me, so I walk with my head hanging low among these souls."

I asked him, "What led you so far from Campaldino, where your body was never found?"

He answered, "At the foot of Casentino, there is a river called Archiano. I reached the spot where its name fades away, pierced through my throat. I ran, bleeding on the ground, until I lost my sight. I died there, calling on Mary, and my body was left empty. I'll tell you the truth—share it with the living. An angel took my soul, but a devil from Hell shouted, 'Why do you take him from me? You carry away the eternal part of him for just one tear, but I will claim the rest!'

"You know how moisture in the air becomes rain when it meets the cold? The devil stirred the fog and wind, covering the valley from Pratomagno to the Apennines. The rain filled the gullies, rushing so fiercely that nothing could stop it. The Archiano found my body near its outlet and pushed it into the Arno, breaking the cross I made over my chest in my final agony. It rolled me along the banks, covering me with mud and debris."

A third spirit then spoke up, "When you return to the world and rest from your journey, remember me. I am Pia. Siena gave me life, and Maremma took it. The one who first put a ring on my finger knows this well."

Chapter 6: Dante's Inquiry on Prayers for the Dead. Sordello. Italy.

When the game of dice breaks up, the one who loses stays behind, feeling sad. He keeps replaying his throws in his mind, trying to learn from them. Meanwhile, the others walk away, some in front, some behind him. A few call out, reminding him of what just happened. He doesn't stop to listen; he hears bits and pieces, but no one crowds around him to help. He tries to defend himself from their words.

I felt just like that in the crowd of spirits. I turned my face this way and that, making promises to free myself from them.

There was the man from Arezzo, killed by the ruthless Ghin di Tacco, and the one who drowned while fleeing capture. I saw Frederick Novello, stretching out his hands in prayer, and the one from Pisa, whose strong will made his father Marzucco proud. I saw Count Orso and the spirit who, filled with hatred and envy, was separated from his body for no crime. It was Pierre de la Brosse, who warned that the Lady of Brabant should pray on earth to avoid joining a worse group in the afterlife.

Once I freed myself from those spirits who only wanted someone else to pray for them, I asked my guide, "You've said before, my light, that prayers cannot change Heaven's will. Yet, these spirits hope for that. Are their hopes useless, or have I misunderstood you?"

He replied, "My words are clear, and their hope is not in vain, if you understand it correctly. Divine judgment doesn't bend because of love's fire; it simply fulfills what it must. I said prayers can't help when they are separate from God's will. In deep matters like this, don't decide on your own. Wait for Beatrice, the one who brings light between truth and the mind. You'll see her soon, smiling and joyful, at the top of this mountain."

I replied, "Good guide, let's hurry! I don't feel as tired as before, and the hill is casting its shadow now."

He answered, "We'll go as far as we can today, but things are not quite as you think. Before we reach the top, you'll see the sun return from behind the hill and shine on us again."

Then, he pointed ahead, saying, "Look! There's a soul standing alone. It will show us the quickest path."

We approached it. This Lombard spirit carried itself with pride, moving slowly and looking at us like a lion lying in wait. It said nothing but watched us as we came closer. My guide spoke to it respectfully, asking for directions, but the soul didn't reply. Instead, it asked about our homeland and life. My guide answered, "Mantua."

At that, the spirit came forward, saying, "I am Sordello, from your city, Mantua!" The two embraced.

Oh, Italy! How low you've fallen! You are a land of suffering, a ship without a captain in the storm. You were once noble, but now you've become a den of wickedness. This noble soul was filled with joy just hearing the name of his home, yet now your people are at war with each other. Look inside yourself, Italy. Is there any part of you at peace?

What's the point of having laws if there's no one to enforce them? Without a leader, your people are out of control. You, who should be devoted and let Caesar lead, have become wild because you try to control the reins yourself.

Oh, German Albert! You abandoned Italy when she needed a leader. May the stars send justice on you, so your successor learns to fear what you have ignored. Your greed for foreign lands has left this garden of an empire in ruins.

Come, and see the Montecchi and Cappelletti, the Monaldi and Filippeschi—these people suffer and are full of doubt. Come, see your noble ones oppressed. Help them, and you will see how safe they can be.

Look at Rome, mourning day and night, crying out, "Why have you abandoned me, my Caesar?" Come see how your people suffer. If you have no pity for us, at least be ashamed of your reputation.

If it is within your power, O Highest God, who was crucified for us on Earth, is Your justice focused elsewhere? Or are You preparing something good for us that we cannot yet understand? Every city in Italy is full of tyrants, and every peasant who takes sides becomes another Marcellus.

Oh, Florence! You might think this does not concern you, thanks to your people's constant meddling. Some value justice but are slow to act. Others refuse to bear the common burden, but your people, always eager, cry out,

"We submit!" You should be proud. You are prosperous, peaceful, and wise—or so it seems.

Athens and Sparta, known for their ancient laws, don't compare to you in making rules. But how often do you change laws, money, and customs? If you reflect, you'll see that you are like a sick woman who cannot rest, tossing and turning to ease her pain.

Chapter 7: The Valley of Flowers. Negligent Princes.

After we exchanged warm greetings several times, Sordello stepped back and asked, "Who are you?"

"My bones were buried by Octavian before the souls of the worthy were called to this mountain to ascend to God," my guide replied. "I am Virgil, and I lost Heaven only because I lacked faith."

Sordello, hearing this, looked amazed. He seemed to struggle between belief and disbelief, saying, "Is it true? Is it not?" Then he bowed his head humbly and embraced Virgil like one embraces a superior.

"O glory of the Latins!" Sordello said, "You showed what our language could do! Eternal pride of the place I come from, what grace allows me to meet you? If I'm worthy to hear your words, tell me: Are you from Hell, and if so, from which part?"

Virgil answered, "I came through every circle of that sorrowful realm, driven by Heaven's power. I lost the vision of the sun you seek, not because of any sin, but simply because I did not have faith. There is a place in Hell that has no torments, only darkness. There, the cries are not wails but sighs. I dwell with the innocent children taken by death before they could be freed from human sin. I also stay with those who, though they did not practice the three holy virtues, lived without vice. But if you know, tell us how we can find the quickest way to where Purgatory truly begins."

Sordello replied, "There is no fixed path for us; I am allowed to move up and around the mountain as I please. I can guide you as far as I can go. But look, the day is ending. It's not possible to climb at night, so we should find a place to stay."

He pointed to some souls on the right and said, "If you allow me, I'll take you to them. You'll find pleasure in meeting them."

My guide asked, "If one wished to climb at night, would they be prevented by others or simply be unable to do so?"

Sordello drew a line on the ground with his finger and said, "You could not cross this line after the sun sets. It's not that anything else blocks the way, but the darkness takes away the will and ability to move upward. We could wander around the mountain during the night, but we couldn't ascend."

My guide, surprised, said, "Take us to the place where we can rest and enjoy the time until morning."

We had walked only a short distance when I noticed that the mountain formed a hollow, much like valleys here on Earth. "Let's go there," said Sordello, "where the hillside makes a small valley. We'll wait there for the new day."

A winding path between the hill and the plain led us to the edge of this hollow. Within, I saw a mix of gold, silver, scarlet, and white, even more beautiful than fine gems and emeralds. Flowers and plants filled the area, more splendid in color and scent than any found in nature.

In the valley, I saw spirits sitting among the flowers, singing "Salve Regina." Their voices floated up before the last bit of sunlight disappeared behind the horizon.

The Mantuan who led us there said, "I won't take you among them just yet. It's better if you observe their actions from here than from up close in the valley."

He pointed to one spirit who sat higher than the others, looking sorrowful. "That's Emperor Rudolph. He had the power to heal the wounds that brought Italy to ruin, but he neglected to act. Next to him is Ottocar, who ruled the land where the Moldau River flows into the Elbe. He was a much better ruler in his youth than his son, Wenceslaus, who now lives in luxury."

Another spirit, who looked tormented and was beating his chest, was there too. "That's Philip, who betrayed the lily of France. See how he sighs, holding his face in his hands? Next to him is his father-in-law, who suffers from the shame of his son's life."

One spirit who appeared strong was singing with another who had a prominent nose. "That is Charles of Anjou," Sordello continued, "wearing the mark of a true ruler. If only his successor had lived up to his legacy, his kingdom would have been far better off. Now Frederick and James possess his realms, but they do not inherit his virtues. Virtue does not always pass down through bloodlines; it comes from Heaven, so we must pray for it."

Sordello also pointed out others: "See the one with the large nose? That's Peter, who sings with Charles. He ruled Provence and Apulia, but his descendants are nothing like him. Then there's King Henry of England, sitting alone. His branches have grown to be better than he was."

The last one, sitting on the ground and looking up, was Marquis William. "He was the reason for the war that brought so much sorrow to Alessandria and Canavese," Sordello explained.

Chapter 8: The Guardian Angels and the Serpent. Nino di Gallura. The Three Stars. Currado Malaspina.

It was now the time of day when people at sea feel homesick and their hearts soften, remembering the goodbyes they said to loved ones. It is also when a traveler, hearing a distant bell, feels a pang of sorrow as daylight fades.

At that moment, I was about to stop listening when one of the souls stood up, raising its hand to get my attention. It brought both palms together and lifted them up, focusing its eyes on the eastern sky as if to say, "I care for nothing else but God."

With great devotion, it began to sing, "Te lucis ante," and its voice was so sweet that it took me out of my own thoughts. The other souls joined in, singing the entire hymn with their eyes fixed on the heavens.

Now, dear Reader, pay close attention, for the scene becomes more meaningful and clear. I saw that noble group of souls silently looking upward, as if they were humbly waiting for something. Then, from above, I saw two angels descending with flaming swords in their hands. The swords were missing their points.

The angels' robes were green, like new leaves in spring. They fluttered behind them as they flew, glowing with the light of their wings. One angel landed just above us, while the other went to the opposite side of the valley, placing the people between them.

I could clearly see their golden hair, but their faces were hard to make out, almost overwhelming to look at.

"These angels have come from Mary's embrace," Sordello explained, "to guard this valley against the serpent that will soon arrive."

Not knowing what road the serpent would take, I turned around and clung to my guide's shoulders, feeling frozen with fear. Sordello then said, "Let's go down to meet the noble souls. It will be a pleasure for them to see you."

I took only three steps before I found myself at the bottom, where I saw a soul looking straight at me, as if trying to recognize who I was. By now, the air was growing darker, but not so dark that I couldn't see the face before me.

As he moved toward me, I moved toward him. "Noble Judge Nino!" I exclaimed. It made me so happy to see that he was not among the damned souls.

We exchanged every greeting we could think of before he asked, "How long has it been since you crossed the waters to the foot of this mountain?"

"I came this morning through the sorrowful realms of Hell," I replied, "and I am still in my earthly life, although I gain life eternal by traveling this path."

As soon as I said this, both Nino and Sordello stepped back from me in surprise, like people suddenly struck by confusion. One turned to Virgil, and the other to a man sitting nearby, calling, "Come, Currado! See what God, in His grace, has willed!"

Then Nino turned back to me and said, "By the grace you owe to Him, who hides His purpose beyond our understanding, please tell my daughter Giovanna to pray for me when you return to the world. Tell her to pray in that place where the innocent are heard.

"I don't think her mother loves me anymore since she has taken off her mourning veil. Poor woman, she'll regret it. A woman's love fades quickly if she doesn't keep seeing or touching the one she loves.

"The viper of Milan may never honor her with a noble crest as much as my family's emblem, Gallura's rooster, would have."

Nino spoke with a passion that reflected his righteous spirit.

My eyes wandered up to the sky, drawn to a spot where the stars were moving the slowest, like a wheel closest to its axle.

"What are you looking at up there?" my guide asked.

"I see those three torches lighting up this part of the sky," I replied.

Virgil said, "The four bright stars you saw this morning have set, and these new ones have taken their place."

As he was speaking, Sordello pulled him aside and pointed with his finger, saying, "Look, our adversary is coming!"

On the side of the valley without a barrier, I saw a serpent slithering toward us. It might have been the same one that gave the forbidden fruit to Eve. It crept through the grass and flowers, occasionally turning its head to lick its back like a cat grooming itself.

I didn't see when the celestial angels moved, but I heard the sound of their wings cutting through the air. The serpent fled at once, and the angels flew back to their stations.

The soul that had approached Judge Nino remained fixed on me throughout the entire encounter with the serpent. Then it spoke, "If the light that guides you has filled your will with as much strength as you need to ascend to Heaven, then tell me if you know anything about the land of Valdimagra or its nearby regions. I once had power there."

"I am Currado Malaspina," it continued. "Not the elder, but his descendant. I loved my family deeply, a love which has now been purified here."

"I have never traveled through your lands," I replied, "but who in all of Europe hasn't heard of your family's fame? It brings honor to your name and tells of your land's nobility. I swear, as I hope for Heaven, that your family's reputation has not diminished. You still possess the glory of both wealth and courage. You are blessed by both nature and tradition. Even when the world loses its way, your family walks the right path."

Currado responded, "Go then. Before the sun sets seven more times in the Ram's sign, what I say will be fixed in your mind even more firmly than now—unless justice fails to take its course."

Chapter 9: Dante's Dream of the Eagle. The Gate of Purgatory and the Angel. Seven P's. The Keys.

The dawn was breaking, casting a soft, white glow on the eastern horizon. The sky was sprinkled with stars, arranged in the shape of a scorpion, which often strikes the nations with its tail. The night had already moved ahead, covering two steps of its journey across the sky, and the third step was about to end. I, with the human weakness of Adam, was overcome by sleep and lay down on the grass. There were five of us resting together.

It was around the time when the sad little swallow begins her morning song, perhaps remembering her past sorrows. It's also the time when our minds, freed from our physical bodies, are more open to visions and dreams. In my dream, I saw a golden eagle flying in the sky, with its wings spread wide and ready to swoop down. It seemed to appear right where Ganymede was taken up to the heavens long ago, leaving behind his family.

I thought to myself that maybe the eagle was just following its instincts, ready to strike, but choosing not to pick up anything this time. Then, it turned sharply and swooped down toward me, as quick as lightning. It grabbed me and lifted me up to a fiery place. In my dream, I felt like I was burning, and the heat was so intense that I woke up suddenly.

I shot up from the ground like Achilles did when he awoke on Scyros, not knowing where he was. His mother had secretly carried him there in his sleep to hide him from the Greeks. I was just as startled, pale with fear, unsure of where I was.

But then I saw my guide standing beside me. The sun was already two hours into the sky, and I was facing the sea.

"Don't be afraid," my guide reassured me. "Everything is fine. Use all your strength now. You have finally arrived at Purgatory. Look at that cliff. That is the wall that surrounds it. And see, there is the entrance where the cliff seems to break apart."

He continued, "Earlier, at dawn, when you were sleeping on the flowers of the valley, a lady came to us. She said, 'I am Lucia. Let me carry this sleeping one and make his journey easier.' Sordello and the other noble spirits stayed behind as she picked you up. As daylight grew brighter, I followed her footsteps as she carried you up here. She placed you where you are now and showed me the entrance. Then she and sleep left you."

Hearing this, my doubts faded away. I felt calm and confident again. When my guide saw that I was at peace, he began to climb the cliff, and I followed him.

Reader, you can see how my story is becoming more intense. If it seems I use greater skill in telling it now, don't be surprised.

As we climbed higher, I saw a crack in the wall that looked like a split in a fortress. Beneath this opening were three steps, each a different color, leading up to a gate. A guardian sat at the top of these steps, saying nothing at first. As I opened my eyes wider to see more clearly, I noticed his face had such a fierce look that I couldn't bear to look at it directly.

In his hand, he held a bare sword that reflected the sunlight so sharply that I had to look away. Then he shouted, "What do you want from here? Where is your guide? Be careful not to cause harm with your arrival!"

"My guide," answered him, "A Lady of Heaven told us to come here. She pointed us to this entrance."

"May she guide your steps in a good way," the guardian replied kindly. "Come forward to these steps."

We approached. The first step was made of smooth, polished white marble, reflecting our images. The second step was a deep purple, rough and cracked along its surface. The third and highest step was bright red, like fresh-spilled blood.

On this top step sat the angel, holding his feet firmly on it. The threshold appeared to be made of diamond. With my guide leading, I climbed the steps, and he urged me to humbly ask the angel to unlock the door. I fell to my knees before the angel's feet, pleading for mercy. I struck my chest three times with my hand in repentance.

The angel traced seven "P"s on my forehead with the tip of his sword, saying, "Make sure you wash these marks when you go inside." His robe was the color of dry earth or ashes, and from beneath it, he pulled out two keys—one gold, the other silver. He used the silver key first, then the gold, to unlock the door.

"If either of these keys fails to turn correctly in the lock," he said, "the door will not open. The golden one is more valuable, but the silver one requires more skill and thought to use. I received these keys from Peter, who told me it is better to open the gate than to keep it closed if the people are repentant."

Then he pushed the sacred door open and warned, "You may enter, but anyone who looks back will be sent out."

The door hinges, heavy and made of metal, creaked and groaned loudly as the door swung open. They made a sound louder and more discordant than when the Roman Temple of Jupiter was looted.

At the first sound, I turned to listen and heard a song. It was "Te Deum Laudamus," sung in sweet harmony. The sound was like hearing a choir sing with an organ; the words came through now and then, sometimes clear, sometimes fading.

Chapter 10: The Needle's Eye. The First Circle: The Proud. The Sculptures on the Wall.

After we crossed through the door that souls, lost in twisted love, ignore because it makes the wrong path look right, I heard it slam shut behind us. If I had turned around to look, what excuse could I have made for my failure?

We climbed up through a narrow, winding crack in the rock. It swayed to the left and right, like a wave rolling back and forth. "We have to be careful here," my guide said. "We must move from side to side with the swaying of the path."

Our progress was so slow that the moon could have completed its whole cycle before we got through this narrow passage. But when we finally emerged into the open, I was exhausted. We both stood uncertain on a plain more desolate than a desert road.

From the cliff's edge to the foot of the steep bank was about three times the length of a human body. As far as I could see in both directions, the ledge stretched on endlessly.

We hadn't moved along the path yet when I noticed the embankment surrounding us. It was a pure white marble, beautifully carved. It was so detailed that even the greatest sculptors—or nature itself—would have been put to shame.

Carved into the marble was the scene of the Angel who came to earth to announce peace, the peace that had been longed for many years. The sculpture was so lifelike that it seemed to say, "Hail." Beside the Angel was the figure of Mary, who opened up Heaven's love. The words "Behold, the handmaid of the Lord" were etched as clearly as if stamped in wax.

"Don't just focus on one spot," my kind guide said. I turned my eyes and saw another scene further down the rock. I moved past Virgil to get a closer look. It was another story carved into the marble: the holy Ark of the Covenant being carried by oxen. There were people in front of it, divided into seven groups. To one sense, it seemed like they were singing; to another, it didn't. There was smoke from burning incense in the scene, and even this smoke seemed both real and not real, confusing both the eyes and the nose.

In front of the Ark, a humble King David danced, his robes tied up, looking both less and more than a king. Opposite, at a palace window, Michal looked down on him, her expression full of scorn and sadness.

I moved forward to look at another scene that came into view after Michal. It was the story of a great Roman Emperor whose kindness moved Saint Gregory to help save his soul. It was the Emperor Trajan, with a grieving widow standing beside his horse, weeping for her dead son.

The scene was crowded with knights, their banners displaying eagles in gold, fluttering in the wind. The widow seemed to plead, "Give me justice, Lord, for my dead son." Trajan replied, "Wait until I return." She protested, "What if you don't return?" He responded, "Then someone who takes my place will do it." She insisted, "Good deeds done by others won't help if you neglect your own." Trajan finally said, "Comfort yourself. I must fulfill my duty before I move on. Justice demands it, and pity keeps me here."

Whoever created these scenes had crafted something entirely new, a visible language that we hadn't seen before. I marveled at these images of humility, beautiful because of who they represented.

"Look," the poet murmured to me, "There are people over there, though they are few. They will guide us to the stairs."

My eyes were still busy taking in these new sights, eager to see more. I turned toward the poet as he spoke.

But I hope, reader, that you do not turn away from your own good intentions because of what I describe. Remember, these torments are just part of the journey. Think of what comes after; the worst of it can't go beyond the final judgment.

"Master," I began, "I see something moving towards us, but they don't look like people. I'm not sure what I'm seeing."

He replied, "The weight of their punishment bends them so low that it's hard to tell what they are. But if you look closely, you'll see how they're suffering under those heavy stones."

Oh, you proud Christians, weak in spirit! Why do you not understand that we are like worms meant to become butterflies, flying towards judgment? Why do you let your spirits float so high, like half-formed insects still trapped in their shells?

Like figures holding up a roof by bending their knees to their chests, these souls were shaped in painful ways that made my heart ache just to look at them. Some were more bent than others, depending on how much they were burdened. The one who seemed to bear his load with the most patience looked like he was weeping, as if to say, "I can't take it anymore!"

Chapter 11: The Humble Prayer. Omberto di Santafiore. Oderisi d' Agobbio. Provenzan Salvani.

When we crossed the doorway that many souls reject because they are fooled into thinking the wrong path is right, I heard it shut behind us with a loud echo. If I had looked back, what excuse could I have given for my failure?

We began climbing through a narrow crack in the rock. It twisted back and forth, like a wave that moves in and out. "We need to be careful here," said my guide. "We must shift our steps from side to side to keep moving forward."

We moved so slowly that the moon could have set and risen again before we reached the end of that narrow path. But finally, we made it to an open area where the mountain rose steeply before us. Exhausted and unsure of the way, we stopped on a wide, deserted ledge. From the edge to the base of the cliff, the distance was as tall as three human bodies stacked on top of each other. As far as I could see, the path stretched out to the left and right, all looking the same.

We hadn't moved yet when I noticed the marble embankment around us. It was so beautifully carved that even the best artists—or nature itself—would have been put to shame.

Carved into the marble was the Angel who brought the message of peace to the world. It was so lifelike that it seemed to be saying, "Hail." The image of Mary was also there, and it looked like she was saying, "Behold the handmaid of the Lord."

"Don't just focus on one spot," my kind guide said. I moved my eyes and saw another scene on the rock nearby. I stepped closer to see it better. It was another story: the Ark of the Covenant being carried by oxen. In front of the Ark were people divided into seven groups. It seemed like they were singing, but it was hard to tell if they really were.

Next to the Ark, King David was dancing, dressed humbly. Opposite him, at a palace window, was Michal, looking down with scorn on his joyful dance.

I moved on to look at another scene. It showed the great Emperor Trajan. A poor widow stood beside his horse, begging for justice for her dead son. The scene was filled with knights, their banners waving in the wind.

The widow seemed to cry out, "Give me justice, Lord, for my dead son." Trajan replied, "Wait until I return." She protested, "What if you don't return?" He said, "Then someone else will do it for me." She insisted, "It doesn't help if others do what you should do." Finally, Trajan said, "You're right. I must do my duty now. Justice demands it, and pity moves me."

These scenes were not just carved art; they felt alive, like a new kind of language. I marveled at their beauty and the humility they showed.

"Look over there," the poet said, "There are some people coming towards us. They will guide us to the stairs."

I turned to see these people, my eyes eager for new sights.

But, dear reader, I hope you don't get distracted from your good intentions by hearing about these torments. Remember, they are just part of the journey. Focus on what lies beyond.

"Master," I began, "I see something moving toward us, but they don't look like people. I can't quite tell what they are."

He replied, "The weight of their punishment bends them so low that it's hard to see them clearly. But if you look closely, you'll see how they're suffering under those heavy stones."

Oh, proud souls! Why do you not realize that we are like caterpillars meant to become butterflies, flying toward our final judgment? Why do you let your spirits float so high, like unformed insects still stuck in their shells?

These souls were twisted into shapes like figures that hold up roofs, knees bent to their chests. Just looking at them made my heart ache. Some were more bent than others, depending on their burden. One who seemed to bear his load with the most patience looked like he was saying through his tears, "I can't take it anymore!"

Chapter 12: The Sculptures on the Pavement. Ascent to the Second Circle.

Side by side, like oxen yoked together, I walked with the heavy soul as long as my gentle guide allowed. But soon he said, "Leave him and move on. It's time for each of us to use our sails and oars to push our boat forward."

I straightened up, as walking requires, though my thoughts still felt heavy and ashamed. I moved on, following my guide, and we both began to show more ease in our steps.

Then he said, "Look down at your feet. It will help you on this path." I did as he said and noticed the ground beneath us,

like the engraved tombs that remind us of the dead.

I saw images of figures carved into the pathway along the mountain. These sculptures were so realistic that they seemed more alive than any grave marker. I saw the one who was created nobler than all other beings, falling from Heaven in a blaze of lightning. I saw the giant Briareus, struck by a heavenly bolt, lying frozen on the ground.

I saw Mars, Pallas, and Apollo, standing in their armor, looking sadly at the fallen giants. Nimrod was there too, looking confused among the people who once followed him in pride.

I saw Niobe with sorrowful eyes, standing amidst her fourteen children, all dead. I saw King Saul, fallen on his sword, lying dead on Mount Gilboa, where no rain or dew would fall again.

There was Arachne, half turned into a spider, mourning over the threads of her web, which had caused her doom. Rehoboam appeared in his chariot, full of fear as he fled, though no one chased him.

I saw the stone pavement display the story of Alcmaeon, who made his mother pay dearly for her jewels. I saw the scene where Sennacherib's sons killed him in the temple, leaving him behind after his murder.

The pavement also showed Tomyris' cruel vengeance on Cyrus, saying, "You thirsted for blood, and now I will quench your thirst." I saw the Assyrians in retreat after Holofernes was slain, and the rest of the scene of their defeat.

I saw the ruins of Troy. Oh, how lowly and destroyed it appeared! I could almost feel the misery that filled those ashes.

Whoever sculpted these images had captured every detail so perfectly that the dead looked truly dead, and the living seemed alive.

Now, you proud ones, lift your heads high and refuse to look at your own wrongs! How foolish you are!

We had already covered more of the mountain and spent more time than I had realized when my guide, who was always watchful, said, "Lift up your head. It's time to stop daydreaming. Look, an angel is hurrying toward us!"

He added, "Fix your actions and appearance with respect so that he will help us move upward. Remember, this day will never come again."

I knew he always meant to make the most of time, so I listened. The angel, dressed in white and glowing like the morning star, approached us. He opened his arms and wings, saying, "Come, here are the steps. The climb will be easier from here."

Hearing this, I thought, "Why do we humans, who are meant to rise, fall so easily before every little challenge?"

He led us to a cleft in the rock. Then he touched my forehead with his wings and promised a safe path.

On our right, to climb the mountain to the church above, is a steep path that was made easier with stairs. In the same way, this rocky bank here was cut to make the ascent less harsh.

As we turned toward the path, I heard voices singing, "Blessed are the poor in spirit." How different these entrances are from those in Hell, where we heard only screams and wails!

We climbed the sacred steps, and I felt it was easier than walking on flat ground. "Master," I asked, "why do I feel like a heavy burden has been lifted? Walking is so much easier now."

He replied, "When all the marks on your forehead are erased, as the first one already has been, you will feel lightness in your steps. Not only will they no longer tire you, but climbing will become a joy."

I then acted like someone who feels something on their head but doesn't know what it is, so they touch it to find out. I used my fingers to check my forehead and found only six marks left. My guide smiled when he saw this.

Chapter 13: The Second Circle: The Envious. Sapia of Siena

We were at the top of the steps, where the second part of the mountain begins. Here, climbing purifies the soul. This level is surrounded by a ledge, much like the first one, but its curve is steeper.

There were no shadows or carvings to be seen. The bank and path seemed smooth and plain, with only the dull color of the stone.

"If we wait here for someone to ask," the Poet said, "I'm afraid we might be delayed for too long."

Then he looked straight at the sun, turning his body so his right side was in the center as he moved his left around.

"O sweet light! I trust in you as I start this new journey," he said. "Guide us as one should be guided here. You warm the world and shine on it; unless another reason tells us otherwise, your rays should always lead us!"

We covered a distance that would be counted as a mile here, and we did so quickly, driven by our strong will. Suddenly, we heard spirits around us, though we could not see them. They called out with kind invitations to Love's feast.

The first voice flew past us, loudly crying, "They have no wine!" It repeated this as it moved behind us. Before the sound faded away, another voice called out, "I am Orestes!" and moved on.

"O Father, what are these voices?" I asked. And just as I asked, a third one cried out, "Love those who have wronged you!"

"This circle punishes envy," said my good guide. "That's why the voices call out words of love to correct it. You'll hear another sound guiding us before we reach the Pass of Pardon."

"Look ahead," he continued, "and you will see people sitting against the cliff."

I widened my eyes and looked ahead. I saw shadows wearing cloaks that blended into the stone. As we moved closer, I heard a cry, "Mary, pray for us!" followed by "Michael, Peter, and all Saints!"

I don't think there's anyone so heartless that they wouldn't feel pity at what I saw next. When I got close enough to see their actions clearly, grief filled my eyes with tears.

They seemed to be wearing rough sackcloth. Each one leaned on the shoulder of the person beside them, all of them supported by the bank. They looked like blind beggars standing at church doors, leaning on each other in need, begging for alms.

Just like beggars, they inspired pity not only with their words but also with their appearance. And just as the blind can't see the sun, these souls were denied the light of Heaven. Their eyes were sewn shut with iron wire, like a wild hawk's eyes are sewn closed to keep it calm.

It felt wrong to walk past them without being seen, so I turned to my wise guide. He knew what I wanted to ask, so he said, "Speak, and be brief and to the point."

I had Virgil on the side of the path where one could fall, as it had no protective rail. On the other side were the souls, with tears flowing from their sewn eyes.

"O people," I began, "certain of seeing the great light that is your only desire, may grace cleanse your hearts so your minds may flow clearly. Tell me, if any of you are from Italy, as it will be dear to me to know."

"O brother," I heard a voice say from nearby, "we are all citizens of one true city. But you mean, who among us once lived in Italy?" I moved closer to see who had spoken. Among the rest, I saw a shade lifting its chin like a blind person trying to speak.

"Spirit," I said, "if you're the one who answered me, tell me your name and where you're from."

"I am Sapia," she replied. "I'm from Siena, and here I cleanse my sinful life by praying to God. I was not wise, though my name means 'wise.' I found more joy in others' misfortunes than in my own success. Let me tell you how foolish I was.

"When I was already old, my fellow citizens fought their enemies near Colle. I prayed to God for what He willed. When I saw our enemies fleeing in defeat,

I felt an unequaled joy. I lifted my face and boldly cried to God, 'From now on, I do not fear you,' like a blackbird after a little sunshine.

"Only at the end of my life did I seek peace with God. If it weren't for the prayers of Brother Pier Pettignano, who was kind enough to care for me, I would still be in debt to my sins.

"But who are you, that you can ask about our state here and still have your eyes open, speaking as you breathe?"

"My eyes will be closed here, too, but not for long," I said. "My sin of envy is slight, but the fear of the torment below still weighs on me."

"And who led you here if you're planning to return below?" she asked.

"The one beside me," I replied. "And yes, I am alive. So, chosen spirit, if you want me to help you when I go back, just ask."

"This is such a rare thing to hear," she said. "It's a sign that God loves you. Please, if you ever go to Tuscany, help restore my family's honor.

"You will find my family among the vain people who hope in Talamone. They will lose more hope there than in finding the River Diana, but the admirals will lose even more."

Chapter 14: Guido del Duca and Renier da Calboli. Cities of the Arno Valley. Denunciation of Stubbornness.

"Who is this one walking on our mountain before Death has given him wings to fly? And he can open his eyes and close them whenever he wants!"

"I don't know who he is, but I do know he isn't alone. Ask him yourself since you're closer. Be gentle so he will speak," said one of the spirits to the other, leaning towards me from the right. Then, they both turned their faces upward to address me.

One of them spoke, "O soul, still bound to a living body, but climbing towards Heaven, please comfort us. Tell us where you come from and who you are, for this is something unheard of."

I replied, "There is a river in Tuscany that flows from Falterona. It's called the Arno. I came from that region. As for who I am, my name means little right now, so it would be pointless to say it."

The spirit who spoke first answered, "If I understand correctly, you're talking about the Arno."

The other spirit asked, "Why does he hide the name of that river as if it were something horrible?"

The first spirit then replied, "I don't know. But it makes sense for the name of that valley to disappear. From where it begins at the mountain's source to where it returns its waters to the sea, virtue is treated like an enemy. It's avoided by everyone there, like a serpent. This may be because of the place itself or the bad habits of those living there.

"This valley's people have changed so much that it seems like the witch Circe turned them into animals. At the start, where the river flows between ugly swine, they seem more fit to eat acorns than human food. As it flows further down, it meets hounds that bark louder than they need to. The river scorns them and turns away.

"As it continues, the deeper it goes, the more it encounters wolves instead of dogs. This cursed ditch then flows through many hollows, finding foxes so full of deceit that they fear no tricks that could trap them.

"I'll keep speaking, even if others hear me. It will be good for them if they remember what I say. I see your grandson becoming a hunter of those wolves along the riverbank. He will terrify them, selling their living flesh and then killing them, robbing many of their lives and himself of honor.

"He will leave that forest covered in blood, and it will take a thousand years for it to grow back to its natural state."

As I listened to these dark words, I saw the face of the other spirit grow disturbed, as if struck by the coming misfortunes. Their words and expressions made me want to know their names, so I asked them.

The spirit who had spoken first replied, "You want me to do for you what you won't do for me. But since God has shown you this grace, I won't be selfish. Know, then, that I am Guido del Duca. My blood burned with envy, so much so that if I saw someone happy, I would turn pale with anger. Now, I reap the harvest of what I sowed. Oh, human race! Why do you put your heart where it can't be shared?

"This is Renier," he continued, pointing to the other spirit. "He is the pride of the Calboli family, a house where no one else has lived up to his worth. It's not just his bloodline that has turned barren; the whole region between the Po River, the mountains, the seashore, and the Reno is full of poisonous roots.

"Where are the noble ones like Lizio, Arrigo Manardi, Pier Traversaro, and Guido di Carpigna? The Romagnuoli have turned into bastards. When will a Fabbro arise in Bologna or a Bernardin di Fosco in Faenza? These families, once noble, have become so corrupt.

"I weep when I think of those times with Guido da Prata, Ugolin d'Azzo, and Frederick Tignoso. The knights and ladies, the joys and hardships, filled us with love and honor. Now, these hearts have grown so wicked.

"O Brettinoro, why haven't you fled when your noble family is gone and so many good people refuse to be tainted? Bagnacaval is wise not to breed anymore. Castrocaro and Conio, however, foolishly try to produce noble counts. The Pagani will be fortunate once their demon departs, though they will never be remembered as pure.

"O Ugolin de' Fantoli, your name is safe since there is no one left to tarnish it. But now go, Tuscan. I'd rather weep than speak, for our talk has pained me deeply."

We sensed that these souls heard us leaving, so they kept silent, making us confident in our path forward.

As we moved on alone, a thunderous voice suddenly broke through the air, shouting, "Whoever finds me will kill me!" It echoed like a burst of thunder, then faded away. Before I could fully grasp the sound, another cry roared, "I am Aglaurus, who turned to stone!"

These words made me step closer to my guide, moving backward instead of forward.

The air grew quiet again. Then my guide said to me, "That was a stern warning meant to keep people within their limits. But you let temptation lure you in, so neither warnings nor discipline seem to work. Heaven calls to you with its eternal beauty, yet you keep looking down at the ground. This is why He, who sees everything, chastises you."

Chapter 15: The Third Circle: The Irascible. Dante's Visions. The Smoke.

The time was now late afternoon, with about the same amount of daylight left as there is between the third hour and dawn. As the sun continued on its path, it seemed to be setting for us, even though it was still shining brightly on the other side of the world. The rays were hitting us straight on because we were circling the mountain and heading westward.

I felt the light getting stronger and more blinding than before, making me raise my hands to shield my face, just like when you block out the sun's reflection from water or a mirror.

As the light reflected in front of me, it hit my eyes, forcing me to turn away. "Father," I asked, "what is this light coming towards us that I can't block out?"

"Don't be surprised if the light still dazzles you," my guide answered. "That is an angel, coming to invite us further up. Soon, this light will not be blinding to you but instead delightful, just as nature intended."

When we reached the angel, he welcomed us joyfully, saying, "Here is the stairway to a gentler ascent than the others." As we began to climb, the song "Blessed are the merciful" was sung behind us, followed by, "Rejoice, you who have overcome!"

My guide and I continued upward alone, and I hoped to learn something from his words. So, I asked him, "What did that soul from Romagna mean when he spoke about envy and sharing?"

My guide answered, "He knows his own greatest flaw and warns us against it so we may avoid the same mistake. Because your desires focus on earthly things, where the more you share, the less each person has, envy grows. But if your love were aimed at heavenly things, the opposite would happen: the more you share, the more each person gains. There, love only grows greater as it's shared."

"I am more curious now than ever," I said, "How can sharing make everyone richer in Heaven, while on Earth, sharing seems to take away from what each person has?"

"That's because you're still thinking only about earthly things," he replied. "In Heaven, divine goodness spreads like sunlight. The more it is shared, the greater it becomes, and the more people love, the more love there is to share. If this doesn't clear your doubts, Beatrice will explain everything when you meet her."

He continued, "Make sure you clear away the remaining five scars on your forehead, like the two already gone. Only then will you find peace."

I wanted to say, "You've answered my question," but at that moment, we arrived at another level of the mountain, and my attention was caught by a sudden vision.

It seemed like I was in a temple with many people, and at the entrance was a woman speaking to her son. She had the tender demeanor of a mother, saying, "Son, why have you treated us this way? Your father and I have been searching for you in sorrow." Then, just as quickly as it appeared, the vision faded.

Next, I saw another scene—a woman with tears streaming down her face, caused by a deep grief and anger. She cried out, "If you are the lord of this city that brought so much conflict among the gods, avenge the man who dared to embrace our daughter!" The lord answered calmly, "What should we do to those who wish us harm, if we condemn even those who love us?"

Then I saw people, burning with rage, stoning a young man to death as they shouted, "Kill him! Kill him!" I saw him fall under the weight of his death but still lift his eyes to heaven, asking God to forgive his killers with a look that inspired compassion.

Once the vision ended, I returned to my senses, aware of the reality around me. My guide, seeing that I had been walking in a daze, said, "What's wrong with you? You can't even stand up straight! For half a mile now, you've been walking as if you're asleep or drunk."

"O my sweet Father, listen to me," I answered. "I'll tell you what appeared to me when I felt so weak."

He said, "Even if you wore a hundred masks, I could still read your thoughts. What you saw was meant to open your heart to the waters of peace that flow from the eternal source. I didn't ask what was wrong with you as if looking at a body without a soul—I asked to wake you up and keep you alert."

We continued walking, peering into the fading light as the sun's rays stretched long and soft across the sky. Then, little by little, a dark cloud of smoke moved towards us, as black as night, leaving us no way to escape. It surrounded us, blocking our vision and stealing away the clear air.

Chapter 16: Marco Lombardo. Lament over the State of the World.

The darkness of hell and a sky without stars, thick with clouds, never made such a heavy veil as the smoke that surrounded us now. It was so dense that I couldn't keep my eyes open, and its texture felt rough against my skin. My guide, wise and faithful, came close to me, offering his shoulder for support.

Just like a blind person follows their guide to avoid stumbling or getting hurt, I moved through the foul air, listening to my guide. He simply said, "Stay close to me and don't get separated."

I heard voices, each one praying for peace and mercy from the Lamb of God who takes away our sins. They all began with "Agnus Dei," repeating it in unison, so their harmony was evident.

"Master," I asked, "are these spirits I hear?" And he replied, "Yes, you understand correctly. They are working to overcome their anger."

Then, a voice spoke to us: "Who are you, who moves through our smoke and speaks as if you still divide time by the calendar?"

My guide said, "Answer them and ask if this path leads upward."

I responded, "O soul, cleansing yourself to return beautiful to your Creator, if you follow me, you'll hear something incredible."

"I will follow as far as I can," he replied, "and if the smoke blocks our sight, we'll stay connected through our voices."

I continued, "I am still wrapped in the body that death will one day unwrap, and I have come here through the suffering of hell. If God in His grace allows me to see His realm in a way uncommon to the living, then don't hide from me who you were. Also, tell me if this is the right path to go further up."

"I was a Lombard," he replied, "and my name was Marco. I loved the world and the virtue that everyone now ignores. You are on the right path to go higher." Then he added, "Please, when you reach the heavens, pray for me."

I promised, "I will do what you ask, but I have a burning question. The world seems to have lost all virtue and is full of sin, as you say. Please tell me the reason for this, so I can understand and share it with others."

He sighed deeply and then began, "Brother, the world is blind, and you come from it! People on Earth blame everything on the stars, as if everything happens out of necessity. If that were true, there would be no free will, no justice for good or evil deeds.

The stars may influence you, but they do not control everything. You have light to know good from evil and free will to choose. Yes, it's hard at first to resist the influence of the stars, but with effort, you can overcome it. You are subject to a higher power and a nobler nature than the stars, which shapes your mind.

So, if the world goes astray, the cause lies in you. Let me explain further. The soul, like a newborn child, comes fresh from its Creator, knowing nothing but joy. It is drawn to whatever gives it pleasure. If it isn't guided, it will chase after trivial things.

That's why there are laws to guide it, and rulers to enforce those laws. But now, while laws exist, no one follows them. The shepherds who should lead only care for themselves, so people seek only what they desire, without any higher purpose.

Clearly, it is bad leadership, not human nature, that has corrupted the world. In the past, Rome had two lights to guide it: the spiritual and the earthly. But now, one light has extinguished the other. The Church holds both the spiritual staff and the worldly sword, which causes it to fear no one. When the Church takes on both roles, it leads to corruption.

In the lands between the Po and Adige rivers, courage and kindness once thrived before Frederick caused conflict. Now, people can travel through that region without encountering virtue, because everyone avoids the good.

Only three old men are left who remember the values of the past: Currado da Palazzo, good Gherardo, and Guido da Castel, whom some call 'the simple Lombard.'

From now on, you can say that the Church has confused two powers in itself, causing it to fall into the mud."

"Marco," I said, "your reasoning is clear. Now I understand why the sons of Levi were kept from owning land. But who is this Gherardo you mentioned as an example of the lost noble class?"

He answered, "Your words seem to test me, for you speak Tuscan, yet you don't know Gherardo? I know him by no other name, unless I call him by his daughter Gaia. Now, I must leave you. Look—the dawn is breaking through the smoke. I must go before the angel appears."

With that, he spoke no more and left.

Chapter 17: Dante's Dream of Anger. The Fourth Circle: The Slothful. Virgil's Discourse of Love.

Imagine, Reader, if you've ever been caught in a thick mist in the Alps, where you can barely see anything, like trying to look through a cloudy film. When the damp fog begins to clear, you might catch a faint glimpse of the sun shining through. Picture that scene, and you'll understand how I first saw the sun again, though it was already setting.

Following my Master's footsteps, I came out of that cloud into the fading rays of sunlight on the low hills.

Imagination can sometimes take us so far away from reality that we don't notice anything around us, no matter how loud it gets. What triggers it? It could be a light in the sky, or perhaps a will guiding it from above.

As I walked, I suddenly imagined the story of a woman who turned into a bird that sings joyfully. My mind got so lost in this vision that I blocked out everything happening around me.

Then, I imagined another scene: a fierce figure on a cross, surrounded by Ahasuerus, Esther, and the righteous Mordecai. This vision shattered like a bubble when the water inside bursts.

Next, I saw a young woman crying bitterly. "Mother," she said, "why did you end yourself in anger? You wanted to avoid losing Lavinia, but now you've lost me."

Just as light wakes you suddenly from sleep, this vision disappeared the moment a bright light struck my face—much brighter than I was used to.

I turned to see where I was when a voice said, "Here is the path upward." This pulled me out of my thoughts, making me eager to find out who had spoken. But just like staring at the sun blinds you, I couldn't see the figure clearly.

"This is a divine spirit who guides us upward without us asking," said my guide. "He hides himself in his own light. He helps us like a man who knows what we need before we ask, showing kindness without waiting for us to beg. Let's hurry up the path before night falls, or we'll have to wait until daylight returns."

My guide and I headed toward a staircase. As I reached the first step, I felt a movement, like wings brushing my face, and heard the words, "Blessed are the peacemakers."

By then, the last rays of the sun were leaving us, and stars were starting to appear. I felt my energy drain away and wondered to myself, "Why is my strength fading?"

We reached a point where the stairway ended, and we stopped, like a ship that has finally reached the shore. I listened carefully for any sounds in this new place. Then I turned to my guide and asked, "What sin is cleansed in this circle? Please explain, even though we have paused here."

He replied, "Here, the love of doing good, which was neglected, is restored. Those who were lazy in their love are now made to act. Focus your mind, and you'll learn something useful from our delay here.

"Neither the Creator nor any creature is ever without love. Natural love is always right, but spiritual love can go wrong if it loves the wrong thing or loves too much or too little.

"When love is directed toward good and kept in balance, it does not cause sinful pleasure. But when love turns toward evil or seeks good in the wrong way, it works against the Creator's plan. From this, you can see that love is the root of every virtue and also every sin that deserves punishment.

"Because love can never turn away from its own well-being, it can't hate itself. And since nothing exists on its own apart from God, we can't desire to hate Him either.

"The evil we love is usually directed at our neighbors in three ways:

"Some wish others to fail so they can appear greater. Some fear they will lose power, honor, or fame when others succeed, so they become envious. Others are so angered by wrongs that they seek revenge, wishing harm on those who wronged them.

"These three forms of harmful love are punished below. Now, I'll tell you about the other kind of love—one that pursues good in a flawed way.

"Everyone has a vague idea of a 'good' that will bring peace, and everyone strives for it. But if your love for this good is weak or misguided, this level punishes you after you repent for it.

"There are other things people love that don't bring true happiness. They aren't the essence of goodness, the root of all joy. Those who love these things too much will find themselves lamenting in the circles above us. But I'll let you figure out the rest for yourself."

Chapter 18: Virgil further discourses of Love and Free Will. The Abbot of San Zeno.

The wise Teacher had finished his explanation and was looking at me to see if I was satisfied. I was silent, though still filled with questions. I wondered to myself, "Am I asking too many questions and bothering him?"

But my true Father, understanding my unspoken worry, encouraged me to speak. So, I said, "Master, your words have opened my eyes, and now I see clearly what you've explained. But please, teach me more about love, which seems to be at the root of every good and bad action."

He replied, "Focus your mind on me, and I'll show you where the blind often make mistakes. The soul, created to love, moves toward anything that seems pleasing. When something pleases you, your mind forms an image of it. That image makes your soul turn towards it. If the soul leans towards it, that inclination is love—a natural reaction tied to pleasure.

"Just as fire naturally rises, so does the soul become drawn to its desire and won't rest until it enjoys what it loves. Now, it should be clearer why some people are wrong to say that all love is good. Love itself might seem good, but what it clings to might not be.

"Think of it like wax; the wax might be pure, but the impression stamped into it might not be."

I responded, "Your words and my own understanding have revealed what love is. But now I'm even more confused. If love comes from things outside of us, and our soul follows it without a choice, how can it be our fault if we go wrong?"

He answered, "I can explain this part, but for anything beyond it, you'll need to wait for Beatrice; that knowledge requires faith.

"Every living soul has its unique abilities, which are not visible unless they act, just like life in a plant is shown by its green leaves. But where our first ideas and desires come from, no one really knows. This first natural desire, like a bee's instinct to make honey, can't be praised or blamed.

"What really matters is the power of your mind that can judge and guide you. This is where you decide whether a love is good or bad. That's where free will comes into play.

"The great thinkers knew about this freedom within us. That's why they gave us ethics. So, while it's true that you can't control what kindles love in you, you do have the power to restrain it.

"When Beatrice talks about free will, this is what she means. Remember that when she mentions it."

By now, the moon was almost at midnight, making the stars around it seem even fewer, like a glowing bucket in the sky. It was moving in the opposite direction of the path the sun travels. My guide, who had lifted the weight of my questions, was now silent.

I stood there, deep in thought, like a person lost in a daydream. But suddenly, I was startled out of my thoughts by a group of people coming towards us from behind.

They moved quickly, like the crowds rushing to see Ismenus and Asopus when Thebes needed Bacchus. From what I saw, they moved with a righteous and loving energy.

In no time, they were upon us, running forward, and two of them called out, "Mary ran to the mountain in haste! Caesar rushed to subdue Ilerda!"

Others cried, "Hurry! Don't waste time on half-hearted love! Passion for doing good refreshes grace!"

"O you eager souls," said my guide, "who might now be making up for past negligence, this one here who lives—yes, it's true—wants to ascend. So, please, show us the nearest way."

One of them replied, "Follow us, and you'll find the path. We are eager to move on, so forgive us if we seem rude for not stopping."

He continued, "I was the Abbot of San Zeno in Verona under the rule of Emperor Barbarossa, who Milan still mourns. Soon, someone will regret putting my monastery in the hands of his sick-minded son."

If he said more, I don't know; he had already moved ahead. But I heard these words, and they stayed with me.

My guide then pointed to two souls coming behind us, saying, "Look, they are condemning their own laziness!"

The two shouted, "Those who died in the desert saw the Red Sea part, but their descendants didn't make it to the Promised Land! Those who couldn't endure with Aeneas chose a life without glory!"

When these souls were out of sight, a new thought entered my mind. One idea led to another, and soon I drifted into deep contemplation. Slowly, my thinking turned into a dream.

Chapter 19: Dante's Dream of the Siren. The Fifth Circle: The Avaricious and Prodigal. Pope Adrian V.

It was the hour when the sun's daily warmth can no longer reach the coldness of the moon. The moon was losing its heat to the earth, or perhaps to Saturn. It was that time of night when fortune-tellers see their "Fortuna Major" in the eastern sky, just before dawn, shining on a path that soon fades.

In a dream, I saw a stammering woman. She was cross-eyed, her feet twisted, and her hands disfigured. Her skin was pale and sickly. I stared at her, and just like the sun warming up frozen limbs, my gaze seemed to give her strength. She began to stand upright, and her face slowly changed into something beautiful, just as love would wish it to be.

When she could finally speak, she started singing so sweetly that I could barely pull my attention away from her. She sang, "I am the sweet Siren who lures sailors into the deep sea. My voice is so pleasant to hear that I make them lose their way. I led Ulysses off his path with my song. Those who stay with me rarely leave because I satisfy them completely."

Before she could close her mouth, a holy and alert Lady appeared at my side, ready to silence her. "Virgil, oh Virgil! Who is this?" she demanded sternly. Virgil approached, his eyes fixed on the Lady.

The Lady grabbed the Siren, tore open her clothes, and revealed her foul, decaying belly. The stench from it woke me up. I turned to look at Virgil, who said, "I called you at least three times. Get up; let's find the way forward."

I stood up. The circles of the Sacred Mountain were already bathed in the morning light, and with the new sun behind us, we began our journey. I followed Virgil, my head bent forward like someone deep in thought, making a half-arch with his body.

Then, I heard a gentle and kind voice say, "Come, here is the passage." I looked up to see an angel with open wings, appearing as white as a swan. He guided us between two walls of solid rock. He flapped his wings, creating a breeze as he blessed those who mourned, saying they would find comfort.

"What troubles you? Why do you keep staring at the ground?" Virgil asked as we climbed past the angel.

I replied, "I just saw something in a vision that fills me with worry. I can't stop thinking about it."

He said, "Did you see that old enchantress? From now on, she is behind us. Did you see how one can be freed from her spell? That is enough; stamp your feet on the ground and lift your eyes to the lure of the Eternal King."

Just like a hawk that first checks its feet, then looks up and flies eagerly towards its master's call, I obeyed. I climbed up the path where the rock gave way, reaching the place where the next circle began.

When I reached the fifth circle, I saw people lying face down on the ground, weeping. I heard them sigh deeply, saying, "My soul clings to the dust."

"O chosen ones of God," Virgil said, "whose suffering is eased by both justice and hope, please guide us to the way upward."

"If you are free from this suffering and want to find the quickest way, always keep your right hand against the outer edge," one of them replied.

Virgil asked them more questions, and I sensed what they meant from their response. I looked into his eyes, and he nodded with a smile, granting me permission to ask them more.

So, I approached one of the souls, who had spoken earlier. "O soul," I said, "who mourns in a way that allows you to turn to God, pause your suffering for a moment and tell me who you were and why you lie face down. Also, is there anything I can do for you on earth?"

He replied, "You'll soon know why we lie face down. But first, know this: 'Scias quod ego fui successor Petri' (Know that I was Peter's successor). Between Siestri and Chiaveri flows a beautiful river. My family takes its name from it. I wore the heavy papal cloak for only a short time—a month and a bit more. And while it felt heavy as mud to carry, every other burden seemed light in comparison.

"My conversion came too late, but when I became the Roman shepherd, I realized that worldly life was a lie. I saw that the heart can never find peace on earth, so I turned my love to God. Before that, I was a wretched soul, greedy and distant from God. Now, as you see, I am being punished for that greed.

"What greed does to the soul is revealed here in the suffering of the converted. There is no more bitter pain on this mountain. As we kept our eyes fixed on earthly things, now justice forces our faces to the ground. Just as greed killed our love for all good things and stopped us from acting, justice here holds us down. We are bound and unable to move until the Lord sees fit to release us."

I had knelt down, wanting to speak, but before I could say anything, he sensed my reverence just by listening.

"Why have you knelt?" he asked.

"For your dignity," I replied. "Standing in your presence makes me feel remorseful."

"Stand up, brother," he said. "Don't make this mistake. I am a servant of God, just like you and everyone else. If you've ever read the Gospel where it says, 'neque nubent' (they will neither marry), you'll understand why I say this. Now go. I don't want you to linger here because your presence hinders my weeping, which helps cleanse my soul.

"On earth, I have a granddaughter named Alagia. She is good at heart, unless our family's evil example leads her astray. She is the only one left to me on earth."

Chapter 20: Hugh Capet. Corruption of the French Crown. Prophecy of the Abduction of Pope Boniface VIII and the Sacrilege of Philip the Fair. The Earthquake.

It is hard for the will to go against a stronger will. So, to please my guide, I reluctantly pulled myself away from that sweet source of knowledge. I followed my Leader along empty paths, walking close to the rock walls, as if we were walking next to battlements. On the other side of us were souls tormented by envy. They were too close to the edge, pouring out their suffering through their eyes.

"Cursed be you, old she-wolf," I thought, "who preys on everything with your endless hunger! Oh heavens, when will the one come to drive you away?"

We walked slowly, barely making any progress. As we moved forward, I could hear the souls around us weeping and lamenting. Among the cries, I heard, "Sweet Mary!" It was said in the voice of a woman giving birth. Then I heard, "How poor you were when you laid your sacred burden in that humble inn."

After that, I heard someone say, "O good Fabricius, you valued virtue with poverty more than wealth gained through vice."

These words moved me so much that I walked closer to find out where they were coming from. The voice continued to speak of the generosity of Saint Nicholas, who gave his riches to help young women live honorable lives.

"O soul who speaks so beautifully," I said, "tell me who you were, and why you alone share these words of praise? You will be rewarded when I finish my short journey in this life."

The voice replied, "I will tell you, not because I expect anything from the world, but because I see such grace shining in you even before your death. I was the root of that evil plant that overshadows all of Christendom, rarely producing good fruit. If Douay, Ghent, Lille, and Bruges had power, they would take vengeance on it. I pray for this to the One who judges all.

"On earth, I was known as Hugh Capet. I was the ancestor of the kings of France, the Louises and Philips who have ruled the country since. My father was a butcher in Paris when all the ancient kings had died, except one who wore a monk's robe in repentance.

"I found myself holding the reins of power and surrounded by so many allies that I could raise one of my descendants to the throne. It was through him that this royal line began. For a while, our dynasty brought little harm, but when the rich dowry of Provence entered my bloodline, it began to thrive on lies and force. It took over Ponthieu, Normandy, and Gascony.

"Charles went to Italy and killed Conradin as payment for his ambition. He then sent Thomas back to heaven. Soon, another Charles will come from France to bring more harm and shame. He goes unarmed, but carries the lance of Judas. He will stab Florence in its belly, bringing sin and disgrace.

"The other, already sailing, will sell his daughter as a pirate would sell a slave. Oh, greed! What else can you do to us? My bloodline is so consumed by you that it has forgotten its own flesh. To make matters worse, I see the French lily entering Alagna, making Christ's Vicar a captive. I see him mocked again, given vinegar and gall, and killed between two thieves. The modern-day Pilate cares so little that he sails his ship into the temple without any thought.

"O Lord, when will I see the vengeance that lies hidden in your divine plan? What I spoke earlier about the Bride of the Holy Spirit made you turn to me for explanation. We pray for her until night falls, and then we chant stories of greed instead. We recall Pygmalion, who was a traitor and thief driven by his endless lust for gold. We speak of Midas, whose greed brought him misery, and Achan, who stole spoils and angered Joshua. We mention Sapphira and her husband, the beating of Heliodorus, and how Polymnestor killed Polydorus.

"Then, we cry out, 'O Crassus, tell us, what is the taste of gold?' We shout these names with different volumes, depending on how much we want to express ourselves. Earlier, I was not the only one speaking of goodness, but now I see no one else raising their voice."

We moved on, trying to go as far as our strength would allow. Suddenly, I felt the ground shake beneath us, sending a chill down my spine like one facing death. I was reminded of how violently the island of Delos shook before Latona gave birth to the two heavenly lights, Apollo and Artemis.

All around us, I heard cries, and my guide turned to me, saying, "Do not fear while I am here with you."

"Glory to God in the highest!" they all shouted. This was what I could make out among the cries around us. We stopped, standing still like the shepherds who first heard that song of praise on the night of Christ's birth. When the trembling ceased, we resumed our journey, observing the souls lying on the ground, returning to their mourning.

Never before had I been so eager to know something. But I was afraid to ask, and I could not figure it out on my own. So, I continued walking, anxious and deep in thought.

Chapter 21: The Poet Statius. Praise of Virgil.

The natural thirst for truth, which can only be satisfied by the grace of God, troubled me as I followed my guide along the rocky path. I was pondering over the just punishment we had seen when, suddenly, just like in the Gospel of Luke where Christ appeared to two disciples after rising from the tomb, a figure appeared behind us. This figure was looking down at the souls lying on the ground. We didn't notice him until he spoke, saying, "Brothers, may God give you peace!"

We turned around quickly, and Virgil, my guide, gave a response that matched the greeting. The figure then said, "May the blessed council grant you peace, though I am banished to eternal exile!"

He continued, "How is it that you, who are spirits that God does not allow into Heaven, have come this far up His mountain?"

Virgil replied, "If you look closely at the marks this one bears, you'll see he belongs among the blessed. However, the one who spins the thread of life has not yet cut his thread, so he cannot travel alone. That's why I was brought from Hell to guide him as far as my teachings can lead."

Virgil then asked, "Can you tell us why the mountain shook and why there was a loud cry from its base?"

The figure answered, addressing exactly what I had wanted to know: "Nothing happens on this mountain without order, and nothing is foreign to its nature. It is free from any disturbances that usually occur on Earth, like rain, hail, snow, dew, or frost. These things never rise higher than the three steps of the holy gate where Peter's Vicar stands.

"The mountain shakes when a soul feels pure and is ready to ascend, which is marked by a cry of joy. The will to be pure gives the soul the freedom to fly upward, surprising it with this new desire.

"I have been lying here in this pain for over five hundred years, but only now did I feel free to rise to a better place. That's why you heard the earthquake and the voices of praise from the spirits on the mountain."

His words relieved me, and I felt less thirsty for answers. My wise guide, Virgil, then said, "Now I understand why the mountain shakes, how souls are set free, and why they rejoice. But please, tell me who you were and why you have been lying here for so many centuries."

The spirit replied, "In the days when Titus, with the help of the Supreme King, avenged the wounds caused by Judas' betrayal, I lived on Earth. My name was famous, though I was not yet a believer. I was known for my sweet poetry. I came from Toulouse, and Rome crowned me with myrtle. People still know me as Statius; I sang of Thebes and the great Achilles, though I stumbled on my second work.

"The flame that sparked my passion for poetry came from the Aeneid. That poem was like a mother and a nurse to me. I would have given anything to have lived during the time of Virgil, even if it meant staying in exile for another lifetime."

Hearing these words, Virgil turned to me, his eyes silently telling me to stay quiet. But sometimes emotions are hard to control; they burst out without our permission. I couldn't help but smile, just a little.

Statius noticed my smile and asked, "Why did you smile just now? If you wish to finish this great journey, please tell me."

I felt caught between staying silent and speaking, so I sighed. Virgil then said, "Speak, do not be afraid. Tell him what he wants to know."

So I said, "You may be surprised by my smile, but there is a reason for it that might astonish you more. This man guiding me is Virgil, the very poet you learned from. If you thought my smile was for some other reason, know that it was because of what you just said about him."

Statius, realizing who Virgil was, bent down to embrace his feet. But Virgil said, "Do not do that, brother. We are both mere shades."

Statius stood up, saying, "Now you can understand the love that burns in me for you. I forgot our current state and treated a shadow as if it were a real, solid being."

Chapter 22: Statius' Denunciation of Avarice. The Sixth Circle: The Gluttonous. The Mystic Tree.

We had already left the Angel behind, the one who led us to the sixth circle and erased another mark from my forehead. Those who desire justice had spoken to us, saying "Blessed," and added "I thirst," but said no more.

Feeling lighter than on the other paths, I moved forward with ease, following the swift spirits. Virgil then began to speak: "Love sparked by virtue always spreads to others, as long as it's shown outwardly. Since the moment when Juvenal came to us in Limbo and told me of your affection, I felt a strong bond with you, even though I had never seen you. So now, these stairs don't seem difficult at all.

"But tell me, and forgive my directness, how could greed find a place in your heart, when you were so filled with wisdom and knowledge?"

Statius first laughed at these words, then answered, "Your words show me your love, and I appreciate that. Often, things seem one way when the true cause is hidden. It seems you think I was greedy in my life, probably because of the circle you found me in. But actually, my problem was the opposite—extravagance. For thousands of months, I've been punished for wasting too much.

"It was only when I read the part where you cry out in anger, 'O cursed hunger for gold, what do you drive men to do?' that I realized how wrong I had been. I realized that my hands were too quick to spend. And I regretted that just as much as my other sins.

"How many people will rise from the dead with their hair cut short because they never repented for this sin, not knowing how serious it was? You should know that the sin opposing greed also withers here. That's why I was among the souls who mourned for their greed—to cleanse myself from being too extravagant."

"Now," Virgil said, "when you wrote about the tragedy of Jocasta's suffering, I noticed that your poems didn't seem to show the faith that is essential for good deeds. If that's true, what brought you to faith later?"

Statius replied, "You were the first to lead me to Parnassus and to the knowledge of God. You were like a man walking in the dark with a light behind him, helping those who follow but not himself. You wrote, 'The world renews itself; justice returns, and a new generation descends from heaven.' That made me a poet and, later, a Christian.

"The world was already filled with the true faith, spread by the messengers of the eternal kingdom. When I saw that your words matched theirs, I began to visit them. I grew to admire them so much that when Domitian persecuted them, I cried for their suffering. I supported their ways and looked down on other beliefs.

"I was baptized even before I wrote my poem about the rivers of Thebes. But out of fear, I hid my Christianity and pretended to be a pagan. That's why I wandered the fourth circle here for more than four centuries.

"Now that you've lifted the cover from what I just confessed, tell me, while we have time climbing this mountain, where our friend Terence is. What about Caecilius, Plautus, and Varro? Are they damned, and where are they now?"

Virgil answered, "These poets, along with Persius, myself, and many others, are in Limbo, the first circle of the dark prison. We often talk about the mountain that our muses love. Euripides, Antiphon, Simonides, Agatho, and many other Greek poets are there with us, wearing their laurel crowns. You will also find characters from your works, like Antigone, Deiphile, Argia, and the mourning Ismene."

The poets then fell silent, looking around as we continued our climb. By now, four hours of daylight had passed, and the fifth was beginning to rise. Virgil said, "I think it's time to turn our right shoulders towards the edge and circle the mountain as we always do."

We followed the usual path, trusting the wise soul's direction. They walked ahead, while I followed behind, listening to their conversation, which taught me more about poetry.

But soon, their conversation was interrupted by a tree in the middle of the road. It had sweet-smelling fruit, but its branches were shaped downward, almost as if to prevent anyone from climbing it. Clear water flowed from the rock and spread over the tree's leaves.

The two poets approached the tree, and a voice came from the leaves: "You shall have little of this food." It continued, "Mary cared more about making the wedding feast complete than satisfying her own hunger. The ancient Roman women were content with water, and Daniel avoided rich foods to gain wisdom. In the golden age, acorns tasted good out of hunger, and every stream was like nectar.

"Honey and locusts were John the Baptist's food in the wilderness. That's why he is honored, as the Gospel reveals."

Chapter 23: Forese. Reproof of immodest Florentine Women.

As I was staring at the green leaves, much like someone wasting time chasing small birds, my guide, more than a father to me, said, "Son, come now; we need to use our time wisely."

I turned around and quickly caught up with the wise ones. They were talking in a way that made the climb easier for me. Suddenly, we heard singing and lamenting: "Labia mea, Domine." It was both joyful and sorrowful at the same time.

I asked, "Father, what is this sound I hear?" He replied, "These are souls, perhaps freeing themselves from their sins."

As pilgrims do when they meet strangers on the road, turning to look but not stopping, so did a crowd of spirits gaze at us as they hurried by. They were silent and devout, each with hollow, sunken eyes, their faces pale and thin. Their skin clung to their bones.

I don't think even Erisichthon, with his terrible hunger, could have been so dried up. I thought to myself, "These are the people who lost Jerusalem, just like Mary who fed on her own son." Their eye sockets were like rings without gems. The face could have spelled out "omo" just by its shape.

Who would believe that just the scent of an apple or water could make them suffer so much without even knowing how? I kept wondering what had made them so starved since the cause wasn't clear yet.

Then, a spirit looked up from the hollow of his eyes and called out, "What grace has come to me?" I wouldn't have recognized him by sight alone, but his voice revealed what his face hid. That spark reawakened my memory of Forese, his features altered but still there.

"Ah, don't look at my skin, dry and discolored like this," he pleaded. "Don't mind how thin I am. But tell me about you, and who those two souls are with you. Please, don't delay."

I replied, "Seeing your face, which I once mourned, now brings me even greater grief. But please tell me, what has made you so thin? I can't speak while I'm still in shock."

He answered, "From the eternal law comes power into the water and the tree we left behind. That is why I am so thin. Everyone here sings with sorrow because they followed hunger and thirst too much. Now, we are purified.

"The scent of the apple tree and the spray of water over the grass ignite our desire to eat and drink. It happens again and again as we circle this mountain. I call it 'pain,' but it should be called 'comfort.'

"It is the same desire that led Christ to joyfully cry out, 'Eli,' when He freed us with His blood."

I said to him, "Forese, it hasn't been five years since you left for a better life. If your sins were erased sooner than the time it takes for true repentance, how did you come here so quickly? I thought I'd find you lower down, where time is spent paying for sins."

He replied, "My Nella, with her tears and prayers, helped me reach this place faster. Her devout prayers freed me from the waiting shore and the lower circles. God finds my little widow even more pleasing because she's so alone in her good deeds. The women of Sardinia are more modest than those she lives among.

"My dear brother, what else can I say? I see a future not far away when Florence's shameless women will be banned from showing off in public. If they only knew what Heaven has in store for them, they'd already be howling in fear.

"If my vision isn't wrong, they will regret their ways before the boy who sleeps in his cradle now grows a beard.

"But enough about me. Who are you? Everyone here is staring at you, wondering why you block the sunlight."

I said, "Forese, if you recall what we once were to each other, this memory will still bring sadness. I was taken out of that life by the one who walks ahead of me. It happened two days ago when the moon was full.

"This one here," and I pointed to Virgil, "led me through the true night of the dead. He guides me now with my living body. He says he will stay with me until we reach Beatrice. After that, I must go on alone. This is Virgil," I said, pointing at him. "The other soul," I pointed again, "is the one for whom your realm trembled when he was freed."

Chapter 24: Buonagiunta da Lucca. Pope Martin IV, and others. Inquiry into the State of Poetry.

We kept moving forward, walking and talking, as if driven by a good wind like a ship sailing smoothly. The spirits around us, who seemed twice as dead, stared at me with hollow eyes, amazed to see someone alive.

I continued the conversation, saying, "Maybe he's moving more slowly for the sake of others. But tell me, do you know where Piccarda is? Is there anyone here I should recognize, anyone of note among these spirits looking at me?"

He answered, "My sister Piccarda, who was both beautiful and good, now rejoices with her crown in Heaven." Then he added, "We can say each other's names here because our physical forms have faded away from fasting." He pointed and said, "That one is Buonagiunta of Lucca, and next to him, with a sharper face, is a man who once held the Church close. He came from Tours and is now purging himself of the eels of Bolsena and Vernaccia wine."

He named many others one by one, all of whom seemed pleased to be called by their names. Not one of them looked angry. I saw some spirits biting the empty air in hunger, including Ubaldin dalla Pila and Boniface, who had been a shepherd to many. I also saw Messer Marchese, who, while in Forli, never seemed satisfied, always thirsty.

Then, like someone scanning a crowd and focusing on one person, I turned my attention to the man from Lucca, who seemed most interested in me. He muttered something, and I caught the name "Gentucca." He felt the sting of justice and was in visible pain.

I said, "O spirit, who seems eager to speak with me, go ahead. Speak, so we can both find some peace."

He replied, "A maiden has been born who hasn't yet worn a veil. She will make my city pleasant for you, no matter what others say about it. You'll see what I mean as you go on your way. If my words were confusing, the truth will soon reveal itself."

He continued, "But tell me, are you the one who wrote the new style of poetry that starts with, 'Ladies, who have knowledge of love'?"

I replied, "Yes, I am. I write and sing whenever love inspires me, using the words it dictates to me."

"Ah, now I see," he said. "I understand what held me, the Notary, and Guittone back from the sweet new style I hear now. I see how your pens follow what you're inspired to write, unlike ours. Those who try to go beyond without seeing this difference will miss it." With that, he fell silent.

Like birds flying south for the winter, sometimes in a flock and other times in a line, the spirits turned and hurried away, moving quickly due to their lightness and desire. Just like a tired runner who lets his companions go ahead while he catches his breath, Forese slowed down and stayed with me. He said, "When will I see you again?"

"I don't know how long I'll live," I answered, "but I know I'll long to return here. The place where I live becomes emptier of goodness each day and seems headed for ruin."

"Go on," he said. "I see the one responsible for it, dragged along by a beast towards the valley where there is no repentance. The beast moves faster with each step, tearing him apart."

Forese looked up and added, "Not long from now, you'll see what I mean. Now, I must leave. Time is precious here, and I can't afford to lose more by walking with you."

Like a rider breaking from a group for the first charge, he left us quickly. I stayed behind with the two who were like leaders of the world. When he was far enough away that I could barely see him, another tree appeared ahead of us, filled with fruit. Beneath it, people reached up, crying out like children begging for something just out of reach. But they were left wanting, as if to make their desire even stronger.

Soon, they walked away, disappointed, and we approached the tree. Someone from the branches called out, "Move along. The tree from which Eve ate is higher up. This tree grew from that one."

At those words, Virgil, Statius, and I moved forward on the rising path. "Remember the creatures from the clouds who, drunk, fought Theseus, and the Israelites who were unfit to fight because they drank too much," the voice reminded us as we walked.

We heard more tales of gluttony as we passed along one side of the path. For a long while, we walked in silence, deep in thought.

Then a voice suddenly called out, startling me, "What are you three thinking?" I looked up to see who had spoken. Never had I seen metal or glass so shiny and red as the figure before me.

"If you wish to ascend, this is the way," the figure said. "Here goes the path for those seeking peace."

Blinded by his brightness, I turned back to my guides, moving forward like someone who can only rely on sound to find their way. Then, like the fresh breeze of May, I felt a soft wind and smelled a sweet fragrance. I heard the words, "Blessed are those whom grace has enlightened so that the desire for taste does not consume them, allowing them to hunger only as is just."

Chapter 25: Discourse of Statius on Generation. The Seventh Circle: The Wanton.

The path ahead was clear for us to climb because the sun had already moved past its highest point, leaving Taurus and heading towards Scorpio. So, like someone in a hurry who doesn't stop for anything, we entered through the gap and began climbing the stairs. The path was so narrow that only one person could go up at a time.

I was like a young bird lifting its wings, eager to fly but not quite ready to leave the nest. I wanted to ask a question, but then I hesitated and dropped the thought. My fatherly guide noticed this and said, "Go ahead and speak. Don't hold back your question any longer."

Feeling confident now, I began, "How can someone get thin when there's no need for food here?"

"If you remember how Meleager wasted away when the burning of a brand took his life," he replied, "this won't seem so strange to you. Or think of how an image in a mirror trembles when you move. If you think about that, what seems hard to understand might make more sense to you. But to fully satisfy your question, I'll call on Statius to help explain."

Statius responded, "If I explain this deeper truth in front of you, Virgil, let my excuse be that I cannot refuse you."

Then he turned to me and said, "Listen, my son, to what I say, and let it answer your question. The perfect blood, which is not used up by the body, stays in the heart. This blood has the power to form all the parts of the body because it flows through the veins to nourish them. After it is digested, it reaches a place where it's best to stay silent about what happens next. Then, it mixes with the other blood in a natural vessel.

"The two bloods come together, one active and one passive, creating a new form. This mixture starts to work, first solidifying, then bringing life to what it has formed. The active power of this mixture becomes like a plant's soul. It begins to grow, sense, and form the organs needed for the body.

"Now, the soul continues to expand, spreading from the heart of its creator. But how this life turns into a human, you do not yet understand. This was a mystery even to wiser men than you, who thought the soul and the intellect were separate. They couldn't see the organ that connects them.

"Be ready to hear the truth. As soon as the brain of the unborn child forms, the First Mover (God) looks upon it with pleasure and breathes a new spirit into it, filling it with life. This spirit blends with what it finds in the body and becomes one soul, able to live, feel, and think for itself.

"To make this clearer, think of how the sun's heat turns grape juice into wine. When a person dies, the soul leaves the body, carrying with it the human qualities: memory, intelligence, and willpower. These abilities are now even stronger than before.

"The soul moves on to either a good place or a bad place, depending on its life. As soon as it reaches its destination, it takes on a new form like air reflecting different colors. The soul creates a new shape for itself, which we call a 'shade.'

"This shade looks just like the person did in life. It has the power to speak, laugh, cry, and feel emotions. That's why, here on the mountain, you hear them sigh and speak. The shape of the shade changes based on its desires and feelings, which is why you see what you see."

By now, we had reached the final circle of the mountain. We turned to the right, where a new challenge awaited us. Here, the edge of the path shot out flames, and the heat rose up to push the flames back, keeping them away from the ledge. We had to walk single-file along the outer edge, away from the fire. I was scared of both the flames and the sheer drop.

My guide warned, "Be very careful here. You need to keep your eyes focused and not make a wrong step."

Then, from within the flames, I heard a hymn: "Summae Deus clementiae" ("God of Highest Mercy"). It made me want to turn and look, and I saw spirits walking through the fire. I watched their steps while also paying attention to my own.

After they finished the hymn, they cried out loudly, "Virum non cognosco" ("I do not know a man"). Then, they started singing softly again. When they finished that song, they shouted, "To the forest ran Diana, driving out Helice, who had felt Venus's poison."

They continued with more songs about virtuous wives and husbands who remained chaste. I believe they sang this way to help themselves endure the fire burning them. They needed to do this until their last wound could heal.

Chapter 26: Sodomites. Guido Guinicelli and Arnaldo Daniello.

As we walked along the narrow path, one behind the other, my wise guide kept saying, "Be careful! It's enough that I warn you." The sun, shining from my right shoulder, made the western sky change from blue to a glowing white.

My shadow made the flames around us appear even redder. I noticed that many of the souls walking there turned their heads to look at me. Seeing my shadow seemed to catch their attention. It made them start whispering, "This doesn't look like a spirit!"

Some of them came closer to me, carefully avoiding the flames. One of them said, "You who walk behind the others, maybe out of respect, answer me. I am burning with thirst and fire. But it's not just me who wants to know; all of us here are thirstier for your answer than a person in the scorching heat of Ethiopia or India is for cool water.

"Tell us, how is it that you cast a shadow as if you are not dead?"

I was just about to answer when something new caught my attention. Another group of spirits appeared in the middle of the burning path, walking toward the ones around me. It was such an unusual sight that I stopped to watch them.

I saw these spirits quickly greet each other, kissing one another briefly as they passed. It was like watching ants that touch heads as they meet, perhaps to share news about their journey or fate.

As soon as their brief greeting was over, they started shouting at each other. One group yelled, "Sodom and Gomorrah!" The others replied, "Look at Pasiphae, lusting after the bull!"

Then, just like birds that fly in two different directions, some avoiding the cold and others seeking warmth, the spirits parted ways. Each group returned to chanting the phrases that matched their shame.

One of the spirits who had spoken to me earlier came closer again, eager to listen to my answer. I had already seen their curiosity twice, so I began, "O souls destined for peace one day, my body is not yet dead. It still carries its blood and bones, which is why I cast a shadow. I am here to see clearly now because a Lady in Heaven granted me this grace.

"But please, to satisfy your longing, tell me who you are and who those others were that passed us."

The spirits were stunned, like a countryman seeing a city for the first time. When they regained their composure, the one who had first questioned me said, "Blessed are you, who bring back news from our land to live a better life. The group that just passed us has sinned in a way that once caused Caesar to be called 'queen' in mockery. They shout 'Sodom!' as a way of shaming themselves and adding to their suffering.

"Our sin was different. We acted against human law, following our desires like animals. That's why, when we part, we shout the name of the woman who became a beast. Now you know our deeds and our crime. You might want to know our names, but there isn't enough time, and I couldn't tell you all of them.

"I will tell you my name though. I am Guido Guinicelli, here to purge my sins because I repented before my final hour."

When I heard his name, I felt the kind of sadness and awe that the sons of Lycurgus might have felt upon seeing their mother. This man was the father of me and my fellow poets who have written sweet and graceful verses about love. For a long time, I walked silently, just staring at him, not daring to approach because of the flames.

When I had looked my fill, I told him I was ready to serve him and promised to honor his legacy.

He replied, "Your words leave a mark on me so clear that even the river Lethe cannot wash it away. But tell me, why do you honor me so much?"

I answered, "Your beautiful verses, which will remain cherished as long as poetry exists, are why I hold you dear."

He then pointed to another spirit and said, "That one there was even better at writing in our language. He mastered both love poetry and romantic prose. People who say otherwise are fools. Many praised the wrong poets before knowing the truth.

"If you are allowed to reach the place where Christ is the abbot, please say a prayer for me. We no longer have the power to sin, but we still need prayers."

170

After saying this, he disappeared into the fire, like a fish sinking to the bottom of a pond.

I moved closer to the spirit he had pointed out. I wanted to honor him, and he responded, "I am Arnaut. I weep and sing as I mourn my past sins but also look forward to the day of hope. I beg you, by the power guiding you to the summit, please remember to ease my pain."

With these words, he too vanished into the purifying flames.

Chapter 27: The Wall of Fire and the Angel of God. Dante's Sleep upon the Stairway, and his Dream of Leah and Rachel. Arrival at the Terrestrial Paradise.

As we walked single file along the narrow path, my wise guide often said, "Be careful! My warning should be enough."

The sun was on my right shoulder, its rays turning the western sky from blue to white. My shadow made the flames around us glow even redder, and I noticed many spirits looking at me with curiosity as I walked by.

They began whispering among themselves, "That doesn't look like a shadow from a spirit!" Some of them cautiously moved closer to me, careful not to step into the flames. One of them called out, "You, who walk behind the others, not out of slowness but perhaps out of respect, answer me! I am burning with thirst and fire, and we all want to know something even more than a person in the heat of Ethiopia craves cool water.

"How is it that you make a shadow like someone still alive?"

I was about to answer when something else caught my eye. Down the middle of the fiery path, another group of spirits appeared, moving towards us. I was so focused on them that I forgot about answering the question.

As the two groups of spirits met, they exchanged quick, brief kisses like ants touching heads as they cross paths. Then they began shouting at each other. One group yelled, "Sodom and Gomorrah!" The other group replied, "Pasiphae lusted for the bull!"

The groups then parted, each going their separate ways. I could hear them crying out their shames as they moved along. Meanwhile, the spirit who had questioned me came closer, still waiting for my answer.

I had seen their curiosity twice now, so I said, "O souls destined for peace one day, my body is not yet dead. It still carries its blood and bones, which is why I cast a shadow. I'm here to see clearly now because a Lady in Heaven granted me this grace. But please, to satisfy your longing, tell me who you are and who the others were that just passed us."

The spirits seemed stunned, like a countryman entering a city for the first time. After they recovered from their shock, the one who had spoken first said, "Blessed are you, who bring news from our world. The group that just passed sinned in the way that caused Caesar to be mockingly called 'queen.' They shout 'Sodom!' to shame themselves and add to their suffering.

"Our sin was different. We broke human laws and acted like animals, so we shout the name of the woman who turned into a beast. Now you know our deeds and our crime. You might want to know our names, but there isn't enough time for that."

Then he added, "But I'll tell you who I am. I am Guido Guinicelli, here to purge my sins because I repented before my final hour."

Hearing his name filled me with awe and sadness. He was the father of those, like me, who have written sweet verses about love. I was so moved that I walked in silence, staring at him without daring to approach.

When I had looked my fill, I told him I was ready to serve him and promised to honor his legacy.

He replied, "Your words leave such a mark on me that not even the river Lethe could wash it away. But tell me, why do you honor me so much?"

I answered, "Your beautiful verses, which will always be cherished, are why I hold you dear."

He then pointed to another spirit and said, "That one was even better at writing in our language. He mastered love poetry and prose, despite what fools say. They often praised the wrong poets before knowing the truth."

He then made a final request: "If you are allowed to enter the place where Christ is the abbot, say a prayer for me. We can no longer sin, but we still need prayers."

After saying this, he disappeared into the flames, like a fish diving deep into the water.

I turned to the spirit he had pointed out, wanting to honor him as well. In his own language, he said, "I am Arnaut, who weeps and sings as I remember my past mistakes. I look forward to the day of hope. I beg you, please ease my suffering when you reach the top."

With that, he too vanished into the purifying fire.

Chapter 28: The River Lethe. Matilda. The Nature of the Terrestrial Paradise.

Eager to explore the heavenly forest, lush and green, I left the riverbank. The forest was so dense that it softened the light of the new day, filling the air with a sweet fragrance.

A gentle breeze brushed my forehead, no stronger than a soft breath. It stirred the branches just slightly, causing them to bow toward the Holy Mountain's first shadow. Yet, the branches didn't sway so much that the birds stopped their songs. They filled the air with melodies, creating music that flowed through the leaves, like the wind passing through a pine forest near the shore.

I walked slowly into the ancient forest, getting so far in that I lost track of where I had entered. Suddenly, a stream crossed my path. Its gentle waves bent the grass along its edge as it flowed to the left. The water was so clear that even the purest waters on Earth seemed muddy in comparison. It moved silently under the thick shade, untouched by sunlight or moonlight.

I paused and looked across the stream at the variety of flowers blooming there. Just then, like something unexpected that catches all your attention, I saw a woman walking alone. She was singing and picking flowers, leaving a colorful path behind her.

"Oh, beautiful lady, warmed by the rays of love," I called out to her, "if your heart reflects the kindness I see on your face, please come closer to this riverbank so I can hear you sing." Her beauty reminded me of the moment when Proserpina was taken from her mother and from Spring itself.

The lady turned towards me, gracefully stepping among the red and yellow flowers, like a dancer who moves with careful, modest steps. My request seemed to please her, and she came closer, her sweet voice carrying the meaning of her song to me as she approached the edge of the river. She stood there, bathed in the light from the beautiful stream, and finally lifted her eyes to meet mine.

In that moment, I don't think Venus herself ever shone so brightly, even when struck by Cupid's arrow. Standing on the other side of the stream, she smiled, holding many colorful flowers in her hands. The river, about three steps wide, separated us. I felt more frustration from that narrow stream than Leander must have felt when the Hellespont divided him from his love, Hero.

"You are new here," she said, smiling. "Maybe that's why you seem so surprised, standing in this place made as a home for humanity. But the psalm 'Delectasti' gives wisdom that can clear up your confusion. Speak, you who asked for my attention. I'm here to answer your questions, as much as you need."

"The water," I said, "and the sounds of the forest make me doubt what I've heard. They challenge my new understanding."

She replied, "I'll explain what you wonder about and clear away the confusion. The Highest Good, who finds joy only in Himself, created mankind pure and placed him here as a taste of eternal peace. But because of man's fall, he only stayed here a short while. He traded his innocence for tears and toil.

"To prevent the disturbances of the world—like storms and heat—from reaching mankind, this mountain was raised so high that it's free from all such disruptions. The winds blow around it, making the forest rustle because it's so dense. The trees absorb this power and spread it through the air, which then carries their scent and seeds to fertile places on Earth.

"That's why plants can grow here without seeds. This land is full of every kind of seed, producing fruit that's never harvested. The water you see doesn't come from natural springs or rain. It flows from a divine source, constantly renewed by God's will, nourishing the land on both sides.

"Here the stream is called Lethe on this side and Eunoe on the other. Drinking from it removes all memory of sin and restores every good deed. This water surpasses any other taste. Even if I stop here, I'll give you an extra blessing, revealing more than I promised.

"Those ancient poets who sang of a golden age and eternal spring might have dreamed of this very place. Here, humanity was innocent, living in an endless spring. This is the true nectar they spoke of."

I turned to my poets, seeing them smile at her words. Then, I looked back at the beautiful lady.

Chapter 29: The Triumph of the Church.

The woman continued singing like a lover, ending her song with, "Beati quorum tecta sunt peccata," which means "Blessed are those whose sins are covered."

She moved forward along the riverbank, like nymphs wandering alone in the woods, sometimes hiding from the sunlight and sometimes seeking it. I walked beside her, matching her small steps with mine. We hadn't taken a hundred steps when the path turned, and I found myself facing east.

Not long after, she turned to me and said, "Brother, look and listen!" Suddenly, a bright light spread across the forest, making me wonder if it was lightning. But it didn't fade; instead, it grew brighter and brighter. I thought to myself, "What is happening?"

A beautiful melody filled the air, reminding me of Eve's mistake in the Garden of Eden. If only she had stayed faithful and obedient, I would have been able to experience these delights much sooner and for a longer time.

While I was lost in this heavenly pleasure, still wanting more, the air under the green branches ahead of us lit up like fire. The sound turned into singing.

"Oh holy Virgins!" I thought, "If I have ever suffered hunger, sleeplessness, or cold for you, now is the time to claim my reward!" I needed help from the Muse Urania and the inspiration of Helicon to describe what I saw, for it was beyond ordinary thought.

A little farther on, I saw what looked like seven golden trees. They seemed to be far away, but as I got closer, I realized they weren't trees. My senses had been tricked. When I finally reached them, I recognized that they were actually seven candlesticks, with flames above them shining brighter than the moon in a clear sky.

Filled with wonder, I turned to Virgil, and his face reflected my amazement. Then I looked back at those bright flames moving towards us. They moved so slowly and gracefully that even newly married brides would have walked faster.

The woman beside me scolded, "Why are you only staring at those lights? Look at what's coming behind them!"

I turned and saw people walking behind the lights. They were dressed in white robes, whiter than anything on earth. The water on my left reflected my image, just like a mirror. When I got to a spot where only the stream separated us, I stopped to watch them more closely.

The flames moved forward, leaving a trail of light behind them, almost like flags. The light above them spread out in seven stripes, each in the colors of the rainbow. These stripes stretched farther than my eyes could see, each about ten paces apart.

Under this magnificent sky, I saw twenty-four elders wearing crowns of lilies, walking two by two. They sang, "Blessed are you among the daughters of Adam, and blessed forever is your beauty."

When they passed, I noticed four creatures crowned with green leaves following them, much like stars follow each other in the sky. Each creature had six wings filled with eyes, just like Argus of myth. I won't describe them in more detail because I have other things to tell, but you can read about them in the book of Ezekiel.

Between these four creatures was a grand chariot on two wheels, drawn by a griffin. Its wings stretched high, almost out of sight. The griffin's front half was golden, and the back half was white mixed with red.

Not even the chariots of ancient Rome could compare to this one—not even the Sun's chariot that was burned up at Earth's request to Zeus.

Three maidens circled the right wheel of the chariot. One was so red she could hardly be seen in the fire. The second was green like emerald, and the third was as white as freshly fallen snow. They followed the lead of the white one, then the red, adjusting their steps to match the song.

On the left side, four women in purple danced. One of them had three eyes on her forehead, guiding the others.

Two elderly men followed behind, walking with dignity. One looked like a disciple of Hippocrates, showing great care for the creatures of nature. The other carried a shining, sharp sword that filled me with fear.

Then I saw four humble-looking people and, finally, an old man walking alone with a sharp, focused expression, as if he were sleepwalking. Like the others, they wore robes, but their crowns were made of roses and other red flowers, giving the illusion that their heads were on fire.

When the chariot reached me, thunder echoed, and the whole procession came to a halt, standing still with their banners at the front.

Chapter 30: Virgil's Departure. Beatrice. Dante's Shame.

As the stars in the highest heaven stood still, those stars that never rise or set and are only veiled by sin, the people there turned toward the chariot with the Griffin. It was as if they found peace in its presence.

One of them, as if given a command from Heaven, began singing, "Veni, sponsa, de Libano" ("Come, bride, from Lebanon") three times. The others echoed the song. Just like the blessed souls who will rise from their graves at the final call, the spirits in the chariot stood up, looking full of life. A hundred of them, ministers and messengers of eternal life, sang, "Benedictus qui venis" ("Blessed is he who comes") while scattering flowers all around.

I've seen dawn break with the eastern sky tinted pink, while the rest of the sky is clear. I've watched the sun rise, its light softened by clouds so that the eye could look at it for a while. This is how it seemed when I saw a lady, clothed in a snow-white veil and a green mantle, surrounded by a cloud of flowers. She wore a dress the color of living flames.

My spirit, which hadn't been in her presence for so long, felt overwhelmed by a powerful, familiar influence. Although I hadn't yet recognized her by sight, something deep inside me, some ancient love, made me tremble.

As soon as her powerful presence struck my senses, I instinctively turned to my left, like a child running to their mother in fear or distress. I wanted to say to Virgil, "I feel the traces of that old flame!" But I found that Virgil had left me. My guide, my beloved teacher, was gone.

I was heartbroken and began to cry. Then I heard the lady say, "Dante, don't cry just yet. You will have more reasons to cry later."

I turned at the sound of my name. It was Beatrice, the lady I had seen earlier, now standing on the left side of the chariot. She spoke to me directly, her eyes looking at me from across the river.

Although her face was partially hidden by a veil, she still carried herself with a regal air, like someone holding back their most important words. "Look at me well," she said. "I am Beatrice. How did you manage to come up to this mountain? Don't you know this is where true happiness lies?"

I felt overwhelmed with shame and looked down into the clear water. When I saw my own reflection, I quickly turned my eyes to the grass, too embarrassed to look up.

She seemed as stern as a mother might to her child. Her compassion was harsh, and it stung. Suddenly, the angels began to sing, "In te, Domine, speravi" ("In you, Lord, I have hoped"), but they stopped before finishing the hymn.

The sound of their singing melted my icy heart, like snow melting in the sunlight. Hearing their voices full of compassion made me cry even harder. The tears streamed down my face and from deep within me.

Standing firmly on the chariot, Beatrice addressed the angels, saying, "You keep watch in the eternal day. You never sleep or lose track of time. That's why I must answer with care so that he who cries before me will understand his sin and sorrow."

She continued, "It wasn't just fate or the stars that shaped his life. Divine grace also played a role, giving him the potential to develop every virtue. But just like rich soil grows more wild weeds if it's not tended, he turned away from his path."

"I guided him for a while with my looks," she said. "I showed him my eyes in my youth to lead him in the right way. But when I crossed into my second life, leaving my body behind, he turned away from me and followed others."

"When I ascended to the spirit realm, my beauty and virtue increased, but he cared for me less and turned to false images of goodness. No prayer or dream could bring him back; he paid no attention to my calls."

"He fell so low that the only way left to save him was to show him the suffering of the damned. That's why I visited the gates of death and asked the guide who has led him here to help."

"God's law would be broken if he drank from the river of Lethe without first feeling the pain of repentance. True cleansing requires tears."

Chapter 31: Reproaches of Beatrice and Confession of Dante. The Passage of Lethe. The Seven Virtues. The Griffon.

Beatrice, standing by the sacred river, turned to me and spoke again. Her words were sharp and direct, cutting into me. "Tell me, is this true?" she asked. "You need to confess if you are guilty."

I was so confused that when I tried to speak, my voice faded before I could even form words. She waited for a moment, then said, "What are you thinking? Answer me. These painful memories should still be clear since the waters haven't washed them away yet."

Confused and full of dread, I barely managed to say, "Yes." My voice was so weak that someone would need to look closely to understand it.

I was like a crossbow that breaks when pulled too hard; my voice cracked under the weight of my sorrow, coming out as a stream of tears and sighs.

Then she asked, "What obstacles did you find that kept you from following the path you knew was right? What temptations or benefits did you see that made you turn away?"

After a heavy sigh, I could barely respond. My voice trembled as I said, "The pleasures of the world distracted me as soon as you were no longer there to guide me."

"If you had stayed silent or denied this, your guilt would still be obvious," she replied. "But when you confess your sins, it turns the punishment into a lesson."

"But," she continued, "I want you to feel even more ashamed of your actions so that you will be stronger the next time you face temptation. Listen to what I have to say. My physical beauty, which is now scattered in the earth, was never meant to be your ultimate goal. If you couldn't be swayed by my passing, what could you find in this world worth chasing after?"

"When the false pleasures of this world first tempted you, you should have resisted. You should not have lowered your wings for anything so trivial as a fleeting desire. Even young birds learn to avoid traps after a few tries."

I stood there in silence, ashamed like a child caught in a mistake. She then said, "If you feel pain hearing my words, look at me and feel an even deeper pain."

Reluctantly, I lifted my head. When I did, I saw Beatrice looking at me with an intense gaze. Her eyes were focused on a two-natured creature, part lion and part eagle, standing nearby. Beneath her veil, she appeared more radiant than ever before, more so than any time I had seen her on Earth.

That realization struck me deeply. The love that once drew me to her now filled me with regret and guilt. I was so overwhelmed that I collapsed. Only she knows what I became in that moment.

When I finally came to, the lady who had been by my side was standing above me, saying, "Hold onto me." She pulled me into the river, leading me through the water as lightly as if she were gliding.

When we reached the riverbank, I heard a sweet song, "Asperges me." I can barely remember the words, much less write them. The lady then wrapped her arms around me and dunked my head underwater, forcing me to drink.

After she pulled me out, I joined a group of four women who began to dance around me, covering me with their arms. They said, "We are Nymphs, stars in the heavens. Before Beatrice came to Earth, we were her handmaids. We will lead you to her eyes, but to see their true light, you will need to sharpen your sight with the help of the three who look even deeper."

As they sang, they led me to the Griffin's chest, where Beatrice was standing. "Don't hold back your gaze," they said. "Look at those emerald eyes that once captured your heart."

I felt a thousand desires hotter than flames drawing my eyes to hers. She kept her gaze fixed on the Griffin. Within her eyes, I saw the reflection of the creature, now showing one of its forms, now the other. It amazed me that the image kept changing while the creature itself remained still.

While I stood there, lost in wonder and joy, my soul felt the satisfaction that comes with longing fulfilled. Then, three more women came forward, singing and dancing like angels.

"Turn, Beatrice," they sang. "Turn your holy eyes to him who has come so far just to see you. Show him the beauty you keep hidden."

In that moment, I was in awe. If anyone had tried to describe her radiance, they would struggle to capture it in words. She stood there, unveiled, glowing with a heavenly light that seemed to make the whole sky rejoice.

Chapter 32: The Tree of Knowledge. Allegory of the Chariot.

My eyes were fixed, steady and focused, as I tried to satisfy a thirst that had been building for ten years. I became so absorbed that my other senses faded, and I felt nothing around me. My eyes were completely drawn to the holy smile before me, like they were caught in an old trap.

Suddenly, I was jolted back to reality when I heard voices on my left. "Too intently!" they warned. My eyes, which had been blinded by the bright light, felt like they had stared directly at the sun. It took a moment for my vision to adjust, but when I finally saw again, the brightness around me seemed dim compared to the light that had captured my gaze.

On the right, I saw a host of angels wheeling around, moving with the sun, their faces glowing with sevenfold flames. They moved like a group of soldiers that turns around in formation, with their shields up for protection. They had passed us completely before the chariot they were guarding turned its pole to follow them.

The maidens who had been singing moved toward the wheels, while the Griffin guided the chariot, carrying his precious burden without flapping a single feather. The graceful lady who had guided me through the river followed alongside Statius and me. Together, we followed the wheel of the chariot as it traced a smaller path.

As we walked through the vast forest, now empty because of the fall of Eve who had trusted the serpent, heavenly music guided our steps. We had moved a distance that an arrow could cover in three flights when Beatrice descended, and I heard the crowd murmur, "Adam!"

We gathered around a tree stripped of its leaves and flowers, its branches stretching out further the higher they reached. It was so tall that even in the forests of India, it would have been a wonder. "Blessed are you, O Griffin, for not plucking these branches with your beak," they said. "This tree led to temptation." The Griffin replied, "This tree holds the seeds of righteousness." Then he moved the chariot's pole beneath the tree and bound it to the trunk.

As the light from above mingled with the glow of the stars, the tree's bare branches began to bloom again. It changed colors, more vivid than violet but less than rose, becoming lush and full. I heard a hymn so beautiful and unique that I had never heard anything like it on earth. I wish I could describe it, but I can't.

If I could capture how Syrinx's story lulled the eyes that watched her to sleep, I would describe how I fell into a deep, dreamless sleep at that moment. But I will move forward and describe when I woke up. I was startled awake by a blinding light and a voice calling out, "Rise, what are you doing?"

It felt like the moment when Peter, James, and John, after witnessing the transfiguration of Christ, woke to find not only that Elijah and Moses had disappeared, but that their Master's clothes had changed. As I regained my senses, I saw the lady who had been guiding me by the river. Confused, I asked, "Where is Beatrice?"

She pointed and said, "Look, she's sitting under the new foliage at the tree's root, surrounded by a group of people. The others are following the Griffin with an even more melodious song." I don't know if she said more because, as soon as I saw Beatrice, I was so focused that I heard nothing else.

Beatrice sat on the ground as if guarding the chariot, which had been tethered by the Griffin. Seven nymphs encircled her, holding torches that neither northern nor southern winds could extinguish. She said, "You will be here for only a short time, but you will be with me forever in the heavenly city where Christ is King."

"For the good of the world that lives in darkness, fix your eyes on the chariot. What you see here, be sure to write down when you return to earth." As she commanded, I turned my gaze to the chariot, ready to obey her every word.

Suddenly, like lightning from a storm, a great eagle swooped down on the tree, tearing away its bark, flowers, and new leaves. It struck the chariot so hard that it rocked like a ship caught in a storm, tilting from side to side. Then I saw a fox jump into the chariot, its fur dull and unclean. Beatrice scolded it harshly, and it fled as quickly as its skeletal body could move.

Next, the eagle returned and left behind some of its feathers, which covered the chariot and its pole. The sight was heartbreaking. Then, the earth beneath the chariot cracked open, and a dragon emerged. It lashed out with its tail, piercing through the chariot's floor, then slithered away, pleased with its destruction.

What remained of the chariot began to sprout feathers, almost like a fertile field growing grass. It was soon covered, as were the pole and the wheels, in an instant. Then the chariot transformed, revealing monstrous heads: three on the pole and one at each corner. The first heads resembled oxen, while the others had a single horn. This was a sight unlike anything I'd ever seen.

Seated high upon this horrifying structure was a shameless woman, her eyes darting around. Beside her stood a fierce giant who seemed determined to keep her by his side. Occasionally, they exchanged kisses. However, when she turned her eyes toward me, the giant grew angry. He struck her from head to toe, then unleashed the monstrous creature. He dragged it through the forest, using it as a shield for the woman and the beast.

Chapter 33: Lament over the State of the Church. Final Reproaches of Beatrice. The River Eunoe.

The maidens began to sing, alternating between three and four voices, their melody a mixture of sadness and beauty. The song was "Deus venerunt gentes," and as they sang, Beatrice listened with a compassionate expression, her face reflecting the sorrow similar to Mary at the cross.

When the other maidens stepped aside to let her speak, Beatrice stood up, her face glowing like fire. She responded with, "'Modicum, et non videbitis me; et iterum, Modicum, et vos videbitis me,'" quoting scripture. She then moved the seven maidens ahead of her, signaling me, the lady, and the wise sage to follow.

We continued walking, and I don't think Beatrice had taken more than ten steps before she turned her eyes to me. With a calm look, she said, "Come closer, so that you can hear me better when I speak." As soon as I was by her side, she asked, "Brother, why don't you ask me questions now that you're walking with me?"

Like someone who is too respectful in the presence of someone great, I struggled to find my voice. I managed to say softly, "My Lady, you already know my need and what would be good for me."

She replied, "You must let go of fear and hesitation. Stop speaking like someone who is still dreaming. The vessel that the serpent shattered is broken, and the guilty ones should know that God's justice is not easily swayed. The Eagle will not remain without heirs forever; it left its feathers on the chariot, which turned into a monster and then fell prey."

She continued, "I see the stars signaling that the time is near when a savior, marked by 'Five Hundred, Ten, and Five,' will come to defeat the sinful woman and her giant partner. My words may seem confusing, like those of Themis and the Sphinx, but soon enough, events will unfold, and you will understand without causing harm to the innocent."

"Pay attention," she said. "Teach these words to those living lives headed toward death. And when you write about what you have seen, do not hide the vision of the plant that has been pillaged here twice. Anyone who harms this plant offends God, who made it sacred. For biting into it, the first soul suffered for over five thousand years, longing for the One who took the punishment upon Himself."

Beatrice paused, then said, "Your mind is clouded like the waters of the Elsa River, clouded with illusions. If not for these distractions, you would have understood the justice behind God's commandment concerning this tree. But since I see you are overwhelmed by guilt and confusion, I will spell it out for you. Keep this knowledge with you, just as a pilgrim carries his staff wrapped in palm leaves."

I responded, "My mind, like wax, is now imprinted with your words. But why does your teaching seem so far beyond my understanding, no matter how hard I try to grasp it?"

Beatrice replied, "This is to show you how far your current beliefs are from the divine truth. You must see how distant your path has become from the divine, as far as the earth is from the highest heaven."

I answered, "I do not remember straying from you, nor do I have any feelings of guilt." She smiled and said, "You may not remember because you drank from Lethe's waters. But the very fact that you forgot shows that your will was focused elsewhere."

"From now on," she continued, "my words will be clear, so you can understand them fully." By this time, the sun had moved higher in the sky. The seven maidens stopped at the edge of a shadowy area, much like the shadows cast by green leaves and dark branches on the Alps' cold slopes.

I saw two rivers, the Tigris and the Euphrates, flow from the same source and slowly part ways, like friends separating. "What river is this that comes from one source and then splits?" I asked.

"You should ask Matilda," was the response. The beautiful lady then explained, "I have already told him this, so it must be that his memory is clouded by greater concerns."

Beatrice added, "Perhaps something else has made his mind forget, but see that other river, Eunoe? Take him there to revive his virtue."

Matilda, without hesitation, took hold of me and turned to Statius, saying, "Come with him." If I had more space to write, I would describe in detail the joy of drinking from those waters, which never fail to satisfy. But since my pages are already full, I must end this part of the story.

From the sacred water, I emerged renewed, like a tree that grows fresh leaves. I was pure and ready to ascend to the stars.

Part 3 Paradiso

Chapter 1: The Ascent to the First Heaven. The Sphere of Fire.

The glory of the One who moves everything shines throughout the universe, more brightly in some parts than in others. I found myself in the heaven that receives His light most fully. There, I witnessed things that cannot be fully described or remembered by anyone who has returned to earth. Our minds become so absorbed when approaching this place that memories cannot capture it all. Still, whatever I managed to keep in my mind of this holy realm will now be the subject of my song.

Oh, Apollo, for this final task, make me a vessel of your power, as those who seek the laurel crown do. Up until now, I have needed only one peak of Parnassus, but now I need both to enter this new arena. Enter into my heart and breathe into me, as you did when you drew Marsyas out of his skin. If you lend me your divine power so I can capture the shadow of that blessed realm in my words, I will go to your sacred tree and crown myself with those leaves, made worthy by this theme and your support.

Father Apollo, we so rarely seek this crown, whether for a conqueror or a poet. This is due to human flaws and weaknesses. If anyone desires the laurel, it brings joy to the god of Delphi. A small spark can ignite a great flame. Perhaps my prayer will inspire others to call upon you with even better voices.

The world's light, the sun, rises for mortals in different ways. But when it aligns with certain stars, it shines brighter and shapes the world more according to its own nature. Just as morning was dawning in one part of the world and nightfall was approaching in the other, Beatrice turned to the left and gazed at the sun. No eagle has ever looked at it so intently!

Like a second ray reflecting off a surface, her gaze infused into my mind. I then turned my eyes toward the sun, drawn by her example. In this heavenly place, I could do things that are impossible on earth. Although I couldn't look at the sun for long, I saw it sparkle, like molten iron fresh from the furnace.

Then, suddenly, it seemed as if another day had begun, as though the Creator had adorned the sky with an extra sun. Beatrice stood with her eyes fixed on the eternal wheels of the heavens. I kept my gaze on her and felt a transformation within me, similar to how Glaucus felt when he tasted the magical herb that made him like the sea gods.

To describe this experience is impossible; it goes beyond words. Only those blessed by grace will understand it. If I was only the new creation that Love had made, then you, who governs the heavens, would know that it was your light that lifted me.

As I was drawn into this vision, the harmony of the eternal spheres captured my attention. It seemed that so much of heaven was lit by the sun's light that it spread far and wide, like a vast lake. This new light and sound sparked in me an intense curiosity about their cause.

Beatrice, seeing my confusion, spoke to calm my troubled mind before I could even ask. She said, "You are distracted by false ideas. If you let go of them, you will see the truth. You are not on earth, as you think. You have moved with the speed of lightning, returning to your true place."

If these few words, more smiled than spoken, freed me from my earlier confusion, they also left me with a new question. I asked, "I am no longer confused, but now I wonder how I could rise above the physical world."

Beatrice sighed and looked at me with the kind of pity a mother has for her troubled child. She began, "Everything has an order. This order makes the universe reflect God. The higher beings see the footprints of the Eternal Power, the ultimate goal for everything. In this order, all things have their place and move toward their destiny. Each creature is given an instinct that guides it toward its purpose.

"Fire rises toward the moon; this force moves the hearts of mortals and unites the earth. This power not only affects non-living things, but also those with intelligence and love. Divine Providence regulates this order, bringing peace to the heaven where the fastest motion occurs. Now, this divine power is taking us to our destined place."

She continued, "Sometimes, though, things don't follow their natural course, just as a fireball can fall to earth if it's redirected. Don't be surprised at your ascent. It's like a stream flowing down from a mountain to the valley. It would be more surprising if, without obstacles, you remained on the ground, like a living flame resting on earth."

With that, she turned her gaze back to the heavens.

Chapter 2: The First Heaven, the Moon: Spirits who, having taken Sacred Vows, were forced to violate them. The Lunar Spots.

O you who have been eagerly following my ship, sailing smoothly with its song, in your small boat, turn back to your shores. Do not venture farther into the sea, or you might lose your way and become lost in my wake.

The sea I sail has never been crossed before. Minerva guides me, Apollo steers, and the nine Muses show me the way. To the few of you who have lifted your eyes early to the bread of angels, which nourishes here without ever making you full, you may sail into the deep sea. Keep following the path behind me, on the water that smooths out as I pass.

Those who sailed with Jason to Colchis were not as amazed as you will be when you witness what lies ahead! The deep and constant desire for the divine realm carried us forward as quickly as you see the heavens moving above you.

Beatrice looked upward, and I looked at her. In the time it takes for a lightning bolt to strike and leave its mark, I found myself in a wondrous place that captured my attention. She, who could sense my every concern, turned to me, as joyful as she was beautiful, and said, "Be thankful in your heart to God, who has brought us to the first star."

A bright, dense, and shining cloud surrounded us, glowing like a diamond reflecting sunlight. This eternal light took us in, just as water receives a beam of light without breaking.

If I had a physical body (though here we do not understand how one dimension could contain another), this only deepens the desire to see the essence in which God and human nature are united. Here, what we believe through faith becomes clear and evident, like the first truth that we all accept.

I replied, "My Lady, I thank Him as much as I can for taking me away from the mortal world. But tell me, what are the dark spots on this star that people on earth say are the mark of Cain?"

She smiled a little and said, "If human opinions are wrong where senses cannot guide, then it shouldn't surprise you if you are also mistaken now. If you trust only your senses, remember they have limits. Now, tell me what you think these spots are."

I answered, "I think the differences we see up here are caused by some areas being denser or lighter than others."

She replied, "You will see how mistaken that belief is if you listen carefully to my explanation. The eighth sphere has many lights, each with its unique qualities and appearances. If the variations were caused only by density, then all these stars would either reflect the same light equally, or be brighter or dimmer based only on how much light they reflect.

"Different qualities must come from different sources. And if your reasoning were correct, it would erase all but one source. Also, if the dimness you see was caused by thinness, this entire planet would have to be uniformly thin, or at least vary like fat and lean parts in a body. If that were true, during an eclipse, the light would shine through as if passing through something thin. But we don't see this, so your theory doesn't hold.

"If the variations were not uniform, there would be a boundary where thinness ends and something else blocks the light. This would reflect the light, like how colors bounce off a mirror backed by lead. You might say that sunlight appears dimmer in some areas because it is reflected back farther. But if you try this with mirrors, you will see that, regardless of the distance, the light will be equally bright in the reflections.

"Imagine placing three mirrors: two equally distant from you and a third farther away. Position a light source behind you so that it shines on all three mirrors and reflects back to you. You'll notice that while the farther image is smaller, it is just as bright.

"Now, let's return to the snow analogy. When snow melts under warm rays, it changes color but retains its original nature. Your mind is like that snow, and I'll shine light on it to help you understand.

"In the heaven of divine rest, there is a body whose power defines everything within it. The next heaven, with its countless eyes (the stars), divides this power into different essences. The other spheres then arrange these distinctions, guiding their effects and purposes.

"Like a craftsman using a hammer, the power and motion of the holy spheres come from their divine source. The heaven filled with stars takes its image from this divine intelligence, imprinting it like a seal. Just as your soul spreads its influence through your body, so this intelligence spreads its power among the stars, revolving within its own unity.

"This power blends with the stars differently, shining through them like joy through a pupil. This is why each light appears different—not because of density or rarity, but because of the divine essence that shapes its brightness and darkness."

Chapter 3: Piccarda Donati and the Empress Constance.

The sun that once warmed my heart with love had revealed the truth to me with such clarity that I felt the urge to speak. I straightened up, ready to express my understanding. But then, a vision appeared, drawing me so close that I forgot my thoughts and words.

Like when we see faint reflections of our faces in clear, still water or through a polished piece of glass, many faces appeared to me. They seemed so faint, almost like shadows, that I couldn't recognize them right away. It was like I had become confused, mistaking these reflections for something real.

When I realized they were not mere reflections, I turned to see who they were. But I saw nothing. I looked back to the light of my guide, Beatrice, who smiled at me, her eyes glowing with kindness.

"Don't be surprised," she said, "that I smile at your childish thoughts. You still do not trust fully in the truth, and instead, you focus on what is not real. What you see here are true spirits. They are here because they broke some vow. Speak with them, listen to their words, and believe. The light that gives them peace will not let them turn away from it."

I approached the spirit that seemed most eager to speak and, overwhelmed with curiosity, I began, "O noble spirit, who tastes the sweetness of eternal life, please tell me your name and your story."

With a warm smile, she replied, "Our kindness never denies a rightful request. I was a nun in the world. If you look closely, you may remember me as Piccarda. Here I am among the blessed in the slowest sphere. We are filled with joy in the Holy Spirit, and we rejoice in being part of His order.

"We are here because we failed to keep our vows fully. The place we are given might seem low, but it is a reflection of our actions on earth."

I replied, "Your divine beauty has transformed you so much that I did not recognize you at first. But your words now make it clearer for me. Tell me, are you and the others here wishing for a higher place to see more or to be closer to God?"

She smiled at the other spirits before answering, her joy so radiant that it seemed like a spark of first love. "Brother, our hearts are content with what we have. We do not desire more because our will is aligned with God's will. If we wanted to rise higher, it would go against His wishes, and there can be no discord here in Heaven. Being in harmony with God's will is essential to this blessed state.

"It is our greatest joy to accept our place in Heaven because it is part of God's plan. His will is our peace, and all creation moves toward this peace."

Now I understood that Heaven is everywhere in the divine realm, even though the grace of the highest good is not the same in every place. Just as someone who is full from one meal may still desire another dish, I found myself wanting to know more about her story.

With words and gestures, I asked what had kept her from fully living out her vow.

"A noble lady in Heaven set the rule for us," she said, "and those on earth take vows to serve the Lord, to watch and pray as His faithful spouse. I followed her path, leaving the world while still a young girl. I took the vows and entered the cloister. But men, more inclined to evil than good, took me away from the sweet life of the convent. Only God knows what happened to me after that.

"The bright spirit beside me went through a similar experience. She was a nun who was also forced back into the world against her will. Yet, she never lost the true veil of her heart. This is the light of Costanza, who continued the royal line of Suabia."

After speaking, she began to sing "Ave Maria," and as she sang, she faded away, like something sinking into deep water. My eyes followed her for as long as I could. When I could no longer see her, I turned back to my main desire—Beatrice.

But when I looked at her, she flashed such a bright light that my eyes couldn't bear it at first. This left me momentarily hesitant, unable to ask more questions.

Chapter 4: Questionings of the Soul and of Broken Vows.

Between two equally tempting meals, a free person would die of hunger before deciding which one to choose. Similarly, a lamb caught between two hungry wolves would fear both equally, just as a dog would hesitate between two deer. So, if I kept silent, I do not blame myself, since my doubts held me back. I was unable to speak, but my desire was clear on my face, more so than any words could express.

Beatrice, like how Daniel had freed Nebuchadnezzar from his fury, looked at me and said, "I see how both your questions are pulling at you. Your mind is caught, unable to decide. You wonder if good intentions remain constant, how can the actions of others reduce one's merit? Also, Plato's idea of souls returning to the stars troubles you. I will address these doubts, starting with the one that is harder to understand.

"Those souls you saw—be it the Seraph closest to God, Moses, Samuel, John, or even Mary—do not have different places in heaven. They do not spend more or fewer years in their existence. All of them beautify the highest circle of Heaven and live a joyful life in varying degrees, based on how deeply they feel God's eternal breath.

"They appeared to you in that specific sphere not because it is where they belong but as a symbol of the lowest celestial order. This explanation fits your mind's way of thinking, which understands things through the senses before grasping them intellectually.

"Scripture often speaks in ways humans can understand, attributing hands and feet to God, even though He does not have them. Similarly, the Church presents Gabriel, Michael, and Raphael in human form, though they are angels.

"As for what Plato argues about the soul, it does not match what you see here. Plato claimed the soul returns to the stars, believing it came from them. He might mean that the soul returns to the influence and impact of those stars, which could contain some truth. This idea was misunderstood for ages, leading people to worship Jupiter, Mercury, and Mars.

"Your second doubt, however, carries less danger, for it cannot lead you away from the truth. The idea that our justice might seem unfair to mortals is a matter of faith, not heresy. But to ease your concern, I will explain it further.

"If violence involves someone not cooperating with the force applied to them, these souls are not excused for their actions. The will is never completely extinguished unless it chooses to be. Just as fire keeps burning no matter how much you try to bend it, so the will always has some power. The more or less it yields to force, the more it shares in the responsibility.

"If their will had been strong, like St. Lawrence on his gridiron or Mutius holding his hand over fire, they would have returned to the path of holiness as soon as they were free. However, such strength of will is rare.

"If you have understood my words, they should resolve your first doubt. But now, another question arises, one you could not answer on your own.

"I have said that a blessed soul cannot lie because it is close to the primal Truth. Yet, you heard Piccarda say that Costanza kept her love for the veil, which seems to contradict me. Often, things are done reluctantly to escape danger, just as Alcmaeon killed his mother at his father's request, though he did not wish to. Remember, when force mixes with the will, the actions are not entirely excusable.

"Absolute will never consents to evil, but it may consent out of fear of a greater harm. When Piccarda spoke, she meant this absolute will, while I referred to the other kind. So, we both speak the truth."

Her words flowed like a holy river from the source of all truth, calming my mind entirely.

"O divine love," I said, "your words fill me with warmth, reviving my spirit more and more. My own gratitude feels inadequate to repay you; may God respond in my place. I now understand that our minds are never satisfied until they are illuminated by the Truth. That is where all desires come to rest, just like a wild beast in its den.

"Yet, as we reach one truth, new doubts arise, pushing us higher and higher. This makes me bold enough to ask you another question. Can a broken vow be compensated by other good deeds in a way that would make the scales balanced?"

Beatrice looked at me, her eyes full of divine love. The intensity of her gaze overpowered me, and I turned away, my eyes cast down.

Chapter 5: Discourse of Beatrice on Vows and Compensations. Ascent to the Second Heaven, Mercury: Spirits who for the Love of Fame achieved great Deeds.

"If I seem to burn with love for you more intensely than anything you've ever experienced on Earth, and if my gaze overpowers you, don't be surprised. This comes from perfect vision, which, once it sees the good, rushes toward it. I can see that the eternal light has already begun to shine in your mind, and once it's seen, it always sparks love. If you're drawn to other things, it's because you've misunderstood the reflection of this divine light.

"You want to know if breaking a vow can be made up for with some other good deed, enough to free the soul from any further consequence." Beatrice began speaking this way, like someone who continues their speech without interruption:

"The greatest gift God gave us in creation, the one most like His goodness, is the freedom of the will. This gift is what makes intelligent creatures unique. Now, think about the value of a vow. When you make a vow, you're giving that free will to God, and He accepts it. This act is a sacred sacrifice.

"What could possibly replace such a gift? If you offer up your free will and then try to use it for something else, it's like trying to do a good deed with ill-gotten gains.

"You now understand the main point. However, since the Church sometimes allows vows to be changed, and this seems to go against what I've just explained, let's explore this a bit more. You'll need to 'digest' this new knowledge to fully understand it.

"Pay attention and keep this in mind. In a vow, two things come together: the content of the vow and the agreement to it. The agreement is binding and cannot be undone unless it's fulfilled. We've already covered this in detail.

"That's why the Hebrews were told to keep their vows, even if what they offered could sometimes be exchanged for something else, as you should know. The substance of the vow can sometimes be changed if the exchange is appropriate.

"But no one should change a vow on their own. They must use both the keys of the Church, the white and the yellow, to do so. Also, any exchange is foolish if the substitute does not fully contain the value of what was originally promised.

"If something holds so much weight that it tips the scales completely, then nothing else can compensate for it. So, never make vows lightly. Keep them faithfully and thoughtfully, unlike Jephthah, who made a rash promise. It would have been better for him to say, 'I was wrong,' rather than to carry out his vow. The same goes for Agamemnon, who caused Iphigenia to suffer.

"Christians, be more serious in your actions. Don't be swayed like a feather in the wind, thinking that any action can wash away your guilt. You have the teachings of the Old and New Testament and the guidance of the Church. That should be enough for you to find salvation.

"If sinful desires tempt you, be strong like men, not like foolish sheep, so that those who don't share your faith cannot mock you. Don't be like a lamb that leaves its mother's milk and fights aimlessly on its own."

Beatrice spoke to me this way, just as I have written it. Then, eager to turn her attention back to where life is fullest, she became silent and her expression changed. Her silence made me quiet, stopping my next question from forming.

Like an arrow that hits the target before the bowstring even stops vibrating, we quickly moved into the second realm. As my Lady entered this new brightness, I saw her grow even more joyful, and the star itself seemed to glow more brightly.

If the star changed and became more radiant, think what happened to me, a being who is so easily affected by everything around him!

In a clear, still pond, fish swim towards anything that touches the surface, thinking it might be food. In the same way, I saw more than a thousand glowing lights coming towards us. Each light said, "Look, this is the one who will increase our love." As they approached us, each one became more vivid, glowing with a clear light.

Reader, imagine how you would feel if this story stopped here, leaving you desperate to know more. You can then understand my desire to learn about these spirits as they became clearer to me.

One of the holy lights spoke, saying, "O blessed soul, to whom Grace allows to see the seats of eternal triumph even before the earthly struggle is over, we are lit by the light that fills Heaven. If you wish to know more about us, feel free to ask."

Encouraged by Beatrice, who said, "Speak freely and trust them as you would the divine," I turned to the light that first spoke to me. I said, "I see how you glow with your own light, shining brightly when you smile. But I don't know who you are or why you are here in this part of Heaven, which hides itself in foreign rays."

When I said this, the light became even brighter. Like the sun, which sometimes hides behind its own brightness, the holy figure seemed to wrap itself in even greater light. Then it spoke to me, as I will describe in the next part of my journey.

Chapter 6: Justinian. The Roman Eagle. The Empire. Romeo.

After Constantine turned the eagle, the symbol of Rome, away from the path it had once followed under the ancient king who took Lavinia, the eagle stayed in the farthest part of Europe for more than two hundred years, near the mountains from where it originally came. Under the shelter of its sacred wings, it ruled the world, passed from one ruler to another, and finally came to rest in my hands.

I was Caesar, and I am Justinian. By the will of the eternal Love that I now feel, I took on the task of revising the laws, removing what was unnecessary. Before I could focus on that work, however, I believed in the idea that Christ had only one nature. I was content with that belief. But then blessed Agapetus, the supreme pastor, guided me to the true faith through his words. I believed him, and now I clearly see the truth of what he said, just as you can see what is false and what is true.

When I turned toward the Church, God, in His grace, inspired me to take on this great task. I then gave the military command to Belisarius, whose actions were so blessed by Heaven that I took it as a sign to rest.

This answers your first question, but I must continue so you can understand why people act against the sacred symbol of the eagle, whether by claiming it for themselves or by opposing it.

Look at the great power that has made the eagle worthy of respect, beginning from when Pallas died to give it sovereignty. You know that it stayed in Alba for over three hundred years, and you know how it was fought over again and again.

You know of its achievements, from avenging the Sabine wrongs to the tragedy of Lucretia. It triumphed over the neighboring nations through seven kings. It fought for Rome's honor against Brennus, Pyrrhus, and other princes and allies.

Heroes like Torquatus, Quinctius (known for his wild locks), the Decii, and the Fabii gained their fame under its symbol. The eagle crushed the pride of the Arabs who followed Hannibal across the Alps. While they were still young, generals like Pompey and Scipio triumphed under its wings, and the city where you were born felt its might.

When Heaven decided to bring peace to the world, Caesar took up the eagle by Rome's will. What the eagle accomplished from the River Var to the Rhine, from the Isère to the Saône, to every valley of the Rhône, is beyond the words of poets.

When it left Ravenna and crossed the Rubicon, it moved with such power that no words could truly capture its feats. It then turned its legions toward Spain and struck down at Pharsalia, spreading its power even to the Nile. It went back to where it had started, to Antandros and the Simois, where Hector lies buried. Then it swept like lightning over Juba and back to the West, where it heard Pompey's clarion call.

What it did under the next leader made Brutus and Cassius howl in Hell. The cities of Modena and Perugia suffered because of it, and Cleopatra, fleeing from it, died by the bite of an asp. The eagle reached the shores of the Red Sea, bringing peace to the world so complete that the temple of Janus was closed.

But what the eagle did before and after these events seems small in comparison when seen with pure eyes in the hands of the third Caesar. It carried out divine justice, exacting vengeance as needed.

Now, listen carefully to what I say: The eagle later flew with Titus to avenge the ancient sin. And when Lombardy attacked the Holy Church, Charlemagne came to her aid under its wings.

Now you can judge those I accused earlier and see their crimes, which are the root of your suffering. One group opposes the eagle with the yellow lilies, while another claims it for a political party. It's hard to say which of these is more at fault.

Let the Ghibellines work under another banner, for those who separate justice from the eagle will always fail. And let this new Charles not try to strike down the eagle. He and his Guelfs should fear its claws, the same claws that stripped the hide from a nobler lion.

Many times the sons have suffered for the sins of their fathers. Let Charles not think that God will change His symbol for the lilies. This little planet, Earth, is decorated with the souls of those who sought fame and honor through righteous deeds. But when their desires turn away from Heaven, their love's light shines less brightly.

Here, joy is given in proportion to one's merits. This is true justice, which makes our love forever align with what is right. Like different voices creating a harmonious melody, each soul here finds peace in its unique place among the heavenly spheres.

In this pearl shines the soul of Romeo, whose great work went unrewarded. The Provencals who wronged him did not laugh in the end. Those who harm others' good deeds will not prosper. Raymond Berenger had four daughters, each of whom became a queen, thanks to Romeo, a poor man and a wanderer. Yet, jealous words led Berenger to demand an account from this just man, who gave back far more than he took. Romeo left, poor and old, and if the world knew his true heart, he would be praised even more."

Chapter 7: Beatrice's Discourse of the Crucifixion, the Incarnation, the Immortality of the Soul, and the Resurrection of the Body.

The holy song rang out: "Hosanna, holy God of Hosts, shining with your light, you bless these happy flames!" The spirit who sang this song glowed with a bright light, and the others joined in, dancing like sparks that quickly moved away, hiding themselves in the distance.

I stood there, uncertain and thinking, "Should I ask her? Should I ask Beatrice?" She quenches my thirst for knowledge with her wisdom. Yet, I felt a deep respect for her that kept me silent, like a child afraid to speak out.

Beatrice noticed my hesitation and didn't let it last long. She smiled at me, a smile so warm it could bring joy even in the midst of fire, and began to speak: "You are wondering how it is possible that a just punishment can be justly punished in return. I will explain, so listen closely; this is a great lesson."

She continued, "When man, who was never meant to exist, failed to obey God, he damned not only himself but all his descendants. Because of this, humanity lived in error for many centuries until God, in His infinite love, chose to descend and unite with human nature.

"Pay close attention now," she said. "When this human nature joined with its Creator, it was pure and good as it was originally made. But by itself, it was exiled from Paradise because it strayed from the path of truth and life. This exile was deserved.

"So, when Jesus took on human nature and suffered on the cross, the punishment was just, considering the human nature he had assumed. But it was also unjust, considering who he was—the divine being who suffered. From this single act, two things happened: God was pleased, and the Jews were satisfied. The earth trembled, and Heaven opened.

"So, it should not be hard to understand how a just punishment was justly punished in return. I can see you are tangled up in thought, trying to figure out why God chose this way for our redemption. This question is still hidden from anyone whose love is not yet fully grown.

"The reason why this was the best way is rooted in the goodness of God. Divine goodness, which has no envy, shines so brightly that it spreads out the beauty of eternity. Anything that comes directly from God is everlasting; it leaves an eternal mark. This gift is free and not controlled by external forces.

"The more something resembles this divine goodness, the more it pleases God. Humanity was created in this divine image, but sin separates us from this goodness, making us less like God. We cannot regain our dignity unless we make up for our sins with righteous actions.

"When humanity sinned, it lost its original dignity and was cast out of Paradise. There were only two ways to make things right: either God could forgive out of mercy, or humanity could atone for its wrongs.

"Now, think deeply. Humans were limited and couldn't make up for their sins by themselves. They couldn't lower themselves enough to correct their disobedience. So, God had to restore humanity either by Himself, or in both ways. But God's goodness wanted to show its generosity, so He chose both ways to lift humanity back up.

"No greater act was ever seen before, nor will there ever be, than when God humbled Himself to become human. This path was more glorious than if He had simply forgiven us.

"Now, let me explain another part so you can understand fully. You say, 'I see the air, fire, water, and earth, and how they eventually decay. If what you say is true, shouldn't they be free from corruption?'

"Listen, brother, the Angels and this heavenly place were created in their entirety. The elements and everything formed from them were made with a created power. The soul of every living thing draws life from the stars and planets, but human life comes directly from God's grace. This divine connection makes the human soul always yearn for God.

"From this, you can understand the idea of resurrection. Think about how human flesh was first created when the first parents, Adam and Eve, were made."

Chapter 8: Ascent to the Third Heaven, Venus: Lovers. Charles Martel. Discourse on diverse Natures.

The world used to believe, in its troubled past, that the goddess of love, Venus, shined down on us from the third heavenly sphere. This belief led ancient civilizations to honor Venus with sacrifices and prayers. They worshipped not only her but also Dione, her mother, and Cupid, her son. They even said that Cupid had sat on Dido's lap.

They named the star that both follows and leads the sun after Venus, from whom my story starts. I wasn't aware when we reached this star, but I knew we were there because I saw my Lady growing more beautiful.

As a spark is seen within a flame or a sound within another sound when one is constant and the other comes and goes, I saw other lights moving in circles within that bright light. They moved at different speeds, perhaps according to their level of understanding. No wind, however strong or fast, has ever moved as quickly as those lights rushing toward us, leaving behind their original circular dance in the high heavens.

I heard "Hosanna!" echoing behind the lights, a song that filled me with a longing to hear it again. Then, one of those lights came closer and began to speak: "We are all ready to bring you joy. We move in circles with the heavenly Princes, guided by the same love. On Earth, you once called us, 'You who move the third heaven with your wisdom.' We are filled with so much love that taking a brief pause to speak with you brings us even more happiness."

After respectfully looking at my Lady, who gave me confidence, I turned back to the light and asked, "Who are you?" My voice was filled with deep affection.

I watched as the light grew brighter with joy at my question. It then answered, "I lived on Earth for only a short time, but if I had lived longer, many evils would have been avoided. I am hidden from you now by the light that surrounds me, just as a creature is wrapped in its own cocoon.

"You loved me dearly, and you had good reason to. If I had stayed on Earth, I would have shown you love beyond just its outer leaves. My land was along the left bank of the Rhône, where it merges with the Sorgue. It awaited my rule.

"The region of Italy with cities like Bari, Gaeta, and Catona, where the Tronto and Verde rivers flow into the sea, was also part of my future. The crown of that land watered by the Danube had already shone upon my brow after it passed beyond Germany's borders. Beautiful Sicily, which lies between Pachino and Peloro and suffers the most from the east wind, was also meant for my rule.

"It wasn't because of a giant monster, but rather because of growing corruption, that Sicily would have kept its kings, descending from Charles and Rudolph through me. However, bad governance caused the people of Palermo to cry out, 'Death, death!' If my brother could foresee this, he would avoid the greed of Catalonia that brings such trouble. He must make sure his ship, already heavy with burdens, takes on no more.

"His nature, which descended from generous ancestors, needs soldiers who don't care about storing wealth away."

I responded, "My Lord, I believe your words bring me joy. I know you see everything as clearly as I do. This makes your words even more precious to me. But tell me, how can something bitter come from a sweet seed?"

He answered, "If I can show you a truth, you will see the answer to your question more clearly. The Good that governs this whole realm shapes the course of events. Not only does it foresee the natures of things, but it also ensures their preservation. Everything that comes from this power is aimed at a specific purpose, just like an arrow shot toward a target.

"If this were not so, the heavens would create random outcomes, like ruins instead of masterpieces. This can't happen unless the guiding spirits of the stars were flawed, and they cannot be flawed because the First Cause, which created them, is perfect.

"Would you like me to explain this more clearly?"

I replied, "No, I understand now. Nature cannot fail in providing what is needed."

He continued, "Would it be worse for people on Earth if they were not organized into communities?"

"Yes," I replied, "and I need no further explanation for that."

"Then," he said, "people must live with different roles and duties. Therefore, the root causes of your actions must be diverse. This is why one person is born a lawmaker, another a king, another a priest, and yet another an inventor. Nature imprints people just like a seal on wax, but it does not distinguish between one type of inn or another. That's why one twin can differ greatly from another, as Esau was different from Jacob, or a man like Quirinus can come from a lowly father and rise to greatness.

"If divine providence did not guide this diversity, all offspring would simply resemble their parents. Now, what was unclear to you should be clearer. But to make sure you understand that I am pleased with you, I will add one more thought.

"Nature struggles when it finds itself in a hostile environment. If people would focus on following nature's path, society would be better. But instead, you force people into roles they were not born for. You make a man, meant for the sword, take up religion, and a man meant to preach into a king. This is why your footsteps stray from the true path."

Chapter 9: Cunizza da Romano, Folco of Marseilles, and Rahab. Neglect of the Holy Land.

Beautiful Clemence, after your Charles enlightened me, he shared the betrayals that his descendants would face. But he said, "Be patient and let time pass." So, I can only say that justified mourning will follow the wrongs you will suffer.

Then that holy light turned back to the Sun, the source of its life, just like all things turn to the source of their goodness.

Oh, deceived souls and sinful creatures, who turn your hearts away from such goodness and focus on empty pursuits!

Now, look, another one of those bright lights approached me, showing its desire to please me by glowing even brighter. The eyes of Beatrice were still fixed on me, giving me her silent approval for my wish.

"Please, satisfy my desire quickly, blessed spirit," I said. "Give me proof that what I'm thinking about you is true!"

The light, which was new to me, continued joyfully from deep within itself, singing as if delighted to do good:

"In that corrupted part of Italy, lying between Rialto and the sources of the Brenta and Piava rivers, there rises a small hill. From this hill, a flame once descended that greatly affected the region.

"From the same root, both that flame and I were born. I am Cunizza, and I shine here because the light of this star won me over. But I gladly accept my fate and do not grieve for it, even though this might seem strange to those who don't understand.

"This precious and bright jewel, which is closest to me in Heaven, still has a great reputation. And it will live on for five hundred years. Consider how one should strive for excellence so that the second life leaves a mark after the first.

"But the people who live between the rivers Adige and Tagliamento don't think this way. They are not even sorry for their sins, despite being punished. Soon, Padua will change the water that bathes Vicenza, as the people continue to defy their duties.

"In the place where the Sile and Cagnano rivers meet, a man rules with pride. But even now, a trap is being set to catch him.

"Feltro will mourn the crime of its wicked pastor, so terrible that nothing like it has ever happened in Malta.

"It would take a huge vat to hold the blood of the people from Ferrara, and whoever tries to weigh it, ounce by ounce, would grow weary. This 'courteous' priest will spill so much blood to show his allegiance, leaving a fitting gift for those still living in the land.

"Above us are mirrors, which you call Thrones, reflecting God's judgment to us, so that these words seem right to us."

Then the light became silent and turned away, carried by the revolving wheel on which it had appeared.

The other joyful light, which I already knew, shone even brighter in my sight, like a fine ruby hit by the sun.

In Heaven, joy makes the light shine, just as a smile lights up a face on Earth. But down below, sorrow darkens the outward appearance as it clouds the mind.

"God sees everything, and in Him, you see all things, blessed spirit," I said. "Nothing of His will can be hidden from you. Your voice, which makes Heaven glad along with the holy flames, could satisfy my longings. But it doesn't. And I wouldn't make you wait for my question if I could see inside you as you see into me."

The light began to speak: "The greatest valley where water spreads out, except for the sea surrounding the Earth, stretches between opposite shores so far that it forms a meridian where it used to form the horizon.

"I lived on the shores of that valley between the Ebro and the Magra rivers, which separate Tuscany from Genoa. The cities of Bougie and the place where I came from share nearly the same sunset and sunrise. My city once heated its harbor with blood.

"My people knew me as Folco. Now, I leave my mark on this Heaven, just as it left its mark on me. Belus's daughter never burned with more passion, betraying both Sychaeus and Creusa, than I did during the time of my youth.

213

Neither did the Rodophean woman, who was tricked by Demophoon, nor even Hercules when he had Iole in his heart.

"But here, we don't dwell on regrets. We smile, not because of the fault that we no longer recall, but at the power that guided and foresaw everything.

"Here, we see the art that decorates the world and the goodness that moves the heavens above and the Earth below. But to satisfy your questions fully, I need to explain more.

"You want to know who is inside this light next to me, shining like a sunbeam in clear water. Know that inside rests Rahab. She was accepted into our order and occupies the highest level here.

"It was fitting for her to be placed in this Heaven, as a symbol of the great victory won by Him who achieved it with both His hands. She supported Joshua's first glorious mission in the Holy Land, a deed that seems to be forgotten by the Pope.

"Your city, which was founded by the one who first turned his back on his Creator, is filled with ambition that causes so much sorrow. It brings forth and spreads the cursed flower that leads both sheep and lambs astray, turning the shepherd into a wolf.

"This is why the Gospels and the great Doctors of the Church are neglected. Instead, the focus is on church laws, which fill the margins of books.

"The Pope and Cardinals are fixated on these laws, not on Nazareth where Gabriel spread his wings. But soon, the Vatican and the other holy parts of Rome, which have been like a cemetery for Peter's followers, will be free of this corruption."

Chapter 10: The Fourth Heaven, the Sun: Theologians and Fathers of the Church. The First Circle. St. Thomas of Aquinas.

The divine power that moves the universe, looking into His Son with all His love, has created everything with such perfect order that anyone who sees it cannot help but admire Him.

Reader, lift your eyes with me to the higher realms, where one motion intersects with another. There, you can start to appreciate the work of the Master, who loves His creation so deeply that He never takes His eyes off it.

Look at how the circle tilts, guiding the planets in their paths to serve the world below. If they did not follow this precise path, many powers in the heavens would be wasted, and almost all life on Earth would cease to exist. If they moved more or less from their current path, both the heavens and the Earth would be thrown out of order.

Now, stay focused on this thought, dear Reader. Stay seated and follow along with what I have begun to explain if you want to find joy in understanding rather than weariness. I've set the scene for you; now, let yourself absorb the knowledge as I focus on the topic that I've been chosen to describe.

The greatest force in nature, which uses heavenly power to shape the world and measures our time, was spinning along the spirals of the universe. It moved towards where its presence is felt sooner each time. I was with it, but I wasn't aware of the ascent, just as someone is barely conscious of their first thought before it fully forms.

Beatrice, who is seen to move from good to even better so swiftly that time itself cannot measure her change, must have been shining with an even greater brilliance. The sunlight I entered was not visible by color but by pure light. No words, art, or skill I possess could describe it; you just have to believe it and long to see it for yourself. It's no wonder if our imaginations fall short, for nothing has ever been able to gaze directly upon the sun's light in its full glory.

Here, in this place, was the fourth family of the Father—the angels who are forever satisfied by seeing how God creates and loves.

Beatrice began, "Give thanks to the Sun of Angels, who has lifted you by His grace to this perceptive level!" No human heart was ever more ready to worship God or give gratitude than mine at her words. My love was so fully absorbed in God that, for a moment, I forgot Beatrice. This didn't upset her; she simply smiled, and the brightness of her smile divided my mind into many thoughts.

I saw many brilliant, triumphant lights circling us, forming a center. Their voices were sweeter than their brightness. They reminded me of how the moon, surrounded by stars, looks when the sky is filled with thin clouds.

In the heavenly court, where I had just returned from, there are many jewels—so beautiful that they cannot be brought back to Earth. The singing of these lights was like those precious jewels. Anyone who doesn't take flight to see this place should be prepared to remain speechless!

After singing, the shining lights circled around us three times, like stars circling the poles. They seemed like dancers who paused in silence, listening for a new melody to begin.

Then, from one of the lights, I heard a voice saying, "When the radiance of grace, which kindles true love, multiplies within you, it leads you up the ladder of Heaven. No one descends this ladder without first ascending. To refuse your thirst for knowledge would be like water refusing to flow toward the sea.

"You want to know what plants bloom in this garland encircling the beautiful Lady who gives you strength for Heaven. I was one of the lambs in the holy flock led by Saint Dominic on the path where those who do not stray become nourished.

"The one closest to me on my right was my brother and master; he is Albert of Cologne, and I am Thomas of Aquinas. If you wish to know who the others are, follow my words as I point them out along this blessed circle.

"The next light is Gratian, who aided both the Church and the world in such a way that he earned his place in Paradise. The one near him, who shines in our choir, is Peter, who gave his treasure to the Church like the poor widow who gave all she had.

"The fifth light, the brightest among us, belongs to someone whose love the world below is eager to learn more about. His mind was so full of deep knowledge that, if the truth is true, there never arose another intellect like his.

"Next, you see the light of that wise man who explored the nature of angels and their duties while still on Earth. The light near him is the Christian advocate whose rhetoric inspired Saint Augustine.

"If you look closely at the next light in this line of praise, you will see the eighth one eagerly waiting. This blessed soul sees every good thing and knows the true nature of the world. His body rests in Cieldauro after enduring martyrdom and exile before finally finding peace here.

"Next, you see the flames of Isidore, Bede, and Richard, who was deeply engaged in contemplation beyond the limits of human thought. The light that draws your attention now belongs to a spirit for whom death seemed slow as he pondered deeply.

"This is the eternal light of Sigier, who gave lectures on the Street of Straw, delving into difficult truths."

Then, like a clock that chimes when it is time for the Bride of God to rise and praise her Groom, I saw the glorious wheel turn. It moved in harmony, producing a sound so sweet that it filled the soul with love, a melody only truly understood in the place where joy is eternal.

Chapter 11: St. Thomas recounts the Life of St. Francis. Lament over the State of the Dominican Order.

Oh, you foolish people! How flawed are the arguments that make you pursue things that lead you away from what truly matters! Some chase laws, some seek wisdom, others follow the priesthood. Some want to rule by force or trickery, others turn to stealing or political power. One is lost in pleasures of the flesh, another becomes lazy and idle. Meanwhile, here I am, free from all these things, lifted into Heaven with Beatrice, surrounded by such glory!

When each soul returned to its place in the circle, they stood like candles in a holder. And from the light that had spoken to me before, I heard a voice. It started to speak again, glowing even brighter as it smiled.

"As I shine in this light," it began, "I can see into the Eternal Light and understand the questions in your mind. You are confused and want me to explain my words in a way you can easily understand. You want to know why I said, 'where well one fattens,' and 'there never rose a second.' We need to be clear about these statements now.

"The Divine Providence, which guides the world with wisdom far beyond any human understanding, set up two leaders for the bride of Christ, the Church. These two leaders were meant to guide her on either side, making her more faithful and confident in her purpose.

"One of these leaders burned with the passion of a seraph, while the other shone on earth with the wisdom of a cherub. I will speak of one, but in doing so, I will praise both, as they worked toward the same goal.

"Between the rivers Tupino and the one that flows down from Mount Subasio, there is a fertile slope. Perugia feels its cold and heat through the Porta Sole, while Gualdo and Nocera suffer under its shadow. From this slope, where it is steepest, a bright sun rose upon the world, just as the sun rises over the Ganges. When people speak of this place, they should not call it Ascesi, for that name falls short. They should call it the East, for it brought a new light to the world.

"Not long after this light appeared, it began to comfort the world with its virtue. As a young man, he faced his father's anger for choosing a 'Lady'—a virtue that closes the door to all pleasures. He married this Lady before the spiritual court, standing firm in his love for her.

"This Lady, called Poverty, had been widowed and scorned for over a thousand years, waiting for a suitor. She remained unmoved, even when powerful forces tried to shake her resolve. She ascended the cross with Christ while Mary was still on Earth.

"To make things clear, I'm talking about Francis and Poverty, the two lovers whose union inspired holy thoughts. Their love and devotion inspired others, starting with Bernard, who ran to follow them, thinking he was too slow. Giles and Sylvester also left everything behind to follow Francis.

"Francis and his followers donned humble robes, without fear of being scorned. Boldly, Francis presented his mission to Pope Innocent, who blessed it. As more followers joined this humble man, Pope Honorius gave the Franciscan Order its second crown, confirming its holy purpose.

"Francis preached before the Sultan, trying to convert the people. But finding them unready, he returned to Italy to continue his mission. Later, on a rocky hill between the Tiber and the Arno, Francis received the final mark of his dedication to Christ, which he bore for two whole years.

"When it was time for him to receive his heavenly reward, he entrusted his beloved Lady Poverty to his followers. His soul left its earthly body to return to Heaven.

"Think of the man who was worthy to guide Peter's ship over the stormy seas. That man was our founder, our Patriarch. Those who truly follow his teachings carry with them great treasure. But many of his followers have wandered off to seek new pastures, returning to the fold with little to show.

"There are a few who stay close to the shepherd, but their numbers are so small that they hardly make a difference.

"If you have listened carefully and understood my words, some of your questions should now be answered. You should see the damage done to the tree and the lesson behind the words, 'Where well one fattens, if he does not stray.'"

Chapter 12: St. Buonaventura recounts the Life of St. Dominic. Lament over the State of the Franciscan Order. The Second Circle.

As soon as the blessed flame had finished speaking, the holy circle began to spin around. It hadn't even completed one full turn before another ring formed around it, joining in the motion, and adding another layer of song to the first. This new song was even sweeter than any music we have on Earth, beyond anything sung by our Muses or Sirens, just as the original light surpasses the reflected one.

It was like seeing two rainbows in the sky, one inside the other, born from the same light. They reminded me of the rainbow that signals God's promise to Noah that there will be no more floods. These eternal rings of light surrounded us, with the outer one mirroring the inner.

After the joyful dance and song ended, both circles stopped at the same moment, like eyes that close and open together. Then, from the center of one of the lights came a voice that drew my attention like a needle points to the star. It said:

"The love that fills me compels me to speak about the other leader, the one who has already been praised here. It's right to honor both, as they fought side by side, and their glory should shine together.

"The army of Christ, which had to be rebuilt at a great cost, was struggling and losing hope. Then, the eternal Emperor came to its aid—not because the army was worthy, but because of His grace. He sent two champions to bring back the scattered people.

"In the land where the gentle west wind blows, where spring begins and Europe blooms again, near the coast where the sun sometimes hides behind the waves, lies the fortunate city of Calahorra. There, under the protection of the powerful shield marked with a lion, was born a true lover of the Christian faith—a warrior devoted to his people and ruthless to his enemies. From the moment he was born, it was clear he had an extraordinary energy that even made his mother a prophet.

"After he was baptized, marrying the Faith at the holy font, his mother dreamed of the great legacy he would leave behind. To show he belonged wholly to Christ, a spirit came to name him Dominic. He was like a farmer

Christ chose to tend His garden. Dominic was a true messenger and servant of Christ, because the first love he showed was for Christ's teachings.

"As a child, he was often found awake and lying on the ground, as if saying, 'This is my purpose.' His parents, Felix and Joanna, were truly blessed to have such a son. He didn't pursue worldly things like many do today. Instead, he longed for spiritual knowledge, the true bread from Heaven. Quickly, he became a great teacher, traveling through the 'vineyard' of the world, which would soon wither if left uncared for.

"Not to seek wealth or power, Dominic went to the Church and asked for the permission to fight against the evils of the world, armed with faith. Then, with his teachings and apostolic mission, he moved with force, like a torrent, cutting through heresies wherever he found the strongest resistance. His teachings created streams that nourished the Catholic garden, keeping its plants alive and thriving.

"Dominic was one wheel of the chariot in which the Holy Church defended itself and won its battles. The excellence of the other wheel, which Thomas spoke of before me, should now be clear to you. But even this circle, which was once so strong, has now broken apart. The followers who once walked in Dominic's footsteps have turned around, putting the wrong end forward.

"Soon they will realize the poor results of their work when the weeds lament that the granary is taken from them. Yet, if you search through the pages of our story, you'll still find some who stay true to their vows.

"Not from places like Casal or Acquasparta, where people distort the Scriptures, but among us are those who hold fast. I am Bonaventura of Bagnoregio, who always put the greater good before any selfish interests. Here with me are Illuminato and Agostino, the first barefoot friars who tied themselves to God with the cord of humility.

"Hugh of Saint Victor is here, as well as Peter Mangiador, and Peter of Spain, who shined below with his twelve volumes. Nathan the seer, Chrysostom, Anselmus, and Donatus, who laid the foundation of grammar, are here. Rabanus is here too, along with Joachim, the Calabrian abbot with the spirit of prophecy.

"I have been inspired to honor this great champion by the kind words and deep insights of Friar Thomas, and the entire company joins me in this tribute."

Chapter 13: Of the Wisdom of Solomon. St. Thomas reproaches Dante's Judgement.

To truly understand what I saw, picture this scene and keep it clear in your mind. Imagine the fifteen stars that shine so brightly in the sky that they outshine all others. Picture the Big Dipper, which circles the sky night and day, never failing in its path. Then, imagine the mouth of a horn that starts at the axis point around which the heavens revolve.

Now, imagine that these stars form two celestial shapes in the sky, like the one made by Minos' daughter when she felt the cold grip of death. Picture these two sets of stars with one set's light overlapping the other. Both sets spin, one moving forward and the other moving backward. This might give you a faint idea of the two rings and the dance I saw around the point where I stood. It was far beyond our usual experience, moving even faster than the heavens that outpace all else.

These lights didn't sing of Bacchus or Apollo. Instead, they sang of the three divine Persons in one God, combining divine and human nature. Their singing and dancing followed a perfect rhythm. As they circled, these holy lights grew happier with each turn.

One of those lights, where the story of God's humble servant was told, broke the silence. It spoke: "Now that we have finished one topic, and its seed has been sown, love compels me to speak of the other."

The voice continued: "You believe that in the heart where the rib was taken to form Eve, and in the heart that was pierced by the lance—the same power that created them filled them with all the light possible for human nature. This explains why I said earlier that no one else had the wisdom that is in this fifth light.

"Now open your eyes to my explanation, and you'll see how my words fit perfectly with what you believe, just like a circle fitting around its center. The things that die and the things that do not are all reflections of the idea that God, in His love, brings into being. This living Light flows from its source and never separates from God or the Love that binds them.

"Through its goodness, this Light reflects in nine different forms, like in a mirror, yet always remains one. It descends to the lowest levels of existence, becoming things that last for only a short time. I call these things 'contingencies'—the things that the heavens create, with or without seeds.

"Neither the material nor the form of these things stays the same. That's why they reflect the divine pattern more or less clearly. That's also why the same tree can bear both good and bad fruit, and why people are born with different qualities.

"If the material were perfect, and the heavens in their fullest power, then the brilliance of the divine stamp would shine through completely. But nature is flawed, working like an artist whose hand shakes despite their skill.

"If the original Love and clear Vision of God's power shape and seal something, then absolute perfection is achieved. This is how the Earth was once made perfect for all living things and how the Virgin Mary became pregnant. So, I agree with your belief that human nature has never been, and will never be, as perfect as it was in these two people.

"Now, if I stopped here, you might ask, 'Then how was he unique?' To answer that, think about who he was and what moved him to ask, 'Request whatever you wish.' He wasn't asking to know the number of the heavenly movers or whether 'necessity' ever aligns with free will. He wasn't asking about abstract questions like the existence of a first movement or whether a right triangle can be formed in a semicircle.

"If you consider what I said, you'll see that his request was for wisdom to rule as a king. And if you focus on 'rose,' you'll understand that it refers only to kings—rare are the good ones.

"Remember this explanation, and it will align with your belief in Adam and Christ. Use this as guidance to move cautiously when you face uncertainties. Wise people do not blindly affirm or deny without careful thought.

"Often, popular opinion can be wrong, misleading the mind. Those who seek truth without the right tools are like fishermen who return empty-handed. This happened to philosophers like Parmenides, Melissus, and Bryson, who wandered without knowing where they were headed. The same goes for Sabellius, Arius, and others who twisted the Scriptures like a blade.

"Don't be too quick to judge, like someone counting crops before they are ripe. I have seen thorn bushes appear stubborn and fierce in winter, only to bloom with roses later. I've seen ships sail smoothly over the sea, only to sink at the harbor.

"Don't assume that just because one person steals and another makes offerings, they will meet the same fate in divine judgment. One may rise, while the other may fall."

Chapter 14: The Third Circle. Discourse on the Resurrection of the Flesh. The Fifth Heaven, Mars: Martyrs and Crusaders who died fighting for the true Faith. The Celestial Cross.

Imagine a round vase filled with water. When struck from either the center or the rim, the water ripples out in waves. This image suddenly came to my mind when the brilliant light of Thomas stopped speaking. His words reminded me of Beatrice, who then began to speak.

She said, "This man has another question that he hasn't voiced, not even in his thoughts. He wonders if the light that surrounds you will stay the same forever. And if it does, how will it not harm your sight when you regain your physical bodies?"

The spirits seemed to be filled with a new joy, speeding up their dance and song. It was as if a prayer had inspired them to move even more eagerly. Whoever mourns that we die here on earth to live in Heaven has never experienced the refreshment of eternal joy.

The spirits chanted, "One and Two and Three, who lives and reigns in Three and Two and One, not confined but surrounding everything." They sang this three times with such beauty that it felt like the perfect reward.

Then, from the most radiant part of the circle of spirits, a gentle voice spoke, perhaps as tender as the Angel's voice to Mary: "As long as the joy of Paradise lasts, so will our love shine like this. The brightness of our light matches the intensity of our love, which comes from how much we see of God's grace. Our vision increases as His grace grows, and with that, our love and light increase as well.

"When we regain our physical bodies, our joy will grow even more because our being will be complete. The Supreme Good will give us more light, allowing us to see Him even better. Our vision will expand, so our love and light will also increase. Just like a glowing coal that becomes brighter but still keeps its form, the light surrounding us will be overpowered by our renewed flesh. But this brightness won't tire us because our new bodies will be strong enough to handle it."

Then both choirs responded "Amen" with such eagerness that it showed their longing for their earthly bodies. This desire was not just for themselves but also for their loved ones—parents, friends, and all who were dear before becoming eternal spirits.

Suddenly, a new light encircled the area like a clear horizon. As the evening sky reveals new stars that seem both real and unreal, I saw new spirits forming an outer circle around the others. How brightly they sparkled! It was the Holy Spirit shining so brightly that my eyes could not bear it.

Beatrice appeared more beautiful than ever, smiling in a way that left all other sights in the background of my memory. My eyes regained their strength and lifted me to even greater heights of salvation, with only Beatrice by my side.

I realized we had ascended because the star we were on now seemed even brighter, like a deep red glow. My heart filled with gratitude, and I prayed in the universal language of love, offering thanks to God for this new grace.

Before my prayer had finished, I saw signs that it was accepted. Brilliant red lights appeared, glowing with a radiance so intense that I exclaimed, "O Sun, how beautifully you light them!"

Like the Milky Way shining between the Earth's poles with its mix of bright and dim lights, these rays formed a sacred symbol—the cross—right in the depths of Mars. This sight was so awe-inspiring that my memory struggles to describe it. But those who follow Christ and take up their cross may forgive my inability to capture the full glory of that vision.

Lights moved along the cross, sparkling and intersecting, much like particles floating in a sunbeam. The movements were swift, slow, straight, and slanted, renewing the sight over and over.

From these moving lights came a melody that wrapped around the cross, a song so enchanting that I couldn't even distinguish the hymn. I only knew it was a song of praise because I heard the words, "Arise and conquer!" even if I couldn't fully grasp their meaning.

I was so captivated by the music that nothing before had ever held me so completely. My words may seem bold, focusing on this new delight instead of Beatrice's eyes. But remember that all forms of beauty grow more intense as one ascends. I had not yet turned back to gaze at Beatrice, so I ask forgiveness if my words seem to ignore her. The joy I felt here is hard to describe because it becomes even purer as one rises higher.

The Divine Comedy

Chapter 15: Cacciaguida. Florence in the Olden Time.

A kind and loving will, which reveals the righteous inspiration behind all good acts, silenced the sweet music and quieted the sacred strings that Heaven's hand plays with both strength and gentleness. How could the spirits, who inspire my desire to pray, ignore my request? They all grew silent as one, encouraging me to speak.

Those who lose eternal love by chasing after things that don't last deserve to mourn forever.

Like a sudden flash in the clear evening sky that catches the eye, a light shot from the right horn of the cross to its base. It was like a shooting star, though nothing seemed missing from the sky, and the light quickly faded. This light moved from the constellation like a star running along a shining band, glowing like a flame behind frosted glass.

The light called out: "O my blood, O the overflowing grace of God, to whom has Heaven ever opened its gates twice as it has to you?"

I listened closely to this voice and turned to look at Beatrice. Her eyes were shining with such a smile that I felt I had reached the depths of grace and Paradise.

The spirit spoke again in a way both lovely to hear and see, but its words were so profound that I couldn't understand them. It wasn't trying to hide its meaning from me; it was just that its thoughts were beyond human understanding.

When the spirit's compassionate tone softened enough for me to understand, the first thing I grasped was: "Blessed are You, O Trinity and One, for being so generous to my descendants!"

The spirit continued: "You have satisfied your deep thirst for knowledge by reading the great book, where nothing ever changes. This thirst has been fulfilled by the light in which I now speak to you, thanks to her who gave you wings for this high journey."

"You think that your thoughts pass through me from the One, just as numbers flow from the number one. And so you don't ask who I am or why I seem more joyful than the others here."

"You're right; both the small and the great here can see into the mirror that reflects your thoughts even before you think them. But to fulfill my sacred love, which keeps me watching with constant longing, you should feel free and joyful to voice your wishes, which I am ready to answer."

I turned to Beatrice. She had already understood my unspoken desire and smiled, giving me the courage to speak. Then I began: "Love and knowledge became equal when the First Equality dawned on you. In the Sun that shines on you, love and knowledge are so perfectly balanced that we mortals can't fully grasp it."

"But for us mortals, the will and the mind are not always in harmony. I feel this imbalance in myself, so I can only offer thanks in my heart for your fatherly welcome. Please, tell me your name, for I wish to know it."

The spirit answered, "O my leaf, in whom I took delight even while waiting, I was your root!" Then he added, "The one from whom your family is named, who has circled the mountain for over a hundred years on the first terrace, was my son and your great-grandfather. It is right for you to ease his long suffering through your actions."

"Florence, within its old boundaries, where it still measures its hours of prayer, was once peaceful, modest, and pure. The city had no golden chains or lavish jewels. People valued the person more than their clothes or accessories. Fathers didn't worry about their daughters' dowries, and homes were not filled with idle wealth. Sardanapalus had not yet arrived to show off his luxury. Montemalo had not yet overshadowed Uccellatojo.

I saw Bellincion Berti dressed in simple leather and bone, and his wife leaving her mirror with her face unpainted. I saw the men of the Nerli and Vecchio families happy with their plain clothes, while their wives worked with spindle and flax.

These women were blessed! They all knew where they would be buried, and none left their husbands' beds for French men. One mother would sing lullabies in the language that first delighted both mothers and fathers. Another would tell family stories of Troy, Fiesole, and Rome as she worked with the distaff.

Back then, seeing a man like Lapo Salterello or a woman like Cianghella would have been as surprising as seeing Cincinnatus or Cornelia now. This was the life of the citizens—safe, peaceful, and filled with community—that Mary gave me when I was baptized as both a Christian and Cacciaguida in the old Baptistery of Florence.

My brothers were Moronto and Eliseo. My wife came from the Val di Pado, and from that place, our surname was derived. Later, I followed Emperor Conrad, who honored me with knighthood for my noble deeds.

I fought against the injustice of those who take what rightfully belongs to you because of the failings of your leaders. There, by that wicked people, I was freed from the bonds of this deceitful world—a world that stains many souls with its false love. And through martyrdom, I reached this eternal peace."

Chapter 16: Dante's Noble Ancestry. Cacciaguida's Discourse of the Great Florentines.

Oh, our poor nobility, You may make people celebrate you here on Earth, where love fades. But that doesn't surprise me. In Heaven, where desires are pure, I once boasted about you. However, you are like a cloak that wears out quickly. If we don't mend it every day, time will cut it with its shears.

I started my words with "You," like they used to in ancient Rome, though families don't hold on to that tradition anymore. Beatrice stood nearby, smiling softly, like someone who laughs at an old story about Guinevere. I spoke, "You are my ancestor. You give me courage to speak, and you lift me up so I feel more than myself. My mind is filled with so much joy, and it's amazing that I can hold it all without bursting."

"Tell me, my dear ancestor," I continued, "who were your ancestors? What were your childhood years like? And tell me about the community of Saint John. How big was it, and who were the most important people?" As I spoke, the light grew brighter, like a coal flaring up in the wind. It then responded in a sweet, gentle voice, though not in today's language.

The light said, "From when my mother, now a saint, first said the 'Ave' to when she gave birth to me, our family line had already returned to the Lion (a symbol of power) 580 times to renew itself. My ancestors and I lived in the outer area of the city, where you now run your annual race. That's all you need to know about my ancestors. Who they were and where they came from, it's better to keep that unsaid."

"Back then," the light continued, "between the symbols of Mars and the Baptist, those fit to bear arms were just one-fifth of the people living today. The community was pure, even among the lowest craftsmen. How much better it would be to have those people as neighbors in places like Galluzzo and Trespiano than to deal with the trickery and stench of some people in the city today!"

"If the people had treated Caesar like a mother instead of a stepmother, some who now trade and barter in Florence would have returned to Simifonte, where their grandfathers were beggars. The Counts would still be at Montemurlo, the Cerchi in the parish of Acone, and the Buondelmonti in Valdigrieve. Mixing people has always caused problems in cities, just like overeating harms the body. A blind bull charges more recklessly than a blind lamb, and one sword often cuts better than five."

"If you look at Luni and Urbisaglia," it continued, "you'll see how they faded away, just as Chiusi and Sinigaglia are now. Hearing how races die out shouldn't surprise you since even cities come to an end. All things have their end, just like you do. It is hidden in some who live longer, while others have short lives. Just as the moon's movement covers and uncovers the shores, fortune changes for Florence too."

"So, what I say about the great Florentines, whose fame is hidden in the past, shouldn't surprise you. I saw the Ughi, the Catellini, the Filippi, the Greci, the Ormanni, and the Alberichi. Even in their fall, they were great citizens. I saw others as powerful as they were in ancient times: those from La Sannella, Arca, Soldanier, Ardinghi, and Bostichi."

"Near the gate, which is now marked with a new crime that will soon be thrown out, were the Ravignani. From them came Count Guido and those who took on the name Bellincione. The family of La Pressa already knew how to rule, and Galigajo's family had gilded weapons in their house. The mighty Column Vair, the Sacchetti, the Giuochi, the Fifant, the Barucci, and the Galli were there too. They were already feeling the weight of the market."

"The family from which the Calfucci were born was already important, and the Sizii and Arrigucci had been chosen for high positions. How I saw those who were ruined by their own pride! Florence celebrated the golden deeds of the Balls of Gold! The ancestors of those who now fatten themselves in the church were there too."

"The arrogant family, who follows others like a dragon, and acts gently to those with money, was already rising. But they came from humble people. Ubertin Donato wasn't happy that his wife's father made him kin with them. The Caponsacco had already come to the market from Fesole, and the Giuda and Infangato families were good citizens."

"I'll tell you something incredible but true," it continued, "a person entered the small circuit through a gate named after the Della Pera family! Each person who bears the noble shield of the great baron, whose name and reputation the feast of Thomas keeps alive, received their knighthood and privileges from him. Now, the one who binds it with a border joins the common people."

"The Gualterotti and Importuni were already there. The Borgo would be much quieter if it wasn't fed by new neighbors. The house that caused your grief, through just disdain, brought death and ended your joyful life. It was honored by both itself and its companions."

"Oh, Buondelmonte," it sighed, "how unlucky you were to flee your wedding on someone else's advice! Many would be happy now who are sad if God had let you drown in the Ema River when you first came to the city. But the broken stone, which guards the bridge, meant that Florence had to find a victim in its last peaceful moment."

"With all these families and others with them, Florence was so calm that it had no reason to weep. These families made the people so just and glorious that the lily (the symbol of Florence) was never placed upside down, nor stained red by division."

Chapter 17: Cacciaguida's Prophecy of Dante's Banishment.

As came to Clymene, to be made certain of what people were saying about him, I felt the same way. He made fathers afraid for their children. Beatrice and the holy light, which had first moved to talk to me, could see my worry.

So, my lady said, "Speak up. Share what you desire. Let it come out clearly. It's not to give us new knowledge, but to get you used to speaking your wishes. That way, we can help you."

I spoke to the light and said, "You, my beloved ancestor, you see things before they happen. Just as no triangle can have two obtuse angles, you see all events in the present. While I was with Virgil on the mountain of healing souls, and later in the world of the dead, I heard troubling things about my future. Although I feel strong against whatever may come, I want to know what is ahead of me. When you know what's coming, the arrow moves slower."

The light answered with love, hidden and shown by its smile. It spoke clearly and not in the confusing way of the past, before the Lamb of God was slain. "Events in your world are all seen in the eternal view," it said. "This doesn't make them necessary, just like a ship is not part of the water it reflects in. From this view, I can see what is coming for you, just like hearing music from an organ."

The light continued, "Just as Hippolytus left Athens because of his cruel stepmother, you will be forced to leave Florence. This has already been decided and will soon happen by those who trade Christ every day. The blame will fall on you, the victim, as it usually does. But the punishment will show the truth behind it. You will have to leave behind everything you love dearly. This will be the first shot from the bow of your exile.

"You will find out how bitter it is to eat another's bread and how hard it is to go up and down someone else's stairs. The hardest part will be the foolish company you'll have to keep. They will turn against you, but soon they will be the ones who are ashamed. Their behavior will show their own cruelty. It's better for you to stand alone.

"Your first refuge will be in the house of a kind Lombard, who carries the holy bird on his crest. He will be so generous that he will help you first, while others only do so last. With him, you will meet someone who was born under a strong star. His achievements will be great, but people don't know him yet because he is still young. Only nine years have passed since he was born.

"Before the Gascon tricks the noble Henry, this person's virtue will show. He won't care for wealth or hard work. His greatness will be recognized, and even his enemies won't be able to stay silent. Trust in him and his kindness. Through him, many people will change, both rich and poor. You will remember him, but you won't speak of it. What I'm telling you might sound unbelievable to those around you."

The light added, "My son, these are the explanations for what you heard. Be aware of the dangers, but don't envy your neighbors. Your life will reach far beyond their betrayals and punishments."

When the light stopped speaking, I felt like someone full of doubt, looking for guidance from a wise and loving person. I began, "Father, I see how quickly time is rushing toward me with this heavy blow. I need to prepare myself, so if I lose my most cherished place, I don't lose everything I have worked for.

"As I traveled through the world of suffering and up the mountain, where my lady's eyes lifted me, and then through heaven, I learned things that will be like bitter medicine to many. If I am afraid to tell the truth, I might lose my life among those who will call this time the 'olden days.'"

The light, which had been smiling at me, flashed brightly like a golden mirror in the sun. It replied, "A conscience troubled by its own or others' shame will find your words harsh. But still, speak the truth fully and let them respond however they want. If your words sting at first, they will become valuable when people reflect on them later.

"Your voice will be like the wind, hitting the highest peaks. That will bring honor to you. This is why you have been shown only the souls known in history. The listener cannot trust or learn from an example without a well-known source or a clear reason."

Chapter 18: The Sixth Heaven, Jupiter: Righteous Kings and Rulers. The Celestial Eagle. Dante's Invectives against ecclesiastical Avarice.

I was alone, feeling joy from the words of that blessed soul. I tasted my own thoughts, both the bitter and the sweet. The Lady, who was guiding me to God, spoke and said, "Change your thoughts. Remember that I am near Him who can free you from all wrongs."

Hearing her comforting voice, I turned around. The love in her holy eyes was so great that I can't find the right words to describe it. My mind can't fully understand it unless someone else helps me. All I can say is that when I looked at her again, my heart was freed from every other desire.

As the eternal joy shone directly on Beatrice, it reflected off her beautiful face and made me feel happy. Her smile filled me with light. She said, "Turn around and listen. Paradise is not only in my eyes."

Sometimes, we can see love in a person's look when their whole soul is taken over by it. In the same way, I saw a holy light shining brightly, and I knew it wanted to speak to me again. It began, "Here, in this fifth resting place on the tree of eternal life, are blessed spirits. On Earth, they were so famous that every poet would want to tell their stories.

"Look at the arms of the cross. I will name some of these souls, and you will see them move across the cross like lightning in a cloud."

I looked and saw a bright light move when the name Joshua was called. I didn't hear the name until after the light moved. When the name of the great Maccabee was called, another light moved and spun around. Joy seemed to push it forward.

I watched closely as lights moved for Charlemagne and Orlando, just as a person watches a falcon flying. Next, I saw lights for William, Renouard, Duke Godfrey, and Robert Guiscard moving along the cross.

The soul that had spoken to me moved among the other lights, showing how skilled it was in the heavenly choir. I turned to my right to look at Beatrice. Her eyes were so clear and full of pleasure that her face looked even more beautiful than before.

Just as someone becomes more aware of their goodness by doing good deeds, I realized that my journey through the heavens had expanded. I felt even more amazed by the miracle I was witnessing.

The change I saw was like when a shy woman suddenly becomes free of her shyness. When I turned back, I saw the white light of the sixth star, Jupiter, which had taken me in.

Within that shining light, I saw the love sparkling in patterns that looked like our human language. Just like birds fly from the shore, forming groups to celebrate their food, the holy creatures in the light moved around, making shapes. They sang while flying and made letters, first forming a "D," then an "I," and finally an "L."

They moved to their own music and then paused, resting in these letters.

I prayed to the divine Muse to help me express what I saw in words. They formed five times seven letters, vowels, and consonants. I watched as the letters seemed to speak to me. The first words spelled out were "Diligite iustitiam," which means "Love justice." The last words were "Qui iudicatis terram," which means "You who judge the earth."

Next, they arranged themselves into an "M," and it looked like Jupiter was inlaid with silver and gold. I saw other lights come down to the top of the "M" and rest there, singing about goodness, which seemed to draw them in.

Then, like sparks flying up from burning logs, countless lights rose. They ascended, some higher than others, as if the Sun had placed each one. When they finally settled, I could see the head and neck of an eagle formed by the glowing lights.

The artist who created this image had no guide. He alone guided it and made it perfect.

The other blessed soul, which had first appeared as a lily on the "M," moved slightly to reveal its message.

O gentle star, how many gems you showed me! You demonstrated that our justice comes from the heavens you illuminate. I prayed to the divine mind that controls your movements to understand the dark smoke that corrupts your light.

I prayed that, once again, the temple—built with signs and sacrifices—would not be tarnished by greed. I looked to the heavenly soldiers and asked them to pray for the people on Earth who have gone astray.

Once, wars were fought with swords, but now they are fought by denying the needy the bread given by the loving Father. And yet, to those who cancel others, remember that Peter and Paul, who sacrificed for this vineyard, are still alive!

You might say, "I am so loyal to the one who lived alone and was led to martyrdom that I do not know the Fisherman or Paul."

Chapter 19: The Eagle discourses of Salvation, Faith, and Virtue. Condemnation of the vile Kings of A.D. 1300.

In front of me appeared a beautiful image with its wings spread out. It was filled with souls, woven together in joy. Each of them glowed like small rubies, shining with the light of the sun. The light was so bright that it reflected into my eyes.

What I saw and heard next is something that no words or writing can fully describe. My imagination can't even grasp it. I saw the beak of the image speak. It used words like "I" and "My," even though it meant "We" and "Our."

It began speaking: "I am here because I was just and merciful on Earth. Now, I enjoy a glory that can't be surpassed. I left behind a memory so strong that even those with evil hearts praise it, though they do not continue my story."

Just as heat from many embers becomes one warmth, the love from all those souls created one voice. I then spoke, "O eternal flowers of joy, you bring many scents together for me to sense. Your presence fills me and breaks the long hunger I've felt. I know that if Divine Justice mirrors another realm in Heaven, you see it without any barrier.

"You know how I pay close attention and listen. And you know the deep question that has troubled me for so long."

Then, the image moved like a falcon coming out of its hood. It flapped its wings, showing its eagerness and excitement. I saw it change, singing with divine grace. Its joy was clear in every word.

The image continued: "The One who designed the outer edge of the world and all that is hidden within it could not create anything that fully contains His power. His Word remains infinitely greater. This truth makes it clear that the first proud being, who was perfect among creatures, fell because he did not wait for the light.

"It also shows that each lesser creature can only contain a small part of that endless good. Our vision, which is just a ray of that greater intelligence, can never see everything. It can only look so far, just as an eye can see the ocean's shore but not its depths. The light is always there, but it's hidden by the deep waters.

"No light comes from anywhere but the pure source. What seems like darkness is just the shadow of the flesh or its poison. The cavern that hid divine justice from you is now open. You often wondered about it.

"You once said, 'A man is born on the shores of India where no one speaks of Christ, reads, or writes. His actions seem good according to human reason. He dies unbaptized and without faith. Where is the justice that condemns him? Where is his fault if he doesn't believe?'

"Who are you to judge such matters from so far away? Your vision is limited to a short span. There would be room for doubt if the Scriptures did not guide you.

"O earthly beings with stubborn minds! The Supreme Good, which is good in itself, never changes. Whatever is just comes from aligning with this good. No created thing draws this goodness to itself; instead, this goodness spreads its light to everything."

Like a stork circling above its nest after feeding its young, I lifted my eyes. The blessed image began to move its wings again, urged by divine wisdom. It circled around, singing, and said, "Just as my words are difficult for you to understand, so is the eternal judgment for all mortals."

The shining spirits grew quiet, still holding their place in the formation that once brought honor to Rome. Then it spoke again: "No one has entered this kingdom without faith in Christ, whether they lived before or after His crucifixion.

"Yet, many cry out 'Christ, Christ!' but will be farther from Him in judgment than some who never knew Him. The Ethiopians, who will stand before the final judgment, will condemn these so-called Christians. The good and the evil will be separated, one group rich forever, the other poor.

"What will your kings say when they see the book where their shameful deeds are recorded? Among them will be Albert, whose actions will soon lead to the desertion of Prague. There will be those who brought misery to the Seine by falsifying coins. They will meet their end by the hand of a wild boar.

"We will see the pride that drives the Scots and English mad, causing them unrest in their own land. We will see the luxurious and weak lives of the rulers of Spain and Bohemia, who neither knew nor wanted to know courage. We will also see the King of Jerusalem, whose virtue is marked with an 'I' while his failings are marked with an 'M.'

"We will witness the greed and cowardice of the one guarding the Island of Fire, where Anchises lived his last days. His sad record will be written in small letters, containing much in a few words. The terrible deeds of a certain uncle and brother who have dishonored a nation and two crowns will also be known.

"The rulers of Portugal and Norway will be judged, along with the one from Rascia who was foolish enough to use Venetian coins.

"O happy Hungary, if she does not let herself be wronged! And Navarre, how fortunate, if she protects herself with the hills that surround her!

"Believe me, Nicosia and Famagusta already suffer and rage because of their leader, who refuses to part from evil."

Chapter 20: The Eagle praises the Righteous Kings of old. Benevolence of the Divine Will.

When the sun, which lights up the world, sets far enough from our part of the sky that all daylight fades away, the heavens light up again with many stars. One of these shines brighter than the others. This scene came to my mind as I watched the eagle of justice, the symbol of the world's leaders, fall silent after its speech. The bright souls, glowing even more than before, began to sing. Their song was so beautiful that I struggled to remember it.

Oh, gentle Love, you hide yourself behind a smile, but in these sparks, you burned so brightly. They were filled with nothing but holy thoughts.

After the bright lights, like jewels on the sixth star, had become silent, I heard a sound like a river flowing down from rock to rock. It carried the richness of its mountain source. It was as if the sound rose up the eagle's neck like a breeze through the hollow of a pipe, becoming a voice from its beak. It spoke in words my heart had been waiting to hear.

It said, "The part of me that sees the sun like mortal eagles now asks for your full attention. Among the lights that form my shape, those that create the sparkle in my eyes are the highest. The one shining in the center of my eye was once the singer of the Holy Spirit. He carried the ark from city to city. Now, he knows the true value of his song, based on his choices, and has received his just reward.

"Out of the five lights forming a circle on my brow, the one nearest to my beak comforted the poor widow for the loss of her son. Now, he understands the cost of not following Christ by experiencing both this life and the opposite one.

"The next light in the circle delayed his death through sincere repentance. Now, he knows that eternal judgment cannot change, even if worthy prayers seem to postpone it.

"The one that comes next worked with the laws and me, but his good intentions led to bad results. He gave in to the church leader and became Greek. Now, he understands that any harm caused by his good deed does not count against him, even though it might have affected the world.

"Further down, you see Guglielmo. His land still mourns him, just as it mourns Charles and Frederick, who are still alive. Now, he knows how Heaven loves a just king. His light still shows this truth.

"Who would believe, down on Earth, that the Trojan Ripheus could be one of these five holy lights? Now, he sees enough of what humans cannot see—divine grace—even if he cannot understand it fully."

Like a lark flying through the air, first singing and then falling silent with joy, the image seemed to be satisfied. It showed the eternal joy that creates everything as it is. Though I was filled with doubt, like glass that takes on the color it reflects, I couldn't stay silent. The words, "What does this mean?" came out of my mouth, pushed by the weight of my curiosity. At that, I saw great joy sparkle around me.

With a gaze that glowed even more brightly, the blessed eagle answered, "I see that you believe what I say, but you do not understand how it is possible. You know the name of what I describe, but not its true nature. The kingdom of Heaven allows itself to be overcome by love and hope. It is not like one man defeating another but rather because it wants to be conquered by kindness.

"The lives of the first and fifth lights in this circle amaze you because they seem like mysteries. You think they were Gentiles, not Christians. But they had faith in the coming Christ, who suffered for them.

"One of them was even brought back from Hell, where no one usually returns to a good will. He came back to life because of the prayers made for him. He believed in the one who had the power to save him and was filled with such love that, at his second death, he was worthy of this joy.

"The other one was saved through grace that comes from a source so deep that no one has seen its origin. He loved righteousness, and through this love, God opened his eyes to the coming redemption. From that moment on, he turned away from the evils of paganism and even rebuked others who followed false paths.

"The three holy women you saw by the right-hand wheel acted as his baptism more than a thousand years before the actual sacrament.

"Oh, how far off is the root of predestination from those who cannot see the First Cause! You mortals should be careful in making judgments. Even we, who look upon God, do not know who all the chosen ones are. And we find joy in this, as it means we are fully aligned with God's will."

The divine voice spoke in this way, helping me to see my own short-sightedness. As a good singer pairs with a skilled musician to make a song more beautiful, the two blessed lights, which I saw flicker together, moved in rhythm to the eagle's words.

Chapter 21: The Seventh Heaven, Saturn: The Contemplative. The Celestial Stairway. St. Peter Damiano. His Invectives against the Luxury of the Prelates.

My eyes were once again fixed on my Lady's face, and my mind followed, letting go of all other thoughts. She didn't smile, but said to me, "If I were to smile, you would become like Semele, who was turned to ashes. My beauty grows more intense as we climb higher in this eternal palace. If my beauty wasn't softened, its brightness would crush your mortal senses like a leaf struck by lightning.

"We have now risen to the seventh level, under the fiery sign of the Lion. Focus your mind and make your eyes a mirror for what you are about to see."

If you knew how much joy I found in looking at her blessed face before shifting my focus, you would understand how grateful I was to obey her guidance, balancing my attention between her and what lay ahead.

I looked into the crystal sphere that revolves around the world and bears the name of its dear leader, under whom all wickedness was defeated. It shone like gold in sunlight. I saw a staircase rise up so high that my eyes couldn't follow it to the top. Many bright lights moved down its steps, and I thought that all the stars of heaven must have gathered there.

The lights moved like flocks of birds at dawn. Some flew away and didn't return, others came back to where they started, and some circled around, staying in place. This is what I saw: the sparkling lights came together as they descended each step.

One light stayed close to us and became so clear that I thought, "I see the love you're showing me." But I hesitated, waiting for a sign from my Lady on when to speak. She, knowing my silence, said to me, "Let your desire be free."

I began, "I am not worthy to hear you speak, but I ask for the sake of her who allows me to ask. Blessed soul, who remains hidden in your joy, tell me why you have come so near to me. And why is it that in this sphere of heaven, I do not hear the sweet music of Paradise, which echoes so beautifully below?"

It replied, "Your hearing is as mortal as your sight. They do not sing here for the same reason Beatrice does not smile. I came down this holy stairway to greet you with words and the light that surrounds me. It was not more love that made me come to you, for even more love burns above. But divine wisdom decides where we should go, and we obey."

"I understand now," I said, "how love in this heavenly court follows the eternal plan. But I find it hard to see why you, out of all your companions, were chosen for this role."

No sooner had I finished speaking than the light became the center of a spinning circle, whirling like a millstone. Then it answered, "A divine light shines on me, piercing through the glow that surrounds me. This light lifts me so high that I can see the supreme source from which it comes. This is the joy that makes me shine. I reflect the brightness as far as I can see it.

"But even the purest soul in heaven, the seraph with eyes fixed most closely on God, could not fully answer your question. What you ask goes so deep into the eternal plan that no created sight can grasp it. When you return to the mortal world, share this truth so that people will not try to reach beyond their limits.

"Here in heaven, our minds are clear. But down on Earth, the mind is clouded and cannot do what it was made for, even when given a glimpse of the divine."

These words set a limit on my questioning, so I humbly asked, "Who are you?"

The light replied, "Between two shores in Italy, not far from your homeland, there are high cliffs called Catria, where thunder rumbles below. There, a hermitage was once dedicated to worship only.

"In that place, I, Peter Damiano, devoted myself to God's service. I lived simply, feeding only on olives, and found peace in my thoughts. That cloister used to give abundant praise to heaven, but now it stands empty, and soon its loss will be revealed.

"I was Peter the Sinner at the house of Our Lady on the Adriatic shore. I had little time left in my mortal life when I was called to wear the cardinal's hat, which only shifted from bad to worse.

"Cephas and the mighty Vessel of the Holy Spirit lived simply, traveling barefoot and taking food wherever they found it. But now, modern leaders need someone to support them on each side, just to hold up their heavy robes. They cover their horses with cloaks, so it seems like two beasts are beneath one skin. Oh, patience, how much you tolerate!"

At this, I saw many little flames descending the steps, spinning and glowing brighter with each turn. They gathered around the one who spoke and let out a cry so loud that it shook me like thunder. I couldn't make out the words, overwhelmed by the powerful sound.

Chapter 22: St. Benedict. His Lamentation over the Corruption of Monks. The Eighth Heaven, the Fixed Stars.

I was overwhelmed and turned to my guide like a little child who runs to the one they trust most. She, like a mother comforting her scared child, spoke to me gently. "Don't you know you're in Heaven?" she asked. "Don't you know that everything here is done with pure love and goodness?

"If you think that cry startled you, imagine how the singing would have affected you. And if I had smiled, you would have been overwhelmed, just like Semele when she was burned to ashes. If you had understood the meaning of their cry, you would know about the justice you will witness before you die. Here, judgment does not act quickly or slowly but strikes at just the right moment, no matter what it seems to those who fear or wish for it.

"Now, turn around," she continued, "because you are about to see some very noble souls. Look as I direct you."

Following her instructions, I turned my eyes and saw a hundred glowing orbs, each reflecting light and making each other shine even more brightly. I stood there, holding back my curiosity, too afraid to ask anything.

Then, the brightest and largest of these lights moved forward, as if to satisfy my unspoken desire. I heard a voice from within it, saying, "If you could see the love that burns within us as I do, you would understand your own thoughts. But so that you don't have to wait too long for your answer, I will explain what you are thinking about.

"That mountain where Cassino stands was once the place of a misled people who worshipped false gods. I am the one who first brought the name of Him who brought truth to the world to that place. The grace I received was so strong that I turned all the nearby towns away from their false worship and toward the truth.

"These other lights around you were all men who devoted themselves to God. They were set on fire by the holy love that brings forth good actions and thoughts. Here is Macarius, here is Romualdus, and here are my brothers who stayed in their cloisters with strong hearts."

I replied, "The kindness you show while speaking to me, along with the good nature I see in all of you, has opened my heart like the sun opens a rose. Please, tell me if I am worthy enough to see you without this veil of light."

The light answered, "Brother, your deepest wish will be fulfilled in the highest sphere, where every desire finds its perfect place. There, every longing is complete, not bound by space or time. Our stairway rises to that place, which is why it fades from your sight. That is the height that Jacob saw, filled with angels. But now, no one climbs it from Earth. My rule has become nothing but empty words.

"The abbey walls that used to be sacred are now like dens for robbers. The monks' robes are like sacks filled with useless flour. The misuse of holy gifts is even more offensive to God than usury because the Church's treasures are meant for those who ask in God's name, not for family or selfish gain. The flesh of mortals is so weak that good beginnings often wither before they can bear fruit.

"Peter began with neither gold nor silver, I began with prayer and fasting, and Francis built his convent on humility. But if you look at how they started and where they ended up, you'll see how the purity turned to corruption. Truly, when the Jordan turned back, and the sea fled, it was less of a miracle than the downfall you see now."

With these words, he withdrew to his group, and they all closed together, rising upward like a whirlwind. My gentle guide urged me to follow them up the staircase with just a glance. Her power was so strong that I followed without hesitation. Nothing on Earth could compare to how quickly I moved, lifted by her will.

Reader, if I were to return to that holy moment—the one that often makes me weep for my sins—you wouldn't have time to dip your finger into a flame and pull it back out before I found myself in the sign that follows Taurus.

O glorious stars, filled with mighty power! It was under your influence that my soul took shape when I first breathed the air of Tuscany. And now, by grace, I had entered your realm. To you, I offer my soul's prayers, hoping to gain strength for the difficult journey ahead.

"You are so close to salvation now," Beatrice said, "that your eyes should be sharp and clear. Before you go further, look down and see how much of the world you have already left behind. Let your heart be joyful as you join the triumphant souls who move through this vast sky."

I looked back through all the seven spheres and saw the Earth. It appeared so small and insignificant that I couldn't help but smile. I now understood how little it really is compared to the greatness of Heaven.

I saw the moon without its usual shadows, which once made me think it was both solid and rare. I then looked at the Sun and saw how the planets—Mercury and Venus—move around it. I also saw how Jupiter sits between the Sun and Mars, and I understood how all these heavenly bodies move in their orbits.

Finally, I turned my eyes back to the beautiful eyes of Beatrice.

Chapter 23: The Triumph of Christ. The Virgin Mary. The Apostles. Gabriel.

Just like a bird sitting quietly on her nest all night, watching over her chicks, waiting eagerly for the morning sun to rise so she can find food for them, my Lady stood there, alert and watchful. She turned towards the part of the sky where the sun moves slower. Seeing her in such deep thought, I felt like someone filled with desire, hoping for something they long for.

I didn't have to wait long. Suddenly, I saw the sky light up more and more. Beatrice cried out, "Look at the hosts of Christ's victory and the harvest gathered by these heavenly spheres!"

Her face seemed to be glowing, and her eyes were so full of joy that I can't even begin to describe it. It was like seeing the full moon on a clear night, surrounded by stars. Above all these lights, I saw a Sun that lit them all up, just like our own sun lights up the sky. The brightness was so intense that I couldn't keep looking at it.

"Oh, Beatrice, my gentle guide!" I thought. She said to me, "The power you see here is so strong that nothing can hide from it. This is where wisdom and power meet. It opened the paths between Heaven and Earth, which people had longed for so deeply."

My mind struggled to take it all in. It felt like a fire breaking out of a cloud, spreading so much that it falls back to Earth. My thoughts were overwhelmed, and I couldn't remember what they had become.

Then, I heard her voice, "Open your eyes and look at me. You have seen so much already that you can now bear to see my smile."

I was like someone trying to remember a forgotten dream but can't quite grasp it. Her invitation filled me with such gratitude that it will always stay in my memory. Even if all the sweetest voices in the world came together to sing, they wouldn't come close to describing her holy smile and the light it brought.

That's why, in telling this sacred story, I must skip over some parts, like a traveler who finds their path blocked. Anyone who understands the weight of this subject will know why my words may fall short. This journey is not for a weak sailor or a careful pilot.

Beatrice noticed my focus on her face and gently said, "Why does my appearance capture you so much that you forget the garden blooming under Christ's rays? There is the Rose where the Word became flesh. There are the lilies that showed the way to goodness."

Hearing her, I quickly turned my attention back to where she directed. I was ready to take on the challenge. Like sunlight streaming through a break in the clouds, casting shadows on a field of flowers, I saw countless bright lights illuminated by beams of light from above. I couldn't see where the light came from, but its glow was powerful.

"Oh, kind and loving power!" I thought. It seemed to stretch itself, giving my eyes more strength to take it in. The name of that beautiful flower, which I call upon every morning and night, filled my soul, making me gaze upon the brightest light.

As I stared, I saw the glory and greatness of the star, shining even more here than on Earth. Suddenly, a small flame descended from the heavens. It moved in a circle, like a crown, and wrapped itself around the light, swirling around it.

Even the sweetest music on Earth would sound like a broken melody compared to the song this flame sang. It was like a beautiful lyre crowning the sapphire light that gives the sky its blue color.

The flame spoke, "I am Angelic Love, circling around the joy that came from the womb where our Desire was born. I will keep circling, Lady of Heaven, as you follow your Son and make this highest sphere even more divine."

With these words, the music quieted, and the other lights began to sing the name of Mary. The grand circle of Heaven spread over us, so vast that I could not see its edges.

My eyes couldn't keep up with the flame crowned with light as it moved upwards to its place. Just like a child reaching out to its mother after drinking milk, every gleaming light seemed to reach upward, revealing their deep love for Mary.

They stayed there, singing "Regina Coeli" with such sweetness that I felt a joy that has never left me.

Oh, what treasures are stored in these holy souls! They once sowed seeds of goodness on Earth, and now they enjoy the fruits of their labor. They gather all that they earned in their time of suffering on Earth. Under the glorious presence of God and Mary, they rejoice alongside the saints of both old and new councils.

And there, among them, is the one who holds the keys to this great glory.

Chapter 24: The Radiant Wheel. St. Peter examines Dante on Faith.

"O chosen souls at the great feast of the Lamb," began Beatrice, "who are fed so fully that your desires are forever satisfied, if by God's grace this man is allowed a taste of what you experience before his death, please consider his deep desire. Shower him with a bit of the knowledge you drink from the eternal fountain, from which his thoughts also flow."

At these words, the blessed souls transformed into glowing orbs, like bright comets fixed in place. They began to move like the gears of a clock: some turned slowly, while others moved quickly, showing their joy in different ways. From the most beautiful of these lights, I saw a flame emerge, brighter and happier than the rest. It circled around Beatrice three times, singing so divinely that my imagination can't recall the song. Words fall short of describing it, so I must leave it out.

The light then spoke, "O my holy sister, your devoted love has drawn me away from my bright sphere." After it stopped, it turned to my Lady and spoke as I have just described.

Beatrice responded, "O eternal light of the great man to whom our Lord gave the keys of Heaven, examine this man on matters of faith, both great and small. You, who once walked on the sea through faith, will know whether he loves, hopes, and believes as he should. But since this kingdom is made of those who believe in the true faith, it is only right that he has the chance to speak about it."

Like a student preparing to answer a question, I gathered all my thoughts, ready for this moment. When she finished speaking, the light said to me, "Tell me, good Christian, what is faith?"

I looked up at the light and then turned to Beatrice. She nodded, signaling for me to share my thoughts.

"May grace help me explain clearly," I began, "to the one who was once a great teacher. Faith is the substance of things we hope for and the evidence of things not seen, as your dear brother once wrote. This is what I believe it to be."

The light responded, "You are correct, but do you understand why faith is described as both substance and evidence?"

I continued, "The things I see here in Heaven are hidden from all eyes on Earth and exist only in belief. This belief is the foundation of our highest hope and becomes a substance. We must reason based on this belief without physical proof, which makes it evidence."

The light replied, "If people on Earth understood this as you do, there would be no room for false arguments." Then it added, "You have correctly described the value of this belief, but do you hold it in your heart?"

I answered, "Yes, I hold it, shining and clear, without any doubt."

The light then asked, "This precious belief, the foundation of all virtues—where did you get it?"

I replied, "The Holy Spirit has poured out the truth through both the Old and New Testaments. This knowledge, proven with such clarity, makes every other argument seem weak in comparison."

The light responded, "You accept the ancient and new scriptures as divine. But why do you believe they are the word of God?"

I answered, "The proof lies in the miracles that followed. Nature alone could not create such wonders without divine power."

The light asked, "But who assures you that these miracles actually happened? Isn't this what you're trying to prove?"

I said, "If the world converted to Christianity without miracles, that alone would be the greatest miracle, greater than all others combined. Remember, you entered the world poor and fasting to plant the good vine, which has now become so corrupted."

When I finished speaking, the holy court echoed through the heavens, singing, "We praise one God!" The melody was so pure and joyful. The light that had questioned me now began to speak again.

"The grace that has guided your thoughts has brought you to this point," it said. "You have answered well. But now, you must explain what you believe and how this belief came to you."

I responded, "O holy father, who sees the truth you once believed in so deeply, I will gladly share my belief and its source.

"I believe in one eternal God, who moves all the heavens with love and desire, yet remains unmoved Himself. This belief is not only supported by logic and physical evidence but also by the truth that has been revealed through Moses, the prophets, the Psalms, the Gospels, and by you and others, who wrote after being inspired by the Holy Spirit.

"I believe in three eternal Persons—Father, Son, and Holy Spirit—who are one essence. This belief has been stamped on my mind by the teachings of the Gospel. This is the spark that grows into a bright flame within me, shining like a star in Heaven."

As I finished, the light embraced my words, like a lord embracing a servant who brings good news. It encircled me three times, singing in joy.

Chapter 25: The Laurel Crown. St. James examines Dante on Hope. Dante's Blindness.

"If it ever happens that this sacred poem, which has taken both Heaven and Earth to create and has caused me so much effort, can overcome the cruelty that keeps me out of the beautiful fold where I once slept as a lamb, safe from the wolves that threaten it, then I will return as a different poet. I will come back with a different voice and new strength. At the baptismal font, I will receive the laurel crown. This is because I entered into the Faith that connects all souls to God, and Peter himself crowned me for this."

As I said this, a light moved toward us from the group of souls who were the first followers of Christ. My Lady, filled with joy, said to me, "Look! Look! Here comes the noble one for whom people make pilgrimages to Galicia."

Just like a dove circling its companion, showing affection, I saw another great light join the first one. They celebrated together, praising the spiritual nourishment they enjoyed in Heaven. When their celebration was over, they both stood still, shining so brightly that it overwhelmed my sight.

Beatrice then said, "O glorious soul, who has described the blessings of our Church, let Hope resound in this realm. You know it well, just as Jesus showed it to the three disciples so clearly."

A comforting voice came from the second light, saying, "Lift up your head and be confident. What comes here from the mortal world must be tested in our light." Hearing this, I lifted my eyes, which had been weighed down before.

The voice continued, "Since our Emperor has granted you the chance to see this court face to face before your death, so that you may strengthen your own hope and that of others, tell us what hope is, and how it fills your mind. Where did it come from?"

Before I could answer, my guide, the compassionate one who helped me reach this high place, spoke for me: "No child of the Church has more hope than this man, as the light of the Sun—our guide—has written. That is why he has been allowed to come to this heavenly city before his earthly journey is over. Now, he will answer the questions you ask and express how dear this virtue is to him."

Like a student following his teacher's lead, I prepared to answer. "Hope," I said, "is the certain expectation of future glory, which comes from divine grace and the merits of one's past actions. This light of hope shines on me from many sources, but it first entered my heart through the words of David, the great singer of God.

"In his sacred song, he wrote, 'Let those who know Your name put their hope in You.' And who doesn't know God's name if they share my faith? The Apostle Paul, too, filled me with this hope in his letters, and now I share it with others."

While I spoke, the light of the soul before me quivered, glowing like lightning. Then it said, "The love I have for this virtue, which carried me to victory, makes me glad to hear you speak about hope. Tell me, what does hope promise you?"

I replied, "The ancient and the new Scriptures reveal that all souls who become God's friends will be clothed in twofold garments in their own land, which is this delightful life. Your brother, too, explained this clearly when he spoke of the white robes given to the saved."

As I finished, the words "Let them hope in You" rang out above us, and all the souls sang in response. Then, one light grew even brighter, so much so that if the constellation Cancer had one such star, winter would have an entire month of daylight.

Like a graceful maiden who joins a dance to honor the bride, that light moved toward the two others, circling around them in harmony. My Lady kept her gaze fixed on this scene, silent and still like a bride herself.

"This is the one who rested on the chest of our Savior, the 'Pelican,' and this is the one chosen for the great mission at the cross," Beatrice explained, though she didn't take her eyes off the scene.

I looked at the bright flame, trying to see more, just as someone might stare at a solar eclipse, but my sight failed. The light then spoke to me, "Why do you try to see what is not here? My body lies on Earth, and it will remain there with the others until the final number of souls is reached. Only two lights from this cloister have ascended to Heaven in both body and soul. Take this knowledge back to the world."

After saying this, the fiery circle grew quiet, and a soft melody filled the air, like oars resting at the sound of a whistle.

I was deeply troubled when I turned to look at Beatrice, only to realize that I couldn't see her, even though I was still close to her in this blessed realm.

Chapter 26: St. John examines Dante on Charity. Dante's Sight. Adam.

While I was confused and unable to see, a voice came from the glowing flame that had blinded me. It made me listen closely as it said, "While you recover your sight, which you lost looking at me, you should speak to make up for it. Tell us what your soul desires. Know that your sight is not gone, just overwhelmed. The Lady guiding you through this holy place has the power to heal you, like the touch of Ananias."

I replied, "Whenever it pleases her, whether soon or later, let my eyes be healed. They were the doorway through which she entered, and I burn with love for her. The Good that brings joy to this place is the beginning and end of all the words that love reads to me."

The same voice that had calmed my fear of being dazzled spoke again, saying, "You need to go deeper. You must explain what has led your heart to this target."

I said, "Through philosophical arguments and divine authority, this love is imprinted on me. Goodness, by its nature, ignites love when it's understood, and the greater the goodness, the stronger the love. Therefore, the mind of anyone who sees the truth must be drawn to that essence. Every good thing in existence is just a reflection of this ultimate Good.

"This truth is revealed to me by the one who explains the origin of all eternal beings. The voice of the Creator Himself confirmed it when He told Moses, 'I will let all my goodness pass before you.' You, too, reveal this truth in the opening of the Gospel that proclaims Heaven's secrets to Earth."

Then I heard, "Your human reason and the authority that supports it show that God deserves your highest love. But tell me if there are other reasons that draw you toward Him, so we can understand just how deeply this love bites into your heart."

I sensed the purpose of the Eagle of Christ; it was clear where this was going. So, I answered, "Every force that can turn the heart toward God has shaped my love. The existence of the world and my own being, the death He suffered so that I might live, and the hope of eternal life have all drawn me away from false loves and placed me on the right path. I love all the things in the garden of the Eternal Gardener as much as He has made them good."

As soon as I finished speaking, a sweet song filled Heaven. My Lady and the other souls sang, "Holy, holy, holy!"

It was like when someone wakes up suddenly from sleep because of a bright light. At first, they hate what they see because they're still half-asleep. But once they adjust, they begin to understand. That's how it felt when Beatrice cleared away all the fog from my eyes with her own radiance, lighting up everything for miles. After that, I saw more clearly than before. I was filled with wonder and asked about the fourth light I saw with us.

Beatrice said, "In that light is the first soul ever created. He gazes upon his Creator."

Just as a tree bends in the wind and then straightens up again, I bent in amazement as she spoke, and then gathered my courage to speak. "O ancient father, the only one created fully mature, the father of every wife, daughter, and daughter-in-law, I humbly ask you to speak to me. You know my desire, even though I do not speak it."

Sometimes an animal struggles under a covering, making its movements obvious. In the same way, the first soul, though hidden in the light, showed its joy in pleasing me. Then it said, "I understand your wish even before you say it because I see it in the mirror of truth, which reflects everything. I will tell you what you want to know.

"You wish to hear how long ago God placed me in the Garden of Eden and how long I stayed there. You also want to know the cause of my exile and the language I spoke. Well, my son, eating the fruit wasn't the true cause of my exile; it was crossing the boundaries set by God.

"For 4,302 years, I longed to be part of this heavenly council, waiting until the right time. I saw the sun return to its position in the sky 930 times before I finally left the Earth. The language I spoke became extinct long before Nimrod's people built the Tower of Babel. Human pleasure changes over time, and so does the way people speak.

"Speech is natural to humans, but the way it's spoken is left to your choice, just as nature allows. Before I descended into Hell, the name of the Highest Good was 'El.' Later, it became 'Eli,' as language evolved, just like leaves on a tree fall and are replaced by new ones.

"I lived on the highest mountain that rises above the sea, pure and innocent, from the first hour of my creation until the second, as the sun moved through its quadrants."

Chapter 27: St. Peter's reproof of bad Popes. The Ascent to the Ninth Heaven, the 'Primum Mobile.'

"Glory be to the Father, the Son, and the Holy Spirit!" all of Paradise began to sing. The melody was so overwhelming that it filled me with joy. What I saw felt like the universe itself was smiling, as happiness flooded my senses through both sight and sound.

Oh, what joy and peace! It was a perfect life, full of love and contentment, with no desire for anything more. In front of me were four bright lights, and the one that had come to us first started to shine even brighter. It glowed so intensely that it

looked as if Jupiter and Mars had exchanged feathers, becoming even more magnificent.

The divine presence that organizes time and purpose in this blessed place brought silence all around. Then, I heard a voice say, "If you see my color change, do not be surprised. As I speak, you will see all of these lights change as well.

"The one who has taken my place on Earth—my place, which should be empty until the Son of God returns—has turned my burial ground into a sewer filled with blood and filth. This pleases the evil one who was cast out of Heaven."

As these words were spoken, the entire sky turned the color of a sunset, glowing red like clouds at dawn or dusk. Beatrice's face changed too; she seemed worried and distressed, much like how the sky went dark when the Almighty suffered.

Then, the voice continued with a tone so changed that it was unrecognizable. "The Church, the bride of Christ, was not built on the blood of Linus and Cletus to be used for the pursuit of gold. Saints like Sixtus, Pius, Urban, and Calixtus shed their blood not for wealth but for this blessed life.

"We never intended that the Christian people should be divided, with some seated on the right side of our successors and others on the left. Nor were the keys of Heaven, entrusted to me, meant to become symbols on a banner used to wage war against fellow Christians. And I was not meant to be a stamp for false privileges that make me blush with shame.

"From up here, I see greedy wolves in shepherds' clothing preying on all the pastures. Why, O wrath of God, do you remain silent? The people of Cahors and Gascony are getting ready to drink our blood. How far has the Church fallen from its noble beginnings!

"But the high Providence, which once protected Rome with Scipio, will soon come to our aid. And you, my son, who will return to Earth, open your mouth and share what I do not hide."

As the voice finished, I saw something like frozen vapor falling from the sky, like snowflakes when the constellation Capricorn touches the sun. The air filled with these shining, victorious sparks, rising to the sky with us. My eyes followed them as far as they could, but eventually, they became too bright for me to see.

Beatrice, seeing that I had stopped looking upward, said to me, "Look down and see how far you have come." When I looked down, I realized that I had moved through the entire arc of the sky, all the way to the edge. I could see the path of Ulysses' journey beyond the Straits of Gibraltar and the land where Europa became a sweet burden.

I would have seen more of this world, but the sun was now directly below my feet. My thoughts, however, were captivated by my Lady, and my eyes turned back to her with more eagerness than ever.

If art or nature has ever created anything to capture the eye and heart, none of it could compare to the divine beauty shining in her face as she smiled. The power of her gaze pulled me from the nest of Leda and sent me soaring into the highest Heaven.

This realm was so full of life and energy that I could not tell where Beatrice chose to place me. But knowing my thoughts, she smiled joyfully, as if God Himself was rejoicing in her face, and began to speak.

"This motion that keeps the center still while everything else moves around it begins right here, in this Heaven. Its source is the Divine Mind, where love and power come together. This Heaven is surrounded by a circle of light and love, and only the One who created it controls it.

"Its motion is not measured by anything else; instead, it measures all other movements, just like how the number ten is defined by halves and fifths. You can now understand how time takes root here and spreads its branches throughout the universe."

She continued, "Greed swallows humans so deeply that they cannot pull themselves out of its grip. Human will starts out pure, but endless desires turn it into something corrupt.

"Faith and innocence can only be found in children. As soon as they grow older, both virtues disappear. One child who follows his mother's teachings later desires her death. Innocence fades as quickly as morning light turns dark.

"So, do not be surprised that there is no one on Earth who governs justly. This is why humanity goes astray. But soon, the circles of Heaven will roar loudly. Before January has fully passed, a great storm will set everything right, turning ships back onto the right course, so that true fruit will follow the blossom."

Chapter 28: God and the Angelic Hierarchies.

After the truth about the lives of suffering mortals was revealed to me by my Lady, who fills my mind with heavenly joy, I felt as if I saw a candle's flame in a mirror. When someone stands behind the candle, they see its light before realizing it's there and turn around to check if the reflection is true. Similarly, I looked into those beautiful eyes that Love used to capture me.

As I turned around, I saw a point of light so bright that it made my eyes shut. No star in the sky could compare; even the smallest star would seem like a full moon next to it. Around this point of light, there was a ring of fire moving so quickly that it outpaced anything else in the universe. This ring was surrounded by another, then another, until there were nine rings in total, each moving slower the farther it was from the center.

The brightest ring was the closest to the central light, and it shone with the clearest flame. I guessed that this was because it was closest to the truth.

My Lady, noticing my confusion, said, "Everything in the universe depends on that point of light. See the ring closest to it? It moves so fast because it is driven by burning love."

I replied, "If the world was arranged like the rings I see here, my questions would be answered. But in the physical world, we see that the farther circles are from the center, the more divine they appear. So, if I am to understand this heavenly order, I need to know why it doesn't match what we observe on Earth."

"It's no wonder you find this difficult," my Lady said. "It is a complex issue. But listen carefully, and I will explain. The physical circles are wide or narrow depending on how much virtue they hold. The greater the goodness, the more influence it has, and the larger the body that contains it.

"The circle that sweeps the universe corresponds to the one that knows and loves the most. If you measure by virtue instead of physical appearance, you will see how the greater things have more power and the lesser ones have less. This is how each level of Heaven fits with its guiding intelligence."

After my Lady's explanation, it was as if the sky had cleared after a storm, revealing all its beauty. I now saw the truth as clear as a shining star. When she stopped speaking, the circles around us began to sparkle like molten metal, their sparks so numerous they surpassed all counting.

I heard them sing "Hosanna" in a choir, praising the fixed point at the center, where they always have been and will remain. Noticing my thoughts, my Lady continued, "These first circles you see are the Seraphim and Cherubim. They move rapidly, trying to be as close to the point of light as possible, depending on how clearly they can see it.

"The other circles are the Thrones, who surround the divine presence. Together, they form the first triad. Their joy is based on how deeply they can perceive the Truth. That's why happiness here comes from seeing the Truth, not just from love.

"The second triad always sings 'Hosanna' with three melodies, creating a joyful harmony. This group includes the Dominions, the Virtues, and the Powers. The third and final triad consists of the Principalities, Archangels, and Angels, all of whom look upward and attract God's presence."

She added, "Dionysius studied these orders with such passion that he named and organized them as I have explained. Gregory, however, disagreed, but once he arrived here, he smiled at his mistake. If you wonder how mortals learned such hidden truths, remember that someone in this place revealed it to them."

Chapter 29: Beatrice's Discourse of the Creation of the Angels, and of the Fall of Lucifer. Her Reproof of Foolish and Avaricious Preachers.

When both of Latona's children, the Sun and Moon, align on opposite sides of the horizon, one in Aries and the other in Libra, they create a perfect balance. During this brief moment, while they are equally divided across the sky, Beatrice kept a gentle smile on her face and stayed silent. She gazed steadily at the point of light that had overwhelmed my senses.

Then she began to speak: "I know what you wish to hear. I don't need to ask, for I see everything in the place where all time and space come together. The Eternal Love created new beings, not for His own benefit, which is impossible, but so that His glory could shine forth and be known.

"In eternity, beyond time and any boundaries, it pleased Him to bring new loves into existence. This creation did not happen because He was idle or inactive before; God's actions have no before or after. Matter and form came into being at the same moment, like three arrows shot from a single bowstring.

"Just as a beam of light instantly fills glass, amber, or crystal, the act of creation happened all at once, without delay. From the Lord, the threefold effect of creation spread out in a single moment.

"Order was created in these substances, with the highest beings being the ones closest to pure action. The lowest were pure potential, and in the middle were those that combined both potential and action.

"St. Jerome wrote that angels were created long before the material world, but the truth is found in many holy writings if you look closely. Even reason supports this, as it wouldn't allow the universe to exist for so long without its guiding spirits.

"Now you know when and how these spirits, these Loves, were created. Three of your questions have now been answered.

"It would be impossible to count to twenty as fast as a portion of these angels fell into chaos and disrupted the elements. The rest stayed loyal and began their work, which they continue to do with endless joy.

"The fall of the angels was caused by the pride of the one you saw crushed under the weight of the world. The others remained humble, recognizing that they were made by a higher goodness. Because of this, they received grace and have a firm, unwavering will.

"Do not doubt; it is a blessing to receive this grace based on how open one is to it.

"Here in this gathering, you can contemplate much if you absorb my words. But since schools on Earth teach that angels have memory, intellect, and will, I need to clarify the truth to clear up any confusion.

"These beings, blessed by God's presence, never turn their gaze away from Him. Nothing is hidden from them, so they do not need to recall things they might have forgotten. Unlike people who dream without understanding, angels always see the truth.

"On Earth, there are many paths of philosophy, driven by appearances and superficial thoughts. Up here, we tolerate this less than when people twist the words of the Holy Scriptures. People do not consider how much blood was shed to bring these teachings into the world or how much God loves those who remain humble.

"Everyone wants to appear wise, creating their own ideas, which preachers then spread while the Gospels remain silent. Some claim the moon turned back during Christ's Passion, blocking the sun's light. This is false. The light faded on its own, creating an eclipse seen by people across the world.

"There are more lies preached each year than there are families in Florence. The sheep return from these sermons filled with nothing but empty words. Ignorance of the harm does not excuse them.

"Christ did not tell His first disciples to preach nonsense. He gave them a true foundation, which they shared loudly, using the Gospels as shields and weapons in the fight for faith. Now, people preach jokes and stories, and as long as the crowd laughs, nothing more is required.

"Today, people hide behind a false piety. If people could see the hypocrisy, they would realize how much trust they place in empty promises. It has gotten so foolish that people flock to indulgences without any proof.

"By this deceit, some enrich themselves, like Saint Anthony fattening his pig. Many are worse than pigs, paying money for things with no true value.

"But enough of this diversion. Let's return to the right path. Remember, this angelic nature multiplies endlessly. No words or imagination can capture how vast it truly is.

"If you look at what Daniel wrote, you'll see that the exact number of angels remains hidden. The original divine light shines in countless ways, depending on how it's received.

"The intensity of love varies according to the ability of each soul to understand. Now, look at the height and vastness of eternal power, which has created so many reflections of itself, yet remains unchanged."

Chapter 30: The Tenth Heaven, or Empyrean. The River of Light. The Two Courts of Heaven. The White Rose of Paradise. The great Throne.

When the Sun and Moon, far from us and positioned on opposite sides of the horizon in Aries and Libra, create a balanced line in the sky, it is a brief moment. During this time, as they are balanced on the horizon before shifting, Beatrice stood with a smile, silently gazing at the bright point of light that had overwhelmed me.

Then she began to speak: "I will tell you what you want to know, for I can see your thoughts in the place where all time and space come together. The Eternal Love created new beings not for its own gain, which is impossible, but so that its glory could shine and be known.

"In its timelessness, without any beginning or end, it chose to create new forms of love. This creation did not come because God was inactive before. His actions have no 'before' or 'after.' Matter and form came into existence together, as if three arrows were shot from one bowstring.

"Just as a beam of light instantly fills glass or crystal, everything came into being in a single moment. From the Creator, everything was created all at once, without delay.

"Order was established in these beings. Those closest to pure action were at the top, while pure potential was at the bottom. In the middle were those that held both potential and action. Some believe that angels were created centuries before the physical world, but if you look at many writings inspired by the Holy Spirit, you'll see this is not true. Even reason shows us that there couldn't be such a delay in the universe.

"Now, you know when, how, and where these beings were created. That should put to rest some of your questions.

"No sooner had they been created than some angels disturbed the elements of your world. The rest remained, delighting in their eternal work. The fall happened because of the pride of one you've seen trapped under the weight of the world.

"The angels you see here recognized their existence as a gift from the Creator. Their humility allowed them to receive the grace of clear vision and a firm will. You should be certain that this grace is a blessing, given to those whose hearts are open to receive it."

As she spoke, my understanding deepened. If I reflect on what she said, I could grasp even more insights.

"On Earth," she continued, "many teach that angels have memory, understanding, and will. But I must tell you the truth, so you are not confused by these teachings.

"These beings always gaze at God. Nothing is hidden from their sight, so they don't need to remember things as humans do. Unlike humans who dream without understanding, angels always see the truth clearly.

"People on Earth have many philosophies, often distracted by appearances. Up here, we see things without distortion, unlike how they're sometimes taught or twisted in the world. The truth is, angels see God directly and are completely content."

As Beatrice finished, a flash of light suddenly surrounded me, leaving me unable to see. "The love that fills this Heaven welcomes you," she said. Then, I felt myself lifted beyond my own power. My sight was now stronger than before, capable of facing any light.

I saw a river of light flowing between two banks filled with beautiful flowers. Living sparks rose from the river and settled onto the flowers like rubies set in gold. They seemed to drink in the scent and then dove back into the water, one after another.

Beatrice spoke again, "I can see your desire to understand what you're seeing. But before you can quench your thirst, you need to drink from this river."

As soon as I heard her words, I leaned forward, eager to see more clearly. As I looked into the water, its shape changed from a flowing stream to a perfect circle.

It was like people removing masks, revealing their true faces. In that moment, the flowers and sparks transformed into something greater, showing me both realms of Heaven.

"O, divine light that allowed me to see this vision of Heaven!" I thought. In this light, God's presence was visible to every soul, giving them peace. It expanded into a circle so vast that it could encompass the entire sun.

Its form was made of rays reflecting the original motion of creation, full of life and power. Like a hill reflected in the water, showing its beauty when it's full of greenery and flowers, I saw countless rows of souls surrounding the light, forming ranks that reached higher than I could count.

If the lowest ranks contained so much light, how immense must the farthest reaches of this vast rose be? My vision took in the vastness and height of this scene, fully understanding the joy and harmony there.

In this place, near and far have no meaning because God directly governs it. The natural laws of space and distance don't apply.

Then Beatrice drew me in closer and said, "Look at this vast gathering of souls dressed in white robes. See how full Heaven is, leaving only a few seats empty.

"That great throne you see will soon be occupied by the soul of Emperor Henry, who will come to set things right in Italy before it is ready. Greed has led people astray, like a child who drives away the nurse and starves.

"There will also be a ruler in Rome who will not follow the right path. But God will not endure this for long; he will be sent to the same fate as Simon Magus, lower than anyone in Alagna."

Chapter 31: The Glory of Paradise. Departure of Beatrice. St. Bernard.

The scene before me looked like a snow-white rose, with the holy souls that Christ had redeemed as its petals. Another group, the angels, flew around, singing and praising God, who made them so noble. They resembled a swarm of bees, dipping into the flower's petals and then returning to where they find joy.

Their faces shone like flames, their wings were golden, and the rest of them was whiter than snow. As they flew from petal to petal, they spread a sense of peace and love, which they had gained by their flight.

The space between the flower and the flying angels was not blocked. The divine light filled the universe so perfectly that nothing could hide it from view. This realm was secure and joyful, filled with both ancient and new souls, all focused on one single purpose.

"O Light of the Trinity," I thought, "that shines in one star and fills all of them with joy, please look down on us here on Earth!"

If people from far-off lands, those who see the sun each day setting in the west, were amazed when they first saw Rome and its wonders, I, who had traveled from human to divine, from time into eternity, felt even more wonder. I had come from a chaotic world to a place of pure peace and justice. In that moment, I could do nothing but silently take it all in.

Like a pilgrim who marvels at a temple, hoping to one day share what he saw, I let my eyes wander through the light. I looked at every part, up and down, seeing faces filled with love, glowing with God's light, and decorated with grace.

I had now seen the general form of Paradise as a whole, and my gaze moved freely, not fixed on one part. I turned with a renewed desire to ask my Lady questions about what I was witnessing. However, when I looked to find her, I instead saw an old man dressed like the holy ones.

His face glowed with kindness, and his posture was like that of a gentle father. Instinctively, I asked, "Where is she?"

He replied, "Beatrice has sent me to answer your questions. Look up to the third circle, the first row of thrones, and you will see her seated in her rightful place."

Without replying, I lifted my eyes and saw her, radiating eternal light like a crown. Though the distance was vast, it didn't matter because her image came to me clearly, not blurred by the great space.

"O Lady, you who are my hope," I prayed, "you who endured the depths of Hell for my salvation, everything I have seen comes from your power and grace. You freed me from being a slave, guiding me in every way possible. Please continue to show me your generosity so that, when my soul leaves my body, it may please you."

She smiled at me from afar and then turned her gaze back to the eternal source of light.

The old man, seeing my focus, said, "To complete your journey, as prayer and love have brought you here, look around this garden. Let your sight be trained by what you see, so you can ascend further into divine light. The Queen of Heaven, whom I love, will grant us her grace. I am her faithful Bernard."

Like a pilgrim visiting Rome to see the famous relic of Veronica's veil, I gazed at the holy man with awe, thinking to myself, "Is this really what the face of Christ looked like?" This was how I felt while looking at the man who had experienced divine peace on Earth through contemplation.

He began to speak, "Son of grace, you won't truly understand this joyful life if you keep your eyes on the lower levels. Look higher, to the most distant circles, until you see the Queen who rules this realm."

I lifted my eyes, and as the sunrise outshines the sunset, I saw a distant part of this heavenly scene shining more brightly than the rest. In the center of this brightness, I saw more than a thousand angels, all glowing and singing with joy. They varied in their radiance, their faces reflecting pure happiness.

At the heart of their song and joy was a beauty that lit up the eyes of all the saints. If I had the words to describe this scene fully, I still would not dare to capture its immense delight.

Seeing where my eyes were fixed, Bernard, the holy man, turned his gaze to her as well, making my own desire to look even stronger.

Chapter 32: St. Bernard points out the Saints in the White Rose.

Absorbed in his joy, my guide took on the role of a teacher and began to explain to me with these holy words:

"Mary healed the wound that Eve caused, and sitting at her feet is Eve herself, the one who first opened that wound. In the third row of seats is Rachel, sitting with Beatrice, just as you see them.

From there, you can see Sarah, Rebecca, Judith, and the ancestor of King David, who once said, 'Have mercy on me,' as you look from seat to seat, going down through the petals of this rose.

Below the seventh row, as with the rows above, are the Hebrew women. They divide the petals of the flower based on their faith in Christ, either before or after His coming. On the side where the flower is full, sit those who believed in the Christ who was to come. On the other side, where there are gaps, are those who looked to Christ who had already come.

The seat of the Lady of Heaven and the seats below her create a great division. Opposite them is the seat of John the Baptist, who lived a holy life in the desert, was martyred, and spent two years in Hell. Below him sit Francis, Benedict, and Augustine, along with the rest, row by row, down to us.

Behold the divine plan at work here! This garden is equally filled on both sides by those of the same faith. Know that, from the middle row down, these souls are not here by their own merit but by the grace of others. They were cleansed before they had the chance to choose for themselves.

You can tell by looking at their innocent faces and listening to their youthful voices. Now, you are silent because you doubt, but I will explain and free you from your confusion.

In this vast realm, nothing happens by chance, just as sadness, thirst, or hunger have no place here. Everything you see has been set by eternal law, perfectly fitting like a ring to a finger.

These souls are here in varying levels of excellence, not without reason. The King, who makes this realm so full of love and joy that no one desires more, creates each mind and grants them different amounts of grace. This is clearly noted in the Holy Scripture, like the story of the twins Jacob and Esau. Their differences are like the shades of their hair, and they are crowned according to the grace they received.

These souls are not here based on their deeds. They are placed in different ranks solely based on the grace given to them at the start. In the early ages, the faith of parents was enough for salvation. Later, circumcision was needed to add virtue. After Christ's time, only baptism could keep innocence on Earth.

Now, look at the face that most resembles Christ. Only its brightness can prepare you to see Him."

I looked and saw such happiness shining on her face, radiating from the holy souls surrounding her. It was greater than anything I had ever seen, revealing God in a way nothing else had.

Then, a voice sang "Ave Maria, gratia plena," and spread its wings in front of her. The whole court of Heaven responded to this divine song, making everything appear even more serene.

"O holy father," I asked, "who is this angel who looks so lovingly at our Queen, shining with joy as if made of fire?"

My guide, who adored Mary like the morning star adores the sun, replied, "He is the angel who brought the palm to Mary when the Son of God decided to take on human suffering. Now, come with me and I will point out the great nobles of this just and merciful empire.

The two seated nearest to Mary are the roots of this rose. On her left is Adam, the father whose bold act brought humanity so much suffering. On her right is Saint Peter, the father of the Church, to whom Christ gave the keys to this beautiful kingdom.

Next to Peter is John the Apostle, who saw the painful days of the Church, Christ's bride, who was won with the spear and nails. Beside him is Moses, the leader who fed the ungrateful people with manna in the desert.

Opposite Peter, you see Anna, Mary's mother, who is so happy to look at her daughter that she never takes her eyes away as she sings Hosanna. Opposite Adam is Saint Lucia, who inspired your Lady to help you when you were in despair.

Since our time is short, we will pause here, like a tailor who makes a garment to fit the cloth he has. Turn your eyes to the First Love so that you can see as deeply into His light as possible. But be careful, for if you rush forward without guidance, you might fall back. You need grace to help you, and you should pray to the One who has the power to grant it. Follow me with your heart, and do not stray from my words."

Then he began his holy prayer.

Chapter 33: Prayer to the Virgin. The Threefold Circle of the Trinity. Mystery of the Divine and Human Nature.

You are the Virgin Mother, the daughter of your own Son. You are humble and yet higher than any other creature. You are the one chosen by eternal wisdom. You gave such honor to human nature that the Creator chose to become one of us.

In your womb, love was reignited. This love is the reason for the eternal peace and beauty of Heaven. Here in Heaven, you shine brightly as a light of charity. On Earth, you are the living source of hope.

Lady, you are so powerful and kind that anyone seeking grace without coming to you will struggle to succeed. Your generosity goes beyond just helping those who ask; often, you reach out before anyone can even ask for help. In you, compassion, kindness, and all forms of goodness are found.

Now, this man who has traveled from the depths of the universe has seen the lives of spirits one by one. He asks for your grace to give him strength so that he can lift his eyes toward ultimate salvation. I, too, pray for him, even more than I do for myself. Clear away the clouds from his mortal sight so he can see the Highest Joy.

I also pray, O Queen, that you protect his soul after this great vision. Help him overcome human weaknesses. Look, Beatrice and all the blessed ones are joining their hands in prayer for him!

The Lady turned her gaze to the speaker, showing how pleased she was with these prayers. Then, she looked up to the Eternal Light, a sight too intense for any creature to see clearly.

Now that I was near the fulfillment of all desires, the fire of longing within me calmed. Bernard signaled to me, smiling, that I should look upward. I was already doing so, for my sight had become purified and was now drawn to the rays of the Highest Light.

From that moment on, what I saw was beyond words and memory. It was like a dream: you remember the feelings, but the details fade. That is how I felt now; my vision was fading, leaving behind only the sweetness it brought to my heart.

O Supreme Light, far beyond human understanding, please lend me just a trace of what I saw. Give my words enough power to convey even a tiny spark of your glory to future generations.

The light I looked upon was so intense that I think I would have been overwhelmed if my eyes had looked away even for a moment. But I grew stronger and dared to gaze into the infinite Glory.

O great grace! It allowed me to focus on the Eternal Light, completely absorbing me. In its depths, I saw everything in the universe bound together by love. Everything—substance, essence, and actions—was woven into one single light.

I believe I saw this unity because I feel immense joy just describing it now. One moment of this vision meant more to me than centuries of past human efforts.

My mind, completely absorbed, remained steady and focused. As I gazed at that light, my passion grew even stronger. There, one becomes so focused that no other desire can pull them away.

From this point on, my words will fall short of what I remember, like a child struggling to speak its first words. Not because the light changed, but because my sight became clearer, revealing more each time I looked.

Within this bright light, I saw three circles of different colors but equal size. One circle seemed to reflect the other, like a rainbow reflecting another rainbow, and the third appeared as a fire coming from both.

Oh, how weak words are to describe what I saw! Even calling them "small" does not fully capture how far they fall short.

O Eternal Light, you alone know yourself, love yourself, and smile upon yourself! That second circle, reflecting the first, seemed painted with the image of a human face. I stared at it, trying to understand how it fit there.

Like a mathematician trying to find the right formula, I struggled to see how this image fit into the circle. But my own thoughts were not enough. Then, a flash of insight struck my mind, giving me the understanding I sought.

At that moment, my vision ended. My desire and will aligned perfectly, moved by the Love that turns the sun and the other stars.

The Divine Comedy

Printed in Great Britain
by Amazon